Ar Chat Chat

牙擦擦

By M Y Lee

ISBN: 978-1-8381724-3-5

DEDICATION

To Friends and the Friendless

DISCLAIMER

This is a work of fiction and, except in case of historical fact, any resemblance to actual persons, living or dead, is entirely coincidental.

Ar Chat Chat

牙擦擦[1]

CONTENTS

[1] Ah Chat Chat is Cantonese slang for blusterer – a bully to their subordinates, a sycophant to their superiors. Get your tones wrong though and you could be saying 'R Seven Seven' - which doesn't mean anything at all.

ACKNOWLEDGEMENTS

I would like to thank the bulbuls, with their tufts and chatter

X+Y = ☺☺

Chapter 1 – Normal Jogging

Cattle Mall

Saturday afternoon. The Mall.

Mewing, gawking, wandering cattle. Every weekend, herds of them, drifting as they browse through the plastic pastures of consumption. They would perhaps use the term stroll, or saunter or amble to make it sound more enjoyable and recreational. Dozy. Why can't they walk in a straight line? They are not even looking at the tat. Why do they have to look at their phone the entire day? What do they look at? More adverts? They list to one side, like badly swamped pedallo boats, as if their tiny, unstable, programmable brains have slipped to the edge of their head and started arcing them off-kilter. Meandering, pacified consumer cattle playing their assigned role in society. There they were, in his way, thousands of fashion drones wasting their vacuous free time in an air-conditioned, faux-marble temple of pointlessness; entranced by handbags, trainers and shirts bearing the sacred brand logos of their consumerist religion. Tossers.

Obediently they traipse along for 'saving' and 'sales'; every week, same sale, same offers, same scams, exchanging their slave-wages for slave-perks they can wear and display to fit-in, on-trend, just like all the other branded beasts. Compliantly they consume their 'can I get' ponsy coffee, and discard their little plastic lids, skinny straws and waxed paper to pile up high in landfills alongside all the trinkets and baubles they wasted their time and money on the previous year. Jonny hated shopping and he hated 'citizens.' One of them was proudly parading their husky through the mall like it was a living badge of honour. What kind of idiot brings an arctic dog to Hong Kong to live in a little, concrete box? They all thought they were cool. Civvy wankers.

Wind-swept, sun-dried and stale with sweat, Jonny Locke tried to stride disdainfully through the throngs of aimless shoppers, so distracted by the window displays and mesmerized by the lifestyle choices that they were entirely oblivious to his quest, his hurry, his purpose: just to get through the Mall, down to the station and get home. Shower. Tram. Pints. Often time he will go up the stairs outside and across the roof just to avoid contact with the zombies, but today his knees hurt, and he couldn't be bothered climbing another step after six hours in the hills. He plotted a course through the machine men with machine minds and machine hearts; they were robo-cattle. Cyber-cattle. Oh, for a repeat action bolt-gun.

The first contact is glancing, a slight brush of forearms as a young bull-zombie, eyes fixed on his phone, almost walks into him. The second bash, slightly more pointed – three Mainland heffers speaking loudly on the escalator and taking up all the space, unaware or uncaring of the polite convention for the pointlessly idle to stand on the right so the meaningfully busy can pass on the left. The 'busy' growled as he forced his way through and up, not turning his head to register their complaints as he deliberately swung his day-sack and shoulder through their paraphernalia of outsize paper and string designer tat-bags.

The third contact is deliberately 'accidently on purpose'; a driven elbow to shopping bag clip for a Chinese man wearing a velour tracksuit with 'Boy London' emblazoned across it – *'I'm proper Boy fucking London'* muttered Jonny under his breath as he bowled past. *'Gold trainers? Wanker.'* Reaching his last corner past the milkers queuing up to get into some handbag shop, he couldn't help himself putting a bit of effort into a solid shoulder to shoulder clash – another mobile phone fixated zombie; legitimate target, easy target, a fat soft-lad who had taken more scoff than his fair share in life. Unlucky tubster.

Jonny wondered to himself, who was the real asshole here? Was it the herd-humans, docile and compliant, gently grazing their way through their procurement pasture, or was it him – the oddball, the misfit, the weirdo? It's a matter of perspective really. Like the time he shouted at the Afghan National Army soldier taking a piss in the fresh air up against the side of the portaloo, only to be shouted back at, *'Why I go in stinky little box to pee? It is you disgusting go in there!'* The slovenly, scrappily bearded ANA boy-man had a point; those turdises stank, a piss with a view was nicer. Jonny was finally through the meandering mob, bipped his Octopus card and smashed into the MTR turnstile with his belt buckle to go down to the train.

It was too busy on the train as well. He knew he smelt, he could smell himself, so the proximity of other passengers was both embarrassing and irritating. One hour ago, he had been alone, wending his way down the steep, scrubby slope having mastered Nam Shan, Sunset Peak and Lin Fa Shan. The peace and serenity of the hills had felt good, revitalized him, but now on the train he felt he had never left the crush of the city. Stress and annoyance swept back into him. His girlfriend couldn't come out to play today either. She never did on Saturdays.

The train was different on a weekend. Instead of the sharp suited office workers, the humpers and dumpers, the sloppy booted builders and belt-pouched tradesmen, at the weekend, the train was full of casuals, couples and shoppers. The 'helpers' were allowed out on a weekend; indentured house servants from the Philippines and Indonesia could escape their domestic drudgery and go meet their friends, stake out a piece of park or walkway with some flat cardboard and fat bags of food, and chat, pray, dance, sing and joke. Jonny normally smiled with them, admired them for their sacrifices and felt some kind of working-class solidarity. They were the good people, the happy people, the kind people, nobly enduring privations and indignity to feed their families back home.

It was therefore with some disappointment and annoyance that he viewed three of these shiny, kind, happy people swearing and threatening another one of their compatriots sat down against the glass partition just three metres from where he leant on the wavering, rubber wall of the inter-coach connection. He could tell that the seated one had said something to arouse their anger. He could tell she was Muslim from her tightly wrapped hiqab. He could tell that the three standing ones were probably not Muslim; two were dressed and made-up like bargirls in tiny denim shorts and bra-tops, all spangles and bangles, whilst the other, with her cropped hair, was clearly proclaiming her sexual orientation by dressing in classic *'the boy one'* style. Dr Martens, chunky watch, Polo shirt, Bomber jacket. Beyond the obvious cultural backgrounds paraded by their dress-states, he had no idea exactly what the problem was, but the three were clearly bullying the one and getting louder and more vicious by the second.

Naturally everyone else on the train was studiously looking the other way, and Jonny really wasn't in the mood, but the boy from London had never looked the other way or walked on by. Jonny had always had thing about bullies; ever since Primary One. He wasn't a big man, so couldn't use his physical presence to smother the aggravation, but he was a bold and direct fellow, so he turned his music off and stepped up.

'Come on girls, be nice ay?' He raised two hands, palms out and tilted his head, impersonating a peaceful, reasonable man, doing the right thing.

The trio gave him a sideways sneer, one advised him to mind his own business, or as she put it, *'Fuck Off!'* The tomboy fronted up to him and one of the gogo girls stepped fast forward and grabbed a chunk of the seated woman's veil and a fistful of hair underneath and gave a firm tug, eliciting a yelp of rage, all the while defiantly staring Jonny in the eyes and daring him to do something about it. This was the Twenty-First Century, they were not going to be told what to do by some short, speccy, sweaty old man. The girls were operating to their understanding of society's norms, where sassy girls acting gangster could shout, pout and intimidate their way through most situations. Men could be intimidated and stared or shouted down just as easily as women these days, girl power mate. Keep up Boomer.

Jonny Locke wasn't interested in society's norms. Jonny had operated alongside women in the Army who were as tough, capable and professional as any bloke and so soldiers were soldiers, and bullies were bullies as far he was concerned. Gender neutral all the way, he saw three physically weaker and over-confident chavs who he reckoned he could take out without too much pain to himself; and they deserved a slap. There was a momentary hesitation, a blip, as a dim recollection that 'boys shouldn't hit girls' flittered up from deep within his memory, but arguably 'girls shouldn't hit girls either' so let's get amongst it, fella ay?

Tomboy was a tough girl. Albeit still half a foot shorter and taken by complete surprise when Jonny was suddenly looming over her and roaring, incomprehensibly, insanely roaring, with an explosive power that shocked her and made her stumble back. Dislocation of expectation achieved rapid effect. The fuck-off-gobby-gogo one saw an elbow and then a fist flashing towards both sides of her face, experienced a discombobulating cognitive overload, shrieked and span away, cowering and covering her head. The third one, still with one fist full of veil and hair, her wrist gripped by her victim's sharp, gold-painted nails, had a bit of distance to evaluate the threat and tried to tug her hand back and go on the attack. The Muslim girl dug in her nails further; she was no pushover either. Tomboy threw a half-cocked kick that may have been impressive in Muay Thai gym class but was unbalanced by the decelerating train and disdainfully forearmed away. The doors opened. The trio fled. Correct choice. Jonny hadn't landed a blow. Result. Could've been messy otherwise. He was, after all, a teacher Loh Si, and supposed to be a pillar of society. He'd be sacked in an instant if he was charged for brawling, whatever the circumstances.

Jonny looked up at the carriage clientele. Nobody looked back. Nobody had seen anything. He looked down at the Muslim lady,

'You OK mate?'

She gave a slight nod but kept her eyes fixed on the floor. She didn't talk to strange men. Especially ones who called her 'mate.'

The Peak

It was the scrunchiest noise. Like a frog in startling drag, spooked mid-burp. Or an exclamatory Yoda trying to suppress a hiccup. Naz went still. He sank his mind into the forest, exhaling his ears out into the scrubby slope, scanning deep, brown eyes, his head traversing mesmerically slow.

'*Ha heeyaa!*' his laughter burst gently from his mouth and bubbled softly out to join the gulps, squeaks, chirps and gabbles of the black faced laughing thrushes that were suddenly evident all around him. How could he not have noticed? Four of them, no six, no twelve, '*Wah salaam aleikum my little friends,*' there's a whole gang bouncing, flitting and bantering their way across the slope, one or two scrunching on the dried leaves, three or four occupying a twisted stemmed rhododendron bush, another four suddenly shooting up to the incense trees then darting back down to the forest floor amongst the hackberries.

Naz grinned to himself and sank down on the trail. '*Your ninja skills are fading old scout*!' he laughed at himself for not picking up the birds instantly. If these were other times, such inattention could have cost him his life. But not now. These weren't other times; these were easy times. Now he could afford to take a knee and pause on his climb to enjoy the cheeky, frantic murmuration of a bush-squabble of itinerant laughing thrushes. Naz took a happy breath, turned and sat down on the stones. He smiled. How rarely in his life had ever actually just stopped, and sat, mid-journey to enjoy the journey? This was a rare gift, the simplest of pleasures to just sit, still, alone and marvel at birds and leaves and flowers and there's a butterfly, two dragon flies, an ant patrol, rhodoleia, iris, bauhinia, maple, shuiying bamboo, camellia, rose myrtle, look at that amazing fern pattern... It's always there, the beauty, the diversity and the wonder. Yet we rarely see it. His mind was suddenly flooded with sensations, smells and evocations of deeply kinesthetic memories. Nazeem Sherazi had spent more time lying still, watching and waiting than most humans ever could imagine, and the world ran deep through his soul.

The thrushes vectored and zagged their way off to his right and he smiled at their departure like he sometimes watched the urchins zoom and race their way home across the city playgrounds down below, their morning mummy-pressed, white uniforms now rumpled and wild; untucked shirts and shrieks letting their spirits soar having been controlled and cowed as they strived to over-achieve in the competitive classrooms of Hong Kong's hot-housed schools. Those thrushes spoke cheeky, irreverent Canto-bird in their freedom. Just like the little rascals in the Mongkok ginnels.

Naz chuckled to himself again as he remembered the four wild boar he had seen further down, under the pagoda, snuffling and troughing their way through the rubbish of plastic pipes, rubble and debris that builders had hoicked over the edge of the wall into the bushes below because they couldn't be arsed to carry it down the slope again. The well-fed snouts made him think of the property tycoons, getting fat shoveling around the trash of a city that inexorably ate up the green spaces; those thrusting visionaries elevating their marvelous pagodas into the sky, built on foundations of a hidden, forgotten blight of crap. In his imagination, the powerful boar spoke measured, deep and powerful Mandarin amongst themselves but gave orders in harsh Cantonese. Naz could follow both tongues, as well as haggle in Punjabi, be polite in Urdu and poetically rude in French. But he thought in English. Sharply focused, clipped-clear English.

Five minutes passed. Five minutes of the hill, the wind, the trees, international politics, street violence and a dark, dusty wadi before he started up and his head twitched. The boys. Time to move on son. He rose, a slight creak in his knee that wasn't there last year and a twinge in his heel which was, and he pushed on. Across the other side of the hill, a proletarian tram hauled itself up a taut cable, an air-conditioned chauffeur smoothly swept a bend and a motorbike began its egotistical, noisy rush to catch up on time. The fifth man was otherwise detained – duty had called. Naz reached the top and spied a familiar, scruffy shape.

'You walked up? Good effort son! Not a proper hill like Sunset as I did this morning but not a bad effort for an elderly fella like you, Nazza!'

Jonny grinned at Naz, who had been stealthily sneaking up on him as Jonny appeared, to the untrained eye, to be dreamily gazing at the skyscrapers below. Naz beamed but couldn't disguise a trace of annoyance that he hadn't been able to execute a firmly spanked slap on his mate's shoulders and make him yelp. Jonny knew exactly what his old mate had been plotting,

'Saw you coming boy! Still got the skills and drills. You're getting old mucker!'

Naz smiled, shook his head and grasped his friend kindly on the upper arm.

'The Force remains strong with this one. But grown chubby belly has.' They laughed and looked down at the city. Naz turned to his buddy,

'Top of the world dad. I reckon we did alright Jonno.'

'Yeah. We're lucky old rogues Nazza. Now, let's go see those millionaire mates of ours and feel like losers again.'

'Ha ha! They had a bit of a five silver-spoon head start on you Jonboy. You'd win in a fair fight.'

'It's never a fair fight mate, not if you do it right. And I bet Micky doesn't buy his round.'

Choi Soei Suits

Friday, 1400hrs. The Boardroom.

Across the water from a wooded glade in Mui Wo, on the magnificent, steely-glazed metropolis of Hong Kong Island, a topic of great developmental significance was about to be discussed. Ranald the banker man gave Micky the property man a firm warm handshake, coming to his feet to as his friend strode into the Reception. Naz the PR man had been there five minutes already and waved from his chair. The three men had been friends since school.

'*Ready?* asked Micky.

'Yep, you got the brief?'

'Yep, on the system, slides are printed out, in colour, good to go. It's very sharp boys, nice work.'

'Yeah, we spent a few evenings on it. Any tips on handling your boss?'

'Big John? Just smile and agree with everything he says. Don't do too much detail, he isn't the brightest and he probably won't be listening. Don't worry if we spend more time talking about rugby and holidays than work. The important thing is to give him enough buzzwords so that he can brief the owners as if it was all his big idea.'

'Mo Liu Do! Typical gweilo boss then?'

Pakistani Naz and Chinese Ranald swapped heavily eyebrowed eyerolls. Micky grinned shamelessly,

'Yep. A corporate Chaat Haai Jai[2] *Just like me!'*

Irish-ish Micky laughed and led Ranald and Naz down the corridor to a sleek, conference room with ceiling-high windows overlooking the

[2] Shoe Shine Boy – Cantonese mockery for a lick-spittle sycophant.

harbor and the Kowloon peninsula. It should have been a spectacular view, but the heat haze and smog were smudging and blurring it into murky mediocrity. Micky showed them in and then vanished again.

Ranald drew out a laminated, ring-bound brief, a slim Moleskine notebook and a Mont Blanc pen. Naz checked that Micky – or rather one of his underlings – had loaded up the presentation properly. He had, it looked slick. Ranald was confident that the financial package he had prepared, with a raft of future projections for some exciting side-projects, were going to convince Micky's boss that his property firm should be investing whole heartedly in the East Lantau Metropolis, supported by loans from Ranald's bank of course. Naz had done the communications work, blending the hard-edged profiteering for internal decision-making with the smushy stuff; mush about community, the environment and innovation so that they could sell it to any audience of shallow-thinking, soft-minded humanoids.

The most difficult factor Ranald and Naz had to consider was what to call the East Lantau Metropolis, or ELM. Branding is, after all, everything. It had been the ELM for quite some time with the original Government Paper being focused on the real estate opportunities and profits that could be made selling the land to developers, who in their turn would make huge gains in rents and sales to businesses and wealthy individuals. However, the project had been a little threatened when the public got to hear of it. The hippies started bleating about the environment, the dolphins, the natural heritage blah blah. The social workers complained about it failing to address the desperate housing needs of Hong Kong's disenfranchised poor; boo-hoo. Most everyone outside the construction and banking industry complained about the incredible cost – $640 Billion and most everyone knew, from experience of every Government project ever, that the actual cost would be many times that.

Metropolis was a bit of brash word too, not very eco with hints of an evil Megamind, so a re-branding had taken place. It had been inspirationally reborn as the Lantau Tomorrow Vision, the LTV, a vision all about 'green' responsibility, 'smart, clean' technology and aspirations for building social housing and an inspired community. Everyone knew the 'green wash' was tokenistic flim-flam and would be brutally ignored by the builders when digger blade hit dirt, but that didn't worry the captains of industry. The boardroom boys knew that the social housing aspect and need for 'people focused' infrastructure would threaten profitability quite significantly – that could all get quietly binned later-on. The Government would do as it was told; a lot of tycoons and Party members stood to make a lot of money from spending all the people's cash. This was capitalism with Chinese characteristics.

Ranald and dozens of quants, surveyors and *'good at maths'* types had consequently been thrashed to death frantically working the numbers to come up with the smartest way to appease the Government's need to assuage the socialist critics but still maintain maximum gain and profit. Ranald was inordinately proud and hugely confident that he had not only done the detail and come up with a sound plan, but that he could sell it with only the least risk of any disinformation being discerned. Ranald was as highly skilled in deception as he was in mathematics – that was the secret of corporate success as far he was concerned. It was a test of one's intellect, a challenge to be relished and, teamed up with his master-chameleon friend Naz (who could sell ice to eskimos), he was going to be lucratively successful on this one. This could be the retirement gig.

Professional Ranald and Precise Naz had arrived exactly on time, knowing they would be made to wait at least 20 minutes so that 'Big John' could demonstrate his status and gain face by arriving last. Ranald knew he had plenty of time for a couple of mental run-throughs and ignored the plastic, mineral water bottles proudly displayed in the centre of the table and leisurely got up and went to the water dispenser to fill one of the little paper cups with warm water. He wondered if anyone else considered the environment. Unlikely. The room was icily chilled by the air conditioning so even with his jacket and tie, his nervousness didn't become sweatiness. He was cool. After five minutes a beautifully, manicured minion opened the door and apologized that 'The Director' (Big John) was running a bit behind time. Another ten minutes and Micky reappeared and took a seat opposite. He smiled at his friends, checked the handout was neatly placed at the head of the table and poured a glass of expensive mineral water from a cheap plastic bottle into a crystal glass, set for his master's arrival.

Ranald had been told this was an informal get-to-know-you meet and had expected just Naz, himself, Micky and John but Micky was swiftly followed by another gweilo (Jaspar – a quantity surveyor) and three Chinese (Timothy, Charles and Sophie who were Projects, Finance and Procurement Plans apparently). Ranald made a careful note of their names as they exchanged cards, two-handed with a small bow. These Chinese – or rather their subordinates – would be the ones doing the actual work and have an understanding of the detail. They all then sat in awkward silence, reading the brief and preparing for any questions, motivated by the dread of not getting the answer exactly right and telling Big John what he was expecting to hear.

Twelve minutes later, the Boss arrived with a crash as he thrust opened the door and boomed his way into the room. Jonathan Theobald Cuthbert McEwan, or J.T.C. McEwan as his business card read. Big John never used his middle names, he didn't think they were dashing enough for a man of his calibre, and he was oblivious to the fact that most people still called him JTC, without any real reference to his middle names at all, the 'C' neither standing for Cuthbert nor Cool.

White, fair haired and tall – inevitably Naz supposed; he remembered the 'Warren Harding Effect' factoid that a third of American CEOs are over 6'2" compared to 3.9% of the general population. Naz was a brown, 5'10" so unlikely to reach the C-suite.

'Hi everybody, sorry I am a bit late' theatrical sigh and eye roll, *'things are crazy, aren't they? Crazy busy! It never stops!'*

He had just been browsing holiday villas that his wife had proposed for

Xmas, and sipping a latte in his office, but only his PA knew that of course.

'Hey!'

He acknowledged Ranald with a grand gesture, gave an alpha-baboon flash of eyebrows, drew himself up to his full height, puffed up his chest and stuck out his hand,

'Hi, I'm John, Senior Director, you must be Ranald, Ran right? And...'

'Nazeem'

'Yeah Noshum, heard lots about you,'

He had been reminded of their names by his PA just as he left his office,

'How was everybody's Easter? We went to Canada – oh fantastic. Did you go to the Sevens? Weren't Fiji magnificent? Great to see them win and not the Kiwis or Saffas for a change hey!'

'Aye indeed, and the Scots won the Challenge Cup.'

Ranald perhaps slightly over-did the brogue, but it seemed to work, John's eyes lit up, Naz gave a little upward glance of admiration for his friend's quick thinking – *'Mamamouchi that was sharp'* he thought to himself. It appears we have Warren Harding and Dunning-Kruger all in the room to play with today.

'You're a Scotland fan? Of course, Ranald! The name, beautiful Scottish name, but you're not a ginger hey! You're a Scot? So, what's the connection?'

Ranald gave a very short explanation of how Chinese Ranald got to be Scottish Ranald, hurrying so as not to lose Big John's attention and let him get back to making manly noises. Naz took a back seat, knowing that the deal was secured. There followed ten minutes of why Scotland is brave, Scots are mighty, everyone else is nesh, the English are all poofs, the French are all corrupt, a ten-minute run through the slides with twenty minutes of side-tracking and rabbit holing at Big John's instigation. Big John didn't give an opinion on the Chinese; he wasn't racist of course, or completely daft. He knew where the power and the money lay.

Naz presented his slides with consummate confidence and style and asked a few direct and important Director level questions at Big John on his way through – all of which were met with variations of,

'Let's just park that there for now' or a *'Great point, we ought to give some consideration to that, work up some options and leverage the learning points from our recent big project over at blah blah blah.'*

At exactly 4:45, the PA appeared on cue to inform Big John that the M.D from Leightons had arrived, terribly sorry to interrupt but his next meeting was due. Jaspar and Timothy were swept up in his coattails as the Big Man dashed off to his next epoch defining, decision making moment of corporate glory.

That left Micky, Naz, Ranald, Finance Charles and Plans Sophie. The three friends looked at each other with great amusement and slight caution as Charles and Sophie were unknown quantities. There was a general puffing of breath.

'Well, that was interesting.' Declared Naz.

'But good, good, he's on side, we are a go.' Ranald quickly jumped in, nervous that Naz was about to make a character assassination of Micky's boss out loud in front of two potential informers.

'Well, yes,' started Finance Charles, *'but there is a lot of detail to work out and plans to be reviewed before we really know this is the right approach.'*

'And he can always change his mind,' added Plans Sophie, *'he often changes his mind. Especially if his Boss isn't convinced, then it is a very*

loud and sudden change of mind!'

At which point she gave a knowing stare towards Finance Charles and without a word Naz realised that their view of their over-bearing boss was probably about the same as his. They were almost certainly two long suffering, highly professional and capable people who should have been John's boss but instead were bullied and berated every day. In a just world, they would be the decision makers and John would have sorted out the projector and got the coffees, but colonial privilege and old-school networks take a long time to die out. There were few nets that Teflon tied suits like John couldn't slip through.

Naz took a risk, switched to Cantonese, shook his head, exhaled, looked out the window and softly muttered,

'Koei loon up, dong bei kup. Hay mong mo yee-ng tsai nido?' (He talks rubbish. I hope there are no informers here), as if talking solely to himself. Charles and Sophie both pretended not to hear him, cast their eyes down in embarrassment, then seemed to both instinctively realise that Micky was unlikely to grass them up and even more unlikely to have picked up the Cantonese and they suddenly snickered like two naughty teenagers, guilty in an act of licentious, insubordinate insurrection. They eyed up Naz, who had presented his slides with such style and panache that they had written him off as another *'Tsoei Seoui Yan'* – good at talking but a triumph of style over substance gained from a privileged education and connections at Kowloon Cricket Club. He spoke Cantonese; maybe he came from a working-class background?

Ranald had already won them over; firstly, he was Chinese, secondly highly technical and accurate on his slides, and thirdly reassuringly serious in his presentation style - boring to John; all professional gravitas to them.

'*I am saying nothing*' whispered Sophie conspiratorially, still in Cantonese and her eyes met Nazeem's with a glimpse of cheeky, subversion in them. They were going to get on just fine.

Micky took the chance to bring things back to his understanding with a quick,

'Gau la, gau la! Back to Ying Mun people please! As Charlie boy says, we have a lot of real work to do. Now, where shall we start?'

'I have a few questions…' and five of the dazzling financial hub's most adept and intelligent business operators focused in on exactly how they could finance and justify the largest and most expensive infrastructure project in the city's history. Six hours and a large Food Panda delivery later, with plastic bags, polystyrene food containers and empty Tetrapak coffee cups strewn around the boardroom, there existed a new 40 slide presentation, an Executive Summary one pager (plus diagrammatic annex, Plans Sophie was sharp at IT too) and a mutual understanding of everyone's role in the plan; the plan to realise a bold, brave new vision of Lantau, for the glory of Hong Kong and the Greater Bay Area.

City Reflections

Friday night. The road.

As he sat and day-dreamed in his Uber through the now almost deserted streets of the sleeping city back to the haven of Kowloon Tong, Naz was feeling equally satisfied and discontent, all at once. The quiet streets, that were normally so calamitously chaotic, gave his mind peace and freedom to wander. He had a gentle smile on his face as working with his old mates Ran and Micky, for the first time since school projects really, was wonderful. Finance Charles and Plans Sophie had turned out to be excellent collaborators; Micky was fortunate to have switched-on operators like that to work with, it explained how his firm was doing so well. Micky was his buddy, but a bit of a bluffer; he needed quality sidekicks.

But Big John? What a legend in his own underpants was that man. He not only cavorted about like Lord Flash Heart, but his off-the-cuff, bigotry, indiscernible though it was to most people, had not escaped the notice of Naz's discerning mind. As an Intelligence Officer, he had been schooled by the adroit linguists, psychiatrists and behaviouralists of the Secret Intelligence Services, plus the occasional showman and magician brought in for the more fun and quirky training sessions he really remembered. He knew a rotter when he met one.

Every choice of word, each emphasis, the volume, inflection, affectation, rhyme, meter, tenor and tone of everything said, and not said, everything revealed or repressed physically, was noted and analysed. Years of attention to what people said or elipted, the literature he read, movies watched, poetry enjoyed and foreign languages mastered, had given Naz a sophisticated understanding of how communications related to the psyche. Almost instinctively now, he knew people for what they were, less those that deceived with an artistry and cunning similar to his own. There weren't many out there who had read The Italian and comprehended every word for its true meaning. Even when he wrote the 'how to' manual, Machiavelli was playing with us after all! Could Naz, with good conscience, support an enterprise that brought advantage to that risible man and his avaricious collaborators? Even though two of his best mates were involved and looked to benefit, could he work for the advancement of the despicable braggart that was Big John and his tycoon buddies? Could he play the corner forever, corporate criminal, for the lucre he had no need of and people he had no respect for?

There was another factor bugging him - his other mates and his own conscience. Was this LTV really progress? Was this development really good for the people and the planet? Time spent lately with Jonny and his hippy mates had shifted his view of the world. The climate change issue was one that resonated with him. He had spent much of his twenties and thirties on bleak hillsides, in dark woods and arid deserts. Spending all that time watching and waiting for the humans to do something, normally something evil he was trying to interdict, the background noise – or more accurately serenity and beauty – of nature had seeped deeply into his soul. Indeed, the nobility of nature, its landscape, the weather, the creatures great and small had all been absorbed into his skin and bones. He had been awed by some incredible weather phenomena, moved to tears and joy by the actions of bugs, birds and creatures that were entirely oblivious of his presence as he sublimated himself into the landscape, waiting for his own prey.

The subtle beauty of it all was running in the background whilst he consciously dealt with some of the ugliest cruelties of human behaviour. But as he got older, the natural stage-drop behind his spot-lit strutting had started to become more prevalent in the foreground of his mind. He was a success, sure, but was he on the right side? He began to fret that, for all his accomplished intellect, he was indeed the idiot, full of sound, fury and nothingness. He loved being part of an elite team, a team of highly skilled, motivated and talented professionals like the one he had just left, but should he actually be playing for the no-hopers, the Sunday league pub team instead of Manchester United? *'Let's be honest,'* he didn't realise, he spoke out quietly but still aloud *'everyone still hates Man United.'*

The Uber driver glanced back, *'We all hate Man City as well now.'* They both laughed.

All Star Hippie Manifesto

Friday, late afternoon. Lantau Island.

Across the water from the magnificent, steely-eyed metropolis of Hong Kong Island, in a soft glade in Mui Wo, nestled in the woods, halfway up a hillside on the old, humble, sleepy backwater of Lantau Island, a topic of huge environmental significance was being discussed. Jonny had arrived first, easily finding the place in a swift 15-minute tab from the ferry. Barry, who lived five minutes downstream arrived 15 minutes late; Arwyn was inbound on the next ferry so fifty minutes late then. They were meeting at Jen's, a long-established nature haven and various activists, entomologists, tree planters, bird watchers and dolphin trackers were ambling in at various intervals to sit round on rickety, lichen-encrusted plastic chairs with wobbly legs, clutching their bamboo cups and tinny reusable thermos mugs filled with steaming green tea.

The trees provided a dark screen wall around their 'eco-boardroom', creepers hung, leaves rustled, and butterflies flittered. Mosquitoes were occasionally slapped down and exterminated – there's a limit to the luv bruv. There was no Powerpoint, laminated briefing pack or mineral water. Everyone did have a mobile phone though and had been shared into the googly-doc which was already a mass of tabs, random comments, obscure hyperlinks and half-baked ideas. Occasionally Jonny felt that a vaguely ordered consensus or disorganized confluence of tangential minds might be emerging from the discourse, but his hopes were swiftly disparaged as the collaborative conversation ebbed, flowed and meandered in an organic miasma that reflected its participants' natural auras.

'*We have to fight this thing though!*' Tree Lorax asserted passionately.

'*Yeah, we must. Resist the man, man!*' Ocean Savior pumped a fist with more than a hint of irony as he played the revolutionary hippy role with a sardonic grin.

'*We need to get people on the streets. March. Protest. Make our voice heard!*' Buffalo Nurturer enjoined them earnestly.

'*It's pointless.*' Veteran-Jaded Campaigner stated firmly. Jonny huffed and backed her up.

'*Protest? Yeah right, like the Government ever listens to protests. Remember Occupy? The leaders are all in jail, not a shred of change. Remember when we all marched against the incinerator? It's virtually built now. Peaceful protest is pointless.*'

'*Ah, but that's not the most terrible way to dispose of our waste.*' Scientist Activist spoke up.

'*What? The incinerator? More carbon and smoke? Climate change anyone!*' Wetland Guardian hit back,

'*It's an environmental catastrophe that incinerator*!' Tree Lorax.

'*Well, actually, compared to landfill, it is quite a sensible way to deal with....*' Scientist Activist tried to present a factually based argument. David Hume nudged David Bellamy in heaven.

'*Woaah! We digress. The ELM people, the E.L.M...*' Jonny tried to restore focus.

'*OK, so we what we intend to do is target Legco and the property tycoons directly and...*'

'*Is it ELM or LTV?*' Ocean Saviour.

'*We need a march.*' Buffalo Whisperer.

Veteran Jaded-Campaigner, looked fierce, '*We have to resist this, to fight it, but non-violent protests never work in China. So, we have to target Legco and the tycoons; or we just start blowing shit up.*' She tried to look revolutionary, as revolutionary as a chubby, white woman with seven cats can look.

Jonny was determined not to be diverted but was losing his cool. This lot couldn't blow up a balloon he thought.

'I like blowing shit up, but we are supposed to be the goodies.' Wilberforce Oddie, Ornithologist. *'And this is China. You'll get shot.'*

'Yeah right. And how do we target Legco tycoons? You'll never get access to Legco. Tycoons won't speak to us – we're scum to them.' Veteran-Jaded Campaigner.

Jonny was fighting through the castrophony, *'We know some people. Barry went to the right school.'*

'Barry?!' Almost everyone, surprised exclamation all round with much comedy facial gymnastics.

'Barry went to school?'

'He's posher than he looks you know,' continued Jonny as they all smiled, a little intrigued as to how big Barry, a hedge-dragged-through-a-man-backwards icon by day and night-time away-with-the-fairies musician, could have gone to private school. They listened to one voice for the first time that evening. Barry smiled bashfully and shrugged, Jonny kept talking,

'Right. What we want to do is get to talk to key members of Legco, small groups not public meetings and choreographed bollocks, and then get in amongst the tycoons, the financiers and the developers. We get rich kids on our team. We use the twenty somethings, university students and people just back from university, those that actually get it and aren't too far corrupted yet to maintain the status quo. The rich, connected but properly educated sons and daughters of the billionaires. We get them to present, persuade, convince and cajole daddy and uncle Rupert to make the right decision. We subvert the system from within the system. Only way.'

'Isn't that a bit manipulative?' asked Wilberforce, the good guy.

'And unrealistic. How do we convince the rich kids, who owe all their privilege to their property portfolios, to turn against their own kind? They owe their wealth to exploiting the people and the planet.' Jaded-Campaigner snorted. Jonny kept trying,

'Well, it isn't really 'turning against'. We just convince them to do the right thing. They know what's right, they have had a modern education. Nobody under thirty denies climate change or wants coal and oil and concrete. They get it. We just need to get them to educate their parents.'

'And use their connections to get us the right meetings.' Barry was in close support.

'And at the meetings we lead with science and finance, not placards and slogans.' Scientist Activist was on board.

'Protesting and marching is all very colourful and great fun, but it does nothing.' Barry and Jonny were on a roll, tag-teaming the group, but it was an assault easily disrupted, Buffalo Whisperer threw her hands up,

'Except get you beaten up by the Popo.' Buffalo Whisperer had scars.

'And you lose your job.' Added Tree Lorax, very sensibly. He carried on,

'Did you see the news? Prison sentences of 3 or 4 years for the Mongkok rioters, the Occupy Central leaders are all being quietly jailed one by one. The Government's revenge is served cold. It's terrible really. Just so you know.'

Jonny gave up, closed his eyes and let it wash over him as he looked at the trees and wondered where to go for a pint.

Jaded-Campaigner was indignant, *'And the tycoon's media lapdogs make you out to be a menace to society, when they are the real threat to society! We are just trying to save the world.'*

'Nobody listens to clever science, polite logic or reasoned arguments,' Right-on Journalist had arrived quietly, been observing carefully, and was now ready to report,

'You need publicity to succeed and protests and violence get publicity. Well-informed briefings don't make the news. Those in power are only ever going to be influenced if public opinion is going to threaten their profits.'

'Yeah, you need to make a noise, or you'll never be heard.'

'And be ignored.'

'Then you get put on ze schwarz list and quietly disappeared a few months later.'

'And how are you going to get the rich kids to help? They're too busy skiing, or running charity fashion shows for Tatler. Giles and Hermione are ever so busy dahling.'

'We could make them swear allegiance to Mother Nature when they buy their weed.'

'That'll work.'

'I know a few dealers. That nice bloke who grows it up in Sai Kung, what's his name?'

'D'ya mean Marky Mark or Drip Fed Fred?'

Laughter all round, except for Jonny. He had given up. How can we ever get anything done when nobody is actually in charge, when nobody actually wants anyone in charge, cos we're a collective consciousness man? Annoying.

'Yakky Dah! What's occurring then?' Arwyn had arrived. Just in time for the group to get up and head for home, the pub or the ferry.

'Blimey. I wasn't going to start singing you know.'

Jonny looked at his watch, looked at Arwyn, and shook his head,

'Got a PeeAitchDee but can't tell the time Prof?' Jonny gave his mate a dead arm and then knocked over two chairs as he sought to avoid a retaliatory kick. Barry shrugged at Jen, the wide-eyed host, who looked at the three tubby middle-aged men acting like naughty five-year-olds and pointed the way to the steps down the path,

'Home time children! Great meeting, great meeting, must do this again soon!'

Jonny gathered his mates in with outstretched arms, *'Right, pack it in you two, you are frightening the hippies. Come on, let's go for a beer. Cheers Jen, laters!'*

'I saw a light on the night when I passed by her window....' Arwyn provided the marching song. Jonny suddenly felt that he needed to get smashed.

Posh Junk

Sunday, late morning. Offshore.

'Wolf of Wall Street!'

'Aaaah Yes! Great film. Not quite Gordon Gecko but a good effort from the young man Di Caprio.'

Big John flared his nostrils and swelled his chest as he bestowed his imperial approval on Ranald's choice of 'W' and Martin Scorcese's film.

'Greed is good!' laughed Micky and raised his G&T, little olive on stick swirling.

'Greed IS good! To the money!' roared John in delight and they all raised their glasses and jeered. All but one.

'Do you know, that film set a world record for the most swearing?' Ranald informed them all sagely.

'Greed is fucking good then!' Roared Micky and they all laughed some more.

'Right, X then, Eva your go!'

Big John grinned as he waved his gin towards Ranald's wife and took the opportunity to rest his eyes on the firm swell of her exquisitely bikinied bosom. Eva looked away from him at the others and arched her back so John could enjoy the view a moment longer. Beneath her, the Captain steered the luxury, party junk expertly around the coast towards Repulse Bay, the engine throbbing gently as the wide bottomed boat splashed its way through the sunshine and waves oblivious to the growing crowds gathering to protest on the Island.

'X-men.' Eva said lingeringly, pouting towards Big John and emphasising the last word vampishly. Everyone groaned as she raised her nose, tilted

her head and reveled in the privilege of being first. First class she thought to herself. The chances of naming five more movies beginning with the letter 'X' were slim and forfeits inevitable.

'X-men, Wolverine,' shouted out Ranald in haste. Everyone groaned again.

'X-Files.' John smiled and swept his head across the sun-glassed faces arrayed around the roof of the junk boat as they all obediently nodded and Mmmmm-ed in admiration. It went quiet. Micky's wife KK was next. She wasn't admiring Big John's big idea; she was looking far away out to sea. They were all looking at her and she felt their eyes. She sighed. Bored.

'Xiu Xiu – The Sent Down Girl.'

They shrugged their collective shoulders and looked blank.

'Is that a real film?' asked John, *'or are you just making it up, KK? Isn't that a Zed, Zoo Zoo?'*

'Joan Chen. Li Xiaolu. Cultural Revolution. Girl gets exploited, raped and shot. International Freedom Award. Not really your thing?' She looked away again, out to sea. Micky looked at his wife, looking lost and irritated all at once. She killed the mood. John was his boss, and his wife wasn't playing by the rules; she hadn't giggled, oozed or coquettishly fawned all day. She kept her wrap tight round her shoulders and her sarong over her knees. KK didn't care; she found his boss insufferable and despised the way her husband acted around him. From Eva's provocative display, Ranald's marriage was as much a sham as their own. The junk suddenly slapped into a wave and wallowed, sending drinks sliding across the slick, white deck.

'Wah hey!' they all roared, snatched up drinks and steadied themselves.

'So, where were we? Aye, Y! Ha har!' KK stared away across the water in disinterest and wondered how to avoid the after-junk BBQ at Big John's.

Chapter 2 – Stand By to Pick Up the Pace

Riot Recce

Sunday morning, the City.

Jonny slung his black daysack over his shoulder and headed out past the dog-piss reeking bench below his 3rd floor walk-up flat, down the slope to PMQ. The shoebox apartment cost a fortune but had a roof space with a rickety barbeque rack and a coffee shop right downstairs. He had packed an umbrella (for symbolic solidarity, and as a sunshade), a bandana and his old army hat-floppy-ridiculous (for shade), a bottle of iced water and first aid kit (be prepared) and a sweat towel (it's June). It was proper redders and he was dripping before he had reached the Mid-Levels escalator. He also had a spare t-shirt so that he didn't have to smell himself when he went for a coffee and a read of the paper once he had got bored of protesting – which wouldn't take long. Hardly Belfast or Brixton izzit?

He was going alone. Sure, some of the teachers from his school would be going, the pro-democracy 'Yellow' Brigade, but they kept it quiet from the 'Blue' teachers who wouldn't hesitate for a nanosecond to report them to the one-man patriotic front that was the Principal. Komrade Principal would inevitably already have a list of imperialist running dogs, ready to respond with alacritous efficiency the moment The Authorities requested information on any deviants that threatened the sanctity of the state's ideological educational programme. This programme was known as Liberal Studies – a patriotic syllabus that had been effortlessly subverted by free-thinking teachers with mischievous relish. The Regime was going to have to reform it again. Anyway, as the foreigner, nobody was going to trust him or invite him along. They probably thought that he was as ignorant of Hong Kong politics as most other ex-pats; who were indeed stunningly oblivious. He was going alone, for himself, for his principles and maybe for a bit of trouble if he happened upon it. God, he missed the Army at times.

He had dressed in black-grey camouflage shorts and a black Beatles' T-shirt he got for HK$40 in Thailand; a classic Yellow Submarine motif, retro dude ☺. This week was 'black' day to symbolize disgust and anger after last week's police 'firm action' overkill and Carrie Lam's lingering stubbornness. Last week a million marchers, all wore white; pure, honest and true; innocent and peaceful. Government intransigence underlined with a surfeit of tear gas and rubber bullets around Legco on Wednesday had changed the mood. This time everyone was in black and the atmosphere had darkened with the costume choice. The MTR and streets were packed with black and there was a sense of drama in the air; it felt like Hong Kong's seething resentment was finally being let out of its cage.

There were police in the open dressed in blue, whilst green uniformed riot police lurked in a backstreet. He used to wear a green uniform himself, he used to work with the police to suppress and control riots. Now he was in black, and the tough guy Police Tactical Unit boys, the Raptors, were in black too. Who were the baddies? Jonny had never really understood as a kid how The Holocaust could have happened and why people didn't just batter the Nazis long before they got their hands on the Schmeissers. In reality, some people did. A few of them tried. Even some of the police fought the Nazis before they became the Gestapo. But the few were not enough; the bulk of the herd complied. Now he was older, he knew exactly where Nazis, the Khmer Rouge and other nasties came from – from right next door. From the Mall. He could identify at least 12 of his school colleagues who would have made enthusiastic informers and concentration camp guards should the PLA roll into town and demand collaboration. His school leaders even called their staff meetings 'collaboration' – it was in their blood.

Jonny had daydreamed his way right across Queen's and Des Voeux Roads before he realised he had passed the bus stops. He had been distracted by the display on the renovation hoardings that gave snippets of Hong Kong history. This was proper governance, some educational material instead of just blank, boring boarding. He had stopped to read much of it; nobody else ever seemed to but he felt huge respect for the mysterious planner who had shown a bit of thought and care over the run-of-the-mill task of putting up hoardings. The IFC was only 50 metres away and promised aircon, it was super-sticky, *'ho chiu sup ngoh ge loh pangyau,'* so the IFC and MTR option made sense. It wasn't until the train was moving that he tuned into the station announcements - Causeway Bay MTR had been closed due to the crowds, so he was going to have to get off at Wanchai and walk. He then registered that pretty much every single person on the platform and the train was in black. Woah, this was going to be a big turnout and his clobber was on-trend. Baaaaah!

He got himself over to the right-hand side of the train as he knew the way the doors opened in every station by now, and so was early out as they hit Wanchai and into the cross tunnel towards the escalators in a trice; only beaten by a Chinese, probably Mainlander, lady who had a little drag along suitcase. As he followed her towards the exit, a heavily built man coming the other way was walking on the wrong side. The MTR is very organized at streaming people into lanes to cope with the numbers at rush hours; small pointers are everywhere to seamlessly nudge punters into orderly lines. This guy though, cut off arms in his vest to show off his protein enhanced biceps and ripped gym physique, wasn't paying attention to the puny pointers. This guy was buff, strutting and imagining the attention his mighty presence and manly mystique was having on everyone else as they parted meekly before him.

The tourist lady hadn't even noticed his magnificent progress and her wheelie-case smacked into his toe. Hunk Man jolted, stepped back and, before she could utter an apology, loomed over her, all shoulders and firm jawline. Jonny had no idea what he said but it was harsh, fast and rude Cantonese. There was no hesitation in Jonny's reaction; his response was viciously instinctive.

'Oi, bully boy! Choo fink you doing? You're on the wrong fuckin' side, not 'er!'

The Michelin man took a step to one side as the commuting crowd swept and rushed around him. He had no idea what Jonny had just said. Open mouthed, Hunk Man stared in disbelief not knowing how to react to a short, angry white man, scrawnier but evidently fiercer than he was. His over developed arms stuck sideways out from his body; veins began to bulge on his neck as he clenched his fists. Jonny took up a fighting stance, not sure if he could get out of the way of one those big arms quickly enough, but willing to try. Strong but clunky he reckoned.

The Chinese lady with the suitcase had vanished, idiot boys. The crowd petered out, space appeared and both idiot boys took the opportunity to step back from a confrontation neither had expected or were convinced they would win. Jonny sneered and set off on his way with a departing *'wanker'* spat from the side of his mouth; Hunk Man still couldn't seem to say anything and hurried on to the platform. Then he stopped. Brain had engaged pride and he suddenly had a lot to say. He spun back, shouted furiously and pointed his finger, jabbing his pointy hand towards Jonny like a riot cop swearing at protesters. Jonny again had no idea what he actually said but he had enough Cantonese and intuition to know that it had something to do with him being a foreigner who had no right to be in Hong Kong and he should fuck off back to his own country. Most likely the reaction the Chinese man would have got on the London Tube from a similarly built local with a comparable hairstyle.

Jonny spun back and advanced three, bow-legged, arms-splayed paces. His shoulders dropped, his arms went wide out to either side and his palms beckoned for the gym queen to come back and say that again.

'What did you fucking say 'ardman? You steppin' to me boy? Come on then, let's fuckin' see ya.'

Protein pill powered He-man took a quick look at the CCTV camera positioned between the two of them, turned tail and vanished quickly into the opening doors of the just arriving next train. A train every 3 minutes at this time of day. Handy. Jonny looked around. Nobody looked back at him. That was a bit unexpected. He hadn't realised he was angry today. He probably shouldn't have been swearing so much, with kids about and all that. But if anyone came kicking at Jonny's front door, he wasn't coming out with his hands on his head, was he? Feedback was a gift, Jonny thought, today he was prepared to give plenty of feedback to planet Earth, he was a teacher, it was his calling after all, and being an ex-soldier meant he could follow that call with a little more conviction than some. Let's see ya Planet Earth, I'll fight the fuckin' lot of ya!

Overwatch

At that moment, Superintendent James Heaviside-Jones was nearby in New Wanchai Police Station, up on the roof, powerful binos in hand, peering down on the marchers. There were thousands of them; hundreds of thousands.

'*What's the number count Fenton*?'

'338,000 Boss.'

'Really? We are going with that? Nobody is going to believe that; we'll look like idiots.'

'Can't have people thinking this is popular. Can't have Carrie not speaking for the majority of the people.'

'Can't have Beijing knowing the truth you mean.'

'Beijing is the truth Boss. The Party is the truth, the light, the way.' Fenton gave a fist in open hand bow.

'Alright, knock it off sarky. He's watching you know...' and James pointed up to heaven.

Fenton grinned and crossed himself like a Catholic. *'Heaven will destroy the Communist Party, ask Falun Gong.'*

'Must really be a million this week.' Chewy, their experienced Sergeant asserted solemnly. Chewy was rarely wrong in anything.

'240,000 last week. 380,000 this week. Numbers approved by Upstairs and the Liaison Office before the march even began. Praise be to Xi, may the blessings of Allah be upon him.' Fenton genuflected, bowed his head, touched his heart and crossed himself all at once.

'Hey no religion. Prohibited. Xi Jinping Thought crime. Please express spirituality with socialist characteristics in accordance with Party

directive one zero five dash seven two. And as the pamphleteers say - Falun Gong must be exterminated.' James continued with a dalek impression that was totally lost on his Chinese colleagues.

They laughed nonetheless at the crazy gweilo and then turned their attention back down to the streets. James pointed:

'There, look, see all those flags again? More this week. I don't get it. Why all the American flags?'

'Dunno Boss. Foreign forces?' quipped Fenton, and he and Chewy laughed. James added,

'There's always Union Jack man, actually Union Jack lady grandma. There is always a Union Jack and an old Hong Kong flag. I like that old flag, dragon and unicorn. Classy. Very Hogwarts'

'I shall have to report you for incorrect disloyalty Sir. Not to mention colonial Imperialist impurity. I do worry about Grandma Wong with that flag though. The spooks will vanish her at some point for being a secessionist traitor.'

'Seriously though Wonger; why the stars-and-stripes? Faith in God, the CIA and the US Government?'

'I'll tell a couple of the boys to mix in with them, ask a few questions.'

'Good call. I'd like to know. I don't think it's the CIA, but you never know – could be spooks, woooooh.'

Inspector Fenton Wong gave a few, precise commands on the radio and four undercover Raptors moved away from the shop doorways they were resting against to stroll along with the flag bearers, make a few friends, slag off the *'huk ging'* (black cops) to prove their rebellious credentials and have a chat.

Public Relations

Jonny came out onto the street on Lockhart and immediately sensed the march over on Hennessey Road. It was packed. There was a tangible 'thrub' of humanity in the air and a little buzz of tension – nice. He considered going across to The Pawn and participating in spirit from the balcony with a cold Guinness, but it was a bit early and he had revolutionary solidarity to honour. He began to walk East, dropping another block onto Jaffe which was quieter, moving from the bar area and into the bathroom, plumbing and furniture shop zone. Man, it was hot. Too hot to go all the way to Victoria Park. He decided to cut back to the march and join it mid-route.

As he got to the junction, he found himself in and amongst the police cordon. They seemed relaxed enough and there were plenty of blue shirts, sleeves rolled up, soft hats, no batons drawn, no helmets worn, not even any shields. He couldn't see any long-barreled weapons here; the bean-bag rounds, pepper pellets, tear gas and rubber bullets hadn't been deployed overtly just yet, but they would be lurking nearby. The police were standing about casually; none of them were pointing fingers or batons, none of them were shouting or pushing or getting wound up. It was just like they were a community police force, there to keep people safe. The crowd were on the far side of the road, crammed in-between the buildings and the traffic island barriers. They were stuck; nobody could move. The North side of the road was empty except for cones and the odd cop or passer-by.

'Hey Sarge' Jonny waved at and approached a police sergeant, relaxed and confident to do so.

'Hi. Why don't you guys let the people onto this side? It's getting dangerous over there.'

The Sergeant smiled back and nodded, *'We looking it. Keep people all safe.'*

A message then came over his radio and four nearby traffic cops strode past and started taking down mine-tape and motioning the crowd to spread out onto the other side. There was a cheer, smiles at the police and people spilled across, stretching their legs and striding out. Jonny looked back at the Sergeant with a wink and a grin.

'*My idea that mate*.' pointing at his own chest. The Sergeant laughed back and shook his head,

'*No. My magic powers*.' pointing at his ear and then his radio clipped onto his lapel. Jonny laughed back,

'*Enjoy the day Sarge!*'

'*You too, Sir!*'

Great thought Jonny, now I can march instead of shuffle along in a sweaty queue, and he joined in the route and started strolling back towards Admiralty. Thirty minutes earlier he had been ready to fight a stranger in the MTR whose body language and manner had provoked an extreme reaction. Now he was trading good natured patter with the police officers he had turned up to protest against. Posture and profile, de-escalation; he thought of his Army lessons and counter-insurgency training. How right it all was now he was the civpop such measures were designed to influence. It's all about attitude; soft skills not tough guy bollocks. No need for The Man to get on your back; kick back and chill a little Popo.

It didn't take Jonny long to get down to Pacific Place and he considered stepping out of the march for an air con break and maybe a chillachino coffee, but the Mall doors had been shut – annoying, what for, where's the riot? Just ordinary, decent, civilised citizens peacefully expressing their views. What's next – '*Do Not Skate*' and '*No Scooters*' signs? Close by was a protester, lounging against a silver fire escape door - grey baseball cap, blue lightweight jacket, grey t-shirt, black, expensive, high quality day-sack. Jonny instinctively knew he was out of place. He had clearly thought about every aspect of his appearance to be unremarkable, and was pretending to be relaxed, but he had noticeably clocked Jonny the instant he stepped up the kerb. Five metres away was another masked 'protester.' Young, fit, jeans, trainers, blue t-shirt, day-sack, grey sweat top hoody, grey baseball cap, cool shades, short hair. Bit warm for a hoody isn't it? Two more casual clones another few metres away, blue and grey casual clothes, baggy jackets. Then two more in the middle of the road at the tram stop, one of whom was looking straight at him, the other was on his phone. Jonny walked on, passing the grey hoody,

'Afternoon officer, didn't you get the memo?'

The lad looked up in surprise,

'Black shirts today, not blue and grey Mr Popo.'

Jonny grinned, waved ciao and kept on walking. Enough marching for the day, where is the closest bit of air con I can get to whilst avoiding this meandering mob?

Eagle's Nest

'Boss, maybe there is CIA down there. Hau Ming reckons he has just been made. Gweilo. Black shirt, combat shorts, black trainers, black daysack.'

'Oh, man in black amongst a million people all in black, great. Throw me a freakin' bone.'

'Grey hair.'

'Ta. That narrows it down then. All the elderlies are out today.'

James knew exactly where young Hau Ming was stationed and swung his binos onto him, then swept past along the street. A flash of grey hair and a familiar gait came into his lenses. He could only see his back, but that skew-whiff waddle was recognizable anywhere. He chuckled.

'Relax Fenton, that's not the CIA, that's just a very naughty boy.'

What is Jonny boy doing in Admiralty on a Sunday afternoon? Certainly not CIA, I fancy, he's a Brit, ex-Army Brit, as was James' own father. Maybe there are foreign forces after all. This might be interesting next time we meet for a beer. A few minutes passed and Fenton piped up again.

'Hong says that the Yankee flag bearers are just naïve, young college kids who think that Trump will come save them if he sees their flag.'

'Seriously? Trump save Hong Kong?' James laughed aloud.

'Yeh, maybe if we paid him enough and built him a golf course hey Boss? We could knock down some public housing for him to open a new hotel on.'

'Only then Spec Wong, only then!'

Chilldown Coffee

It took a while to find a place that wasn't shuttered up in anticipation of the collapse of civilization. Jonny found it all a little bit panic-stricken, people were flapping as far he was concerned over some pretty modest, minor-aggro. In fact, he hadn't even seen any aggro. He had headed uphill, or up escalator, to the serene surroundings of the hotels atop Pacific Place. He found a bathroom and splashed water over his face in a swanky, attended washroom. As the attendant motioned to where the towels were, Jonny wondered if there was anywhere else on earth where he would feel that he was the one, too grubby and too filthy, to be in the public toilets? A little less sticky and sweaty, with his reserve T-shirt on, he found himself a comfy corner of a plush coffee shop where he could de-melt with a frappachino under some savage aircon. Thankful for the chilled air, he looked at his phone.

The Telegram icon had a little red number. He tapped it and read the message from KK. 'MJ.' He tapped in 'MK2'. There was a surge of melancholy and loneliness; he suddenly missed her terribly and had to express it. He typed:

I dream your touch and

Smile your kisses

The warmth of your passion

And delight of infectious giggles

Dispel my solitude

He hit the little blue arrow and went to put the phone down, but as he did, he saw the title bar expand and the word *'typing....'* The message came through,

'Ooh poetry. Well, almost ;) What doing?'

'Saving the world. Protest. U?'

'Wasting my life with the idle rich. Need help saving the world? Where U?'

'PP.'

'Meet me.'

'Where? When?'

'15 minutes. Asia Society.'

'K.'

'*Wow!*' he thought. His enigmatic lover had surprised him again, and on a Sunday. That was unheard of. He felt like just a boy. Life was good, but he really needed some deodorant right now.

Staunton's Steps

'I have your picture on my wall Mr Locke, well mugshot anyway.' James gave Jonny a big grin.

'Why? What for? I know I am something of a pin-up mate but...'

'Saw you down at the march, bothering my boys.'

'Oh! So, they were your lot. Their fancy dress is crap mate, you wanna wise 'em up.'

Micky jumped into the conversation,

'You went to the protests? What for? You ain't got a dog in that fight.'

Micky was looking at Jonny with incredulity, sitting on the street steps outside Staunton's in SoHo - Jonny's Bohemian-slash-Gentrified uber-cool, skinny-legend white 'hood. By rights, it was Ranald's turn to host the pub night, but nobody ever wanted to go to D.B where Ran lived. Ranald also referred to their meetings as 'The Durbar' which was all a bit Indian Raj dull and a trifle pretentious. Instead of a grand, panopolied gathering amongst silken pavilions on chiffon pouffes, they were instead sat on the wobbly, cobbled floor, next to an escalator and a kebab shop – much more Loya Jirga than Durbar.

'*Good Lord.*' Said Ranald, '*We went on another junk trip, didn't we Micky? Beautiful day.*'

'*Well, I believe in protest more than cocktails matey. Freedom isn't free bruv, gotta stand up and fight for the right, to party you know?*'

'*I went too.*' Naz piped up.

'*Really? You should have said.*' Jonny was surprised. 'Mr Writer' was rasping itself out from the pub sound system, set down and to their left, the bar dug into the hillside, jam packed with middle-class punters.

'*Course he went, you're a fucking terrorist Nazza!*' snorted Micky.

'*You're all doped up on religion and sex and TV, Micky. You need to get woke bruv.*'

Jonny looked at Naz, '*I didn't think anyone else would go; I went to both of them, million and two million.*'

His numbers referred to the estimated attendance at the marches over the past two weekends, a sizable proportion of the 7 million population in the Territory.

'*240,000 and 380,000.*' James stated, with absolute conviction and factual correctness.

'*Woah! Fact checker, get on Google.*' Jonny beamed at the copper.

'*240,000? People's Police numbers*!' Naz waded in. James smirked rakishly,

'I am the policeman of the people, for the people, loved by the people, my people.'

'Ho Ho Popo!'

'Proper Popo propaganda! You boys ain't good at sums are you? I was there, mate, no way it was only 240,000, the streets were packed for hours, you couldn't even get into the Park. Fuck off with your mickey mouse numbers.' Jonny was not going to be kind this evening.

'Hey, I have a degree in Sports Science, good at football and maths me, it's an ology. Did you even go to University Jonny boy? Did you even go to school? What is it they call your alma-mater – YOCI, Young Offenders' Correctional Institute?'

James was in a feisty mood as well and Jonny was the one oik who hadn't gone to University straight-off. After surviving a comprehensive school in England, he did a part-time degree as an adult learner, whilst working, paid for by himself. In truth, the others admired him the more for it – but weren't ever going to resist taking the mickey regardless. Especially as Jonny never failed to wear his working-class hero credentials like a badge of honour on his salt-and-vinegar chipped shoulder.

James needed to kick off steam. The past few weeks had been difficult for the police, and James could sense things were going to be getting worse. His unit, in fact all police units, had been warned not to book a summer holiday and that overtime was going to be the norm not the exception. Intelligence suggested that there were a lot of subversives, rabble rousers and troublemakers out there. Nobody quite believed the communists' mantra of 'foreign forces' – the intel boys laughed out loud but then quickly started talking about 'foreign funding streams' in case they were under surveillance themselves. But the Police were certain of the strength of feeling and fear of China out there amongst the population; they operated under an invisible shadow themselves, so they knew that the 'Occupy spirit' was abroad again and policing was going to be tricky for a while – young, old and increasingly angry actors of all shades and intentions were emerging. Consequently, despite quietly sympathizing with the protesters, James was a tad tense this evening and getting punchy with his old mates was safe-ish.

Micky was oblivious, *'Sports science? Fucking P.E mate! 5 points for a try, 2 for a conversion, 11 in a football team, a 6 if it hits the boundary. Math ends.'*

'Maths – sss.' James bit back.

All laughed. Micky had gone to Cornell in the States. James had gone to Loughborough in UK, which may be a world-famous sports university, but Sports Science was still P.E as far as the more academically pompous were concerned. They were all a little bit academically pompous, truth be known, pride and pomposity – it's a man-ting. Posh man-ting, actually.

Ranald asked, *'What are you protesting about anyway? The price of avocado toast? How does this affect you?'*

Ranald was bemused that two of his friends were so anti-Government, anti-establishment, anti-Chinese and Q.E.D. anti-Hong Kong. He couldn't fathom that they would actually go out on a hot, summer's afternoon and protest on the streets rather than go on a junk trip or to a beach barbeque. He had had a lovely time on the junk, with Micky and Big John.

'It affects everyone. Listen to the lawyers.' Naz replied. Micky decided to change the subject,

'Listening to lawyers costs a thousand dollars a minute mate. It's the price of a pint in this place affects everyone. I protest. Who picked this place? Not even a fucking decent happy hour?'

Micky was trying his best to avoid politics. It bored him. He liked rugby, girls, motorbikes, and money-making opportunities to be the topics of their conversations. Jonny suddenly waved his phone in Micky's face,

'Check this out – right in my 'hood.' Jonny pressed play on the video capture; a riot cop with a shotgun in one hand had hold of a protester by his daypack strap. The two were tugging in different directions, the protester's girlfriend was also pulling on an arm, when from out of shot came a black-clad ninja, literally flying through the air with an immaculate kung-fu kick to hit the cop centre-clavicle and knock him flat, sprawling backwards and trying not to lose his weapon. Another two youths charged in and rained blows on the downed cop, kicking and whacking with fists, feet and a stick.

'What a kick eh? Should put that boy on a T-shirt.' marveled Jonny.

'Wooah. Nice but mental. That gun could've gone off.' Ranald worried about such things. Jonny liked violence,

'The cop deserved it.'

James felt he ought to stick up for his own side,

'For what? You don't know what that kid had done. You're just anti-establishment, you'd protest against anything.'

'Even the lawyers are protesting. If the lawyers and judges say this is a bad law, then this is a bad law. Come on, they aren't anti-establishment, they are the establishment, all those DBS swots. Even they are against this.' Naz decided to back Jonny up,

'If this bill goes through then any one of us could be spirited away to China and disappeared James.'

'Yeah, like what are the chances?'

Naz was happy to expand,

'They took those booksellers. The two Canadian hostages. A million

Uighurs in brain-washing camps, concentration camps.'

'Oh behave. They aren't concentration camps, there's no gas chambers. That's ridiculous. There are Islamic terrorists up there. Nothing to hide, nothing to fear and the commies aren't going to start messing with everyone. It's bad for business.' James was digging in.

'Exactly. To get rich is glorious comrade – remember your Deng Xiaoping.' mocked Ranald.

'Oh yeah. Deng Xiaoping. The man who ordered Tiananmen. There's a role model. You don't get it because you are the 1 percent. We are the 1 percent. But the rest of the people here, they are terrified. They feel the hand of big brother getting heavier every day. The facial recognition, the mainlanders pouring in...' Jonny was getting agitated. Naz had suddenly lost his chill vibe too and took up the baton,

'Yeh and it ain't just the surveillance; the press are self-censoring more and more, nobody is allowed to criticize China. They banned Winnie the Pooh for fuck's sake! What kind of psychotic, paranoid regime bans a cuddly bear? And Peppa Pig, Peppa the terrorist pig?!'

Naz was fixing Micky and Ranald with a glare,

'And I don't like that Islamic terrorist shit – Uighurs just want freedom to go to Mosque, being a Muslim is not being a terrorist. Don't buy into that racist bullshit boys.'

Jonny continued the assault on James:

'Yep, since Xi got in, things have changed. A mate at my school just came down from Shanghai. His Kiwi mate was disappeared. Just didn't turn up to school one day. He was arrested as he left home, taken to a windowless cell where the lights were always on, not told anything, why he was there or anything. No pillow. Bunk bed, squat bog. Then, after three days they started on him. Shouting at him in Chinese and hitting him. Then he gets a piece of paper, all in Chinese, and told to sign. He

says 'I aint gonna sign that, I dunno what it says.' Then they shouted at him and told him if he signs it, he gets to go home. If not, he stays. He signed it. He left. Back to New Zealand.'

'What had he done?'

'Well, he was single, divorced right, and he used to go see a special lady, a working lady you might say, for a massage and happy endings. Same woman for years. They got on, you know? He liked her. That is what they charged him with. Visiting a prostitute.'

'Well then, he broke the law. Fair enough.' James was resolute.

'Exactly. Nothing to hide, nothing to fear.' Ranald was conventional and conformist – in public.

'No pillow? Bit harsh.' Micky was enjoying himself. Jonny ignored him,

'Really? You fink dat is fair enuff.' Jonny's accent changed with his mood and he glowered at Ranald. Ranald fought back,

'Absolutely. This is China. You know the score, you take the money, you follow the rules, or you go home.'

'Right. Ok then. Kowtow to the greed of The Party.'

'How do we know that is even true? A mate of a mate? Fake news!' Micky delighted in arguing against Jonny; Ranald and James agreed,

'Yep.'

'Well, I believe it. I know full well how people are disappeared.' Naz came alongside Jonny,

'And you are happy for that to be Hong Kong too? What about 'One Country, two systems?'

James and Ranald both laughed scornfully. James opined,

'That stopped the moment the QE2 sailed over the horizon. China is China. This is China. There's money and there's power and there's guns – and the Party own all of the above.'

'So, we just give up?'

'Yep. Give up. Serenity to accept what you can't change and all that. Just keep your head down and carry on. You can't change anything. You aren't even Chinese, it's not your fight.'

'You are Chinese Ran, don't you want to fight?' Jonny asked.

'I can't see the benefit. I can see the risk, I can see the cost, but benefit analysis suggest sub-optimal outcome my friend. Not a wise investment.'

'Wow.'

Naz and Jonny puffed their cheeks and rolled their eyes in exasperation. Jonny gave his verdict,

'Banker. Silent 'double ewe.' Ran was, to be honest, a little miffed at this.

'Don't be too down mate, property prices are holding up.' said Micky with a wink to bolster Ran's morale. This time everybody groaned at the property manager and tension relaxed a smidgeon. But not Jonny. Jonny was in a punchy mood. He fixed James with a stern eye and leant in.

'So, Plod, what are the instructions from Beijing? When are the live rounds coming out? We've all seen the exercises over the border, the PLA getting all manly.'

A trace of a sneer played quickly across his face. There was aggression there and Jonny wasn't feeling the need to disguise it.

'What do you mean by that rubbish? We make our own decisions.'

James was calm. He dealt with aggro every day. He instinctively raised his chin as he spoke, tilted his head, so Jonny got the message that he was being looked down upon, down a self-assured nose that was confident that if things came to blows, James would easily win. Jonny was feisty enough to take that risk; stuck-up Ruperts can't fight nearly as well as they imagine from their rigorous training regime of a few jolly japed dorm raids and a rugger scrum.

'Really? All that new kit, those shiny new toys. All the gear and no idea it looked like to me. I saw the video of that fat cop pump-action pepper spraying a bloke sat on a wall by City Hall.'

'He was told to move, he didn't. Tough. Should have moved.'

'Really? You don't think that was excessive force?'

'Well...'

'And firing tear gas 200 metres away down range? You couldn't even see the protesters, let alone decide if they were a threat to life or even property.'

'They were rioting.' James was digging in.

Jonny had put his beer down, to the side, and shifted himself round, still on a lower step to James but preparing a bit of space for when he needed to move. Once again, the rage was growing from that dark space behind Jonny's temples,

'Fuck off! They were peaceful protesters. There was absolutely no need for tear gas. Your lot had a bunch of new toys, got tooled up for a riot and then started one.'

'The rioters were warned. It was an illegal assembly. Public order and ...'

James had picked up on the cues and mirrored them. His beer had been put aside, his weight shifted back and up, and he was halfway from his butt to his knees. Jonny kept going,

'Bollocks! You lot decided to go in hard and crush everything early because you waited too long for Occupy and your generals had gotten a bollocking over the border for being too soft. So, you turned up as hard men this time around. You are robocop puppets, the PLA are pulling your strings!'

Jonny was on one knee now, right shoulder back, left forward, left arm jabbing a pointed fist to emphasise his point.

'We don't have generals pongo, and we don't take orders from China, and they were throwing bottles...'

James suddenly stood up, the 'puppets' jibe had taken a few seconds to hit but now it did. It provoked a violent reaction and James' calm, steady composure vanished in a flash. He was no puppet. He was an officer of The Force. His sudden rise surprised Jonny who had been sub-consciously leading the escalation up to this point and so had been confident he was in control. He was outflanked but reactive enough for an old geezer. Jonny was swiftly up and onto his toes, as he had been in the local Thai boxing gym a thousand times,

'Bottles? Plastic, water bottles and umbrellas? Ever heard of minimum force? Courageous restraint?'

James was now the one taken aback.

'And who the fuck are you working for?'

'What?' Jonny was put off his stride by that. Who am I working for? What does that mean? James decided that he was not going to expound on that question.

The whole boozy street crowd were waking up to a bit of a drama happening amongst them. The rest of the boys had tuned in and Naz was rising; Ran had scooted to his left to avoid being hit in the impending melee. Naz was swiftest to act decisively, bottle of beer in left hand was across James chest, right hand palm raised was in front of

Jonny's eyes.

'Steady boys. Calm down, calm down.' In the obligatory Scouse Harry Enfield style.

'Courageous restraint required ourselves, ay, ay, ay?'

Both James and Jonny immediately took the opportunity to climb down, gave a shrug, a yeah, yeah and a shy smile. Both men were inured to violence and as comfortable backing down as stepping up. Violence wasn't a matter of prestige or honour, it was just part of a job. Wax on, wax off. Spectators' heads turned away.

'True, true. But you have to admit...'

Jonny continued, but this time looked round at all the boys for mutual support,

'... you have to admit that plod have been a bit heavy handed. Clearly the whole city supports this protest.'

'Well, maybe not the whole city. I think the silent majority wants rule of law, back to normality, good for the economy et cetera,' started up Micky, all serious, Ran was nodding.

'The police have been heavy handed; they were right bully boys to us the other week.' came back Jonny, gentle in tone if not lexis,

'They have over done it James. Tear gas is not weapon of first resort you know. But I do accept, it's a bit of both. The students have been stupid and unnecessary too. Why smash the place up?'

James nodded. *'Yeah, some troopers could have been a bit cooler. But the boys aren't used to it you know? It's been a while since most of them have done riot training and, you know, it's hot and...'*

Jonny relaxed, took a swig of beer, burying the hatchet, *'Yeah, being in all that kit in 30 degrees is proper shit, I get that some of the boys lose it sometimes, everyone has a bad day.'*

'*Yeah.*' Said James.

Truce restored. But both sides knew it was a temporary truce. Battle lines had been drawn down the Shelley Street steps. Jonny looked surreptitiously down at his phone, there was a message from KK. She was sat at home on her generous penthouse balcony, kids in bed, looking half at the sky and half at the reflection in the patio doors of the pretend fire which flickered away in the air-conditioned lounge, giving no heat but plenty of mood.

The alacrity and dismissiveness of the fire

Thoughts entwine, sunder, desire

The spiritual intensity of a torn, despairing heart

Faded ... tarnished

Lovers apart.

'*I'm hungry.*' said Jonny. '*Burger boys? I know a great place just down here.*'

'*Good plan.*' Naz agreed.

'*I am not hungry, ate earlier.*' said James, '*Me too.*' '*And me.*' Micky and Ranald picked their side. Which left Naz, thinking to himself, 'it always leaves Naz, why do I have to be the grown-up?'

'What about a Lebanese? There's a good one just down there on the right, we can sit up on the roof and do the hubbly-bubbly thing if you don't want to eat.'

'Yeah alright. Maybe space for a fa-la-fell or too.'

'Isn't it fal-oh-full?'

'Feel awful mate.'

Unanimous. Thank Allah for the grown-up.

Escalation

'What is wrong with you? You been, you been, you stand on the right!'

Jonny spat his words out at low volume but high intensity. The bemused Mainland Chinese at first ignored him and then glared at him, but they didn't move aside. It is a custom, a matter of manners, that in Hong Kong, as in London, one stands on the right on an escalator and one walks on the left. Want to go faster? Go left and walk. Want to go slower? Go right and stand still. The confusing thing for visitors is that every escalator has a female, robot voice repeating the mantra

'*To be safe on the escalator, hold on to the handrail. Stand firm and don' t walk.*'

To a Mainland Chinese, instructions from the authorities, even pre-recorded and plainly unnecessary ones, are to be obeyed. To do otherwise can invite severe repercussions and negative social credit ratings. When these instructions are also clearly displayed on information posters at every MTR station, then disobedience is simply reckless.

Jonny's frustration was not only puzzling therefore, but a direct insult to China and an assault on its supremely harmonious society. The ignorant barbarian needed to be taught a lesson and the round-faced, crew cut leader of this party of six, wheeled-suitcase toting tourists felt it his duty to scold the ruffian. He was an official back in Wuhan, an important traffic control officer and would use the foreigner's own tongue to correct his behaviour. He drew himself up to his full height, enhanced by the inch-high soles of his red, white, orange and yellow, eye-stunning

Balenciaga trainers, and launched into Jonny with a jabbing forefinger waggling in front of his face.

'Don' t walk! Obey rule. This China!'

'This is Hong Kong Commie!'

'Hong Kong is China!'

'Not yet!'

They had disgorged from the top of the escalator and were facing off in the Mall, creating a minor blockade to the escalator traffic with the ring of six suitcases and their heavily set owners staring in outrage at this arrogant, imperialist running dog.

'China! You get out! Go home!'

'I am home. Ngoh hai Heung Gong yan, lei hai Heung Ha yan!'

Jonny's cockney Cantonese made the rubber-necking locals walking past smile broadly and a few stopped, stood themselves off to his shoulder and stood ready to back up the gweilo against their designer-clad, bling-blinged oppressors – even if his Cantonese was execrably bad.

The Mainlanders were not only outraged by this foreigner who didn't know the rules but now they were being challenged in their own country by a bloody wog. It was their patriotic duty to put this savage in his place, and educate any of the treacherous, mutinous Cantonese scum who were siding with the foreign spies like the deviant lapdogs they were.

'You get out!' 'This China!'

The mainlanders all started shouting and waving their fingers and fists, their Gucci and Burberry paper bags wafting crunchily, their Coach handbags shuddering with indignation. They were aggressive and confident, six patriots, one ignorant foreigner. They quickly ran out of

English and carried on in Putonghua, this is China after all, and it is others' duty to learn the language if they want to be there. Mandarin has united China as one people.

They were so incandescently furious, that six, chubby tourists in a comical kaleidoscope of colours and 'luxury brands' instantly shifted from being threatening to annoying, to ridiculous. Jonny's mood changed quickly, and his initial discomfort about being out-numbered evaporated as he knew they had drawn a crowd and the Putonghua shouting was guaranteed to bring him more allies by the second, not them. 1.4 billion Chinese people might be insulted, but the thirty odd bystanders were enjoying this. He started to mock,

'Nice manbag fat boy, did you get special cheap-cheap number-one, bargain?'

pointing at the lead scolder's purse. It wasn't a wallet, it was a purse and whilst the logo on it may have impressed the owner and his friends, it meant nothing to Jonny except that the man was carrying a pretentious purse to show off just how gloriously rich he was. The crowd, many youngsters amongst them, started joining in, three teenage girls started in on the three females,

'Love what you have done teaming tracksuit and high-heels darling. Wah, are those Jimmy Choos shoes? Oooohs!'

Noting incomprehension, they quickly shifted from English to Mandarin, with Cantonese asides thrown in liberally to share more cutting and profane observations.

'Are those eye lashes by Givenchy? Lush!'

'Butt by Shanghai Babang?'

'Chav suit by Gooey Chi?'

'Such a short skirt, collagen by Chanel!'

The tourists realised that one, enemy white man had been incomprehensibly reinforced by Chinese people. Whose side were they on? They didn't appear to be on theirs. There were suddenly about twenty, jeering young Hong Kongers, who were relishing the chance to pour scorn on these representatives of the vulgar wealth and bullying power of Big Brother Xinnie the Pooh's Communists. The three Strongese men were all Party affiliated, big shots in their jobs back home and determined not to back down to these counter-revolutionary deviants, surely reinforcements from the People's Police would be here in seconds? Back home any altercation like this would be surrounded by whistle blowing, baton wielding security personnel in a matter of minutes, all faces would have been identified by surveillance and a world of pain would be visited on the culprits and their families. Forever. Accordingly, this just wouldn't happen back home, in civilised, harmonious China where people knew how to behave. At all times.

'*Get back!*' screamed one of the tourist ladies feeling threatened now by the pressing crowd encircling them,

'*You punish by Police*!' yelled another.

'*You criminal!*' the third.

They were used to their privilege and obedience; they were not used to being defied and certainly not used to impudent inferiors.

The lead tourist shouted in Putonghua '*It is him you should be beating!* and pointed at Jonny who was now really enjoying the way things had turned out. A Cantonese jeered back,

'Speak real Chinese this is Hong Kong, we don't speak Communist here.'

Closed umbrellas were appearing and being raised in fists, surgical masks were being put on, hoods raised, young scouts were looking out for cops and preparing to unfurl umbrellas to the flanks and blind the cameras, a shopkeeper opposite was already looking for the metal, kinked latch-pole to pull down the shutter. The lead tourist launched himself forward towards Jonny, his left hand still clutching his purse, his right raised in a fist and he threw a clumsy blow towards Jonny's head. To his officially empowered mind, there was no alternative for him but to use force and he had beaten many transgressors back in China. Well slapped them, he wasn't really very tough at all, but everyone knew who he was.

It was well telegraphed, easily read force and Jonny contemptuously batted it aside. Jonny stepped back, considered a counter punch but as two, young local lads had the assailant by the arms, simply leant forward and gave two, swift, little open-handed slaps to the cheek.

'Behave Commissar, you are in the free world now boy, and we stand on the right on our imperialist escalators.'

The other two men had gone forward to attack Jonny too but were instantly grabbed by their arms, shoulders and shirt collars and pulled sideways as several blows from closed umbrellas hit them in the face. There was a pop as umbrellas were raised around the edges of the melee by the teenage girls whilst the teenage boys surged forward with wild, rapid punches. One of the mainland women dropped all her bags and started swinging her fists in unbalanced fury like a Glaswegian berserker full of whiskey. The other two launched into ear-splitting screams. It was the screams that worked best and, as swiftly as the mob had attacked, the youths dissipated and dispersed. Jonny was walking casually away, a glassy dude stepping out the Mall's swing glass doors before the tourists had even noticed he had gone. They were left surveying a scattered, battered mess of bags and clothing that they had been so proud of just five minutes before. What is happening here? This is China. They looked shell-shocked.

Statement of Intent

Jonny was on his way to a riot and had enjoyed the unscheduled warm-up in the Mall. He hadn't been to a proper riot yet. He had been to plenty of protest marches and sit-ins. He had walked through Wanchai with a million or two others on a couple of occasions, at least it felt like millions. He had gathered with tens of thousands at the Cultural Centre and made new friends as they strolled up to the new station at Kowloon West, only to have to work his way back to Canton Road again as the cops had cordoned off every route away. He had chatted with 'extremists' and 'radicals' in Mongkok and found them to be mild-mannered, conventionally sane and eminently reasonable. He had seen plenty of trouble on TV though, watched the police provoke violence and start firing tear gas and pepper rounds and all their other macho weapons, but he hadn't ever gone to a protest with any real intent to riot himself. He feared he was missing out.

Today was a bit different. He fancied it. After being stared at, shouted at, blocked and intimidated by the police on five separate occasions now, with no aggro offered on his part, his sympathy had gone and turned to contempt and, whilst not yet hatred, his blood was up. He had always stood up to bullies and it was evident to him which side the bullies were on. As a soldier he had worked alongside police all over the world. He knew how stressful it was to be abused, to have to deal with chaotic situations, to cope with all that heavy, sweaty kit and not to know exactly what was going on or what to do about it. He knew how important it was to be 'firm, fair and friendly' and how difficult it was sometimes to show 'courageous restraint' or apply only 'minimum, appropriate force' when you were having a bad day. He knew how 'de-escalation' was often the polar opposite of what a man felt like doing – which was to smack the gobby oik and teach the hooligans a lesson. That wasn't bullying, that was keeping order, protecting public safety and restoring a safe and secure environment.

However, after the umpteenth time of watching social media clips of yet another totally unnecessary pepper spray to the face, out-of-control baton wielding and an obscene amount of tear gas being fired, Jonny had made his mind up. He was out of solidarity for his former colleagues in the forces of law and order. Frankly the police conduct offended his professionalism; they were brutish and excessive more often than self-disciplined, measured and astute in their actions. At least on the social media clips he had increasingly been finding appearing in his online echo-chamber of public information. Micky and Ran were watching very different clips of course; savage hooligans and violent mobsters who needed to be restrained and disciplined before they destroyed Hong Kong. The echo chambers had been built and were filling up with hooting and hollering acolytes of Blue or Yellow.

Jonny could perhaps have remained neutral by telling himself that the 'Yellow' sites, the Be Waters, Stands, Apple Dailys et al were only showing the bad cops and never the good cops. But his personal experience was confirming his liberal prejudice that the Hong Kong police had been the PLA in disguise for months now. The officers and the top brass had been thoroughly indoctrinated. The Torquemadas had created an Inquisition within the Institution previously known as the Hong Kong Police. That clever Facebook algorithm was working perfectly to reinforce Jonny's prejudices, responding to his 'likes' and 'views' to deliver tailored content that increasingly fed his Weltanschauung. What a clever thing AI was, artificial intelligence creating artifice in an organic brain.

He had swung back to sympathy for the hard-pressed forces of law and order when he saw a clip of an enraged police officer who was so wound up that he launched himself into the air against a shuttered shop-front, bounced off and landed on the street. This wasn't the keystone cops' moment when an officer had thrown his water bottle at a handful of bemused protesters thinking it was a tear gas grenade. That officer then sheepishly went and picked it up again, obviously under zero threat, so it wasn't clear as to why he threw anything in the first place. Rather, this shop-front assault was a moment of rage and frustration that was hilariously stupid – but endearingly human and no one had got hurt except perhaps the officer himself. Certainly, his pride smarted. But it did highlight the mental stress, violence and lack of control that was becoming evident amongst the police. Jonny wondered if PTSD was infecting the police already. Unlikely though. He had been in the Army years and he had no rage or PTSD issues, did he?

It seemed community policing was dead, their motto of *'We Serve with Pride and Care'* was now a risible joke to most of the people. How long before it was replaced with *'Duty, Honour, Country'* or *'Be Pure, Be Vigilant, Behave*?' Or simply *'Obey*!' The police press conferences were more damning evidence of that; never admitting fault even when a *'that's a fair cop guv'* admission and commitment to conduct some internal restorative justice should have been an obvious choice. The Police seemed hellbent on denying and whitewashing their mistakes rather than learning from them. Society was too critically intelligent and well-informed for the old PR tactics of blanket denial and blame shifting to wash anymore. Sometimes it was just plain embarrassing as they further alienated themselves from the society they were supposed to serve and protect.

That was why, instead of just his water bottle and a sweat towel that usually comprised his minimalist protest kit, today his bag contained an umbrella, mask, goggles, change of shirt, first-aid kit, gloves and a plain black, peaked cap. He also had some spare glasses. Spectacles were awkward for revolutionaries and enforcement authorities alike. They steamed up, hampered a gas mask and were easily knocked off. However, contact lenses were not compatible with tear gas – the gas stuck to them and you couldn't wash out the pain. Moreover, for an aging rebel like Jonny, he couldn't read his phone messages with his lenses in, as his arms weren't long enough to cope with the twin indignity of somehow being chronically short-sighted and near sighted all at once. Bifocals may help physically but mentally he still couldn't get his head around the lens diagrams and physics of that latest erosion of his physical powers.

He was also quite conscious of his combat capabilities; a persistent knee injury and old codger's hamstrings gave him the sprinting ability of a stunned slug. His reaction speed and muscle power, once hawk like in precision and lethality in his mind, were now more akin to a grumpy penguin, which his slightly potted-belly and diskily-slipped spine made him considerably resemble. As he contemplated the less-than-mighty warrior that peered dejectedly back at him in the shop window reflection, he wondered if fronting up to heavily armoured, lean, fit, twenty something riot cops wasn't a recipe for the kind of pathetic comedown that the shop-shutter bouncing policeman had experienced. It evidently was. He looked like Ernold Same, not Robin Hood.

However depressing that conclusion may have been, it was still likely to be more fun than marking the Year 9 common formative assessment papers sat on his desk, so lay on Macduffer, let's see what these rozzers are really made of. He double tapped his ear-pod for some inspiration and prepared himself to chuck a few eggs at a few junctions. Besides, he had a lady to impress.

Express Yourself

Jonny was positively bouncing past Chungking Mansions, almost at the Ferry now having decided that was the best route home as the MTR had once again colluded with the evil Government and Gestapo to turn off the public transport it was their job to provide. They didn't care, the MTR bosses had chauffeur driven limousines to get around town. He laughed when he remembered Carrie Lam's famous publicity trip to a new MTR station where it was evident that she didn't even know how an octopus card turnstile worked! Woman of the people my arse! Anyway, he had had a great afternoon.

First up, he had met his girlfriend. From *'not really sure what it is all about'* last week, this week KK had arrived with two daysacks full of beautifully crafted posters to hand out to the faithful. Not only had she the art-school skills to design them, but she evidently had the commitment and funds to get them printed. KK then proved herself to be far better at revolution than her 'used to be a tough-guy' boyfriend by producing a tin of spray paint and a sharp cut stencil before swiftly tagging various surfaces with '5 demands not one less' graffiti. His job was to shake the can and keep watch. He was mostly distracted - she looked great in black, protest gear.

They had a wander around Nathan Road, admired the protesters as they hauled roadside railings to form blockades. They cable-tied them together in triangles which were both easy to push about and made an effective block. Many had brought pliers and spanners to unscrew them from their fastenings; some had hammers and chisels and crowbars to lever up the bricks and cobbles from the pavement and Mongkok now had a splay of roadside sandpits, devoid of paving. As well as their tools and laser pointers, the protesters had proper, industrial respirators, cool looking goggles and facemasks, a sign language system, medics, water replen-man, these kids were well prepared. Hong Kong people are well organised, they always have all the gear.

Jonny felt slightly embarrassed by his own kit-prep. Some of the makeshift shields made from road-signs, or the way nobody seemed to be able to throw a decent petrol bomb, was a bit amateur but overall, he was impressed. They hung around a bit for some casual missile throwing and watched the Popo lines in the distance until they started raising the black flag and he thought a coffee break might be wise to wait out the tear gas. He chucked a token half-brick himself, got a telling off and an arm-drag away from his girlfriend. Chucking bricks was vulgar, nihilistic hooliganism – her graffiti was art, there's a difference. About four-thirty, Jonny's phone rang. Naz was nearby and wanted to meet up. KK said that she had to go and would leave the boys to it, not giving in to Jonny's entreaties to meet his best mate. He rarely mixed his mates and his love-life, but he thought Naz might get along well with her. Naz was as circumspect a man he knew when it came to secrets.

She never wanted to meet his friends. He had no idea she'd met them all.

Jonny hugged her goodbye then darted off to find Naz, who had been treating himself to a foot massage, or that was all he was admitting to, and they went for a coffee. Not their usual Starbucks with its street chic décor on Sai Yee Gaai, as Starbucks was now tainted as 'Blue,' so they went to a non-chain, ultra-cool student hangout in a grubby looking building with a cruddy lift that he would never find again unless Naz took him. They raised the average age in there by about 20 years. After their fancy coffees and nancy snacks, they had come back down to the street and the smell of tear gas and some furiously running students told them that it was all kicking off. Naz had no mask, and Jonny's swimming goggles were decidedly not 'ally' so they both decided to thin out and go home. A stream of vans going past down Nathan Road told him that the day's action was over anyway, or at least The Filth had changed shift.

Jonny would like to get more involved but, not being Cantonese and sticking out as a 'foreign force' it was going to be tricky. His own students were a bit young and he couldn't well riot with youths he was supposed to mentor. His fellow teachers were living in fear of the Principal and EDB Inquisitors and his mates were all far too middle class for a riot. His old mates Arwyn and Barry might be up for it, but not too seriously, they were non-violent Gandhi types. Despite both of them being hard-as-nails, both were decidedly built for comfort, not speed, these days. Plus, they might not have the cells equipped for fellas with diabetes and gout he laughed. Naz was up for it though. He was a dark horse that lad and lived for a bit of skulduggery and shenanigans. He had indeed been for a foot massage but had earned that by slashing a few police van tyres beforehand whilst they were all looking the other way at the protesters. The boys decided they ought to take up protesting more professionally. It would liven things up, as long as they didn't get arrested by James – the humiliation would be unbearable.

Kit was an issue though. Jonny began to wonder where he could get a decent face mask as he thrust through the slim, metal turnstile and walked down the gangway towards the ferry, then lost concentration as he heard that distinctive buzzer that told him that the gates were closing. Back to the safety of Soho for the evening, no riots up there, just some damn fine hangouts and over-priced ale. Naz would follow him up after a shower and change. Life was good - Jonny liked the protests, a bit of aggro had brightened up this dull old town.

Chapter 3 – Get Amongst It

Pub Quiz

'Oy Oy! Over here Damps.'

Jonny waved and beckoned across the crowded pub; Micky and Naz were already there.

'Ah, you got us a table, good skills. Is there enough space for us all?'

Micky answered, *'Yeah, we'll be alright, James ain't coming - busy protecting the Realm.'*

'Beating up teenage girls and tear gassing puppies. He wotzapped earlier – another overtime shift.' Naz rolled his eyes and wobbled his head as he said it.

Micky had more sympathy for their absent friend, *'He must be knackered.'* Naz and Jonny had zero empathy,

'He must be loaded! All that overtime pay!'

'I heard he was at all night poker game with the Triads.'

'Ah yes, Yuen Long.'

'Have we entered?' asked Ran as he reappeared from the bar and sat down with his pint.

'Yep. Team Name – Chewbacca The Net. Twenty dollars please.'

'Do you think the cops did deliberately stay away from Yuen Long?' Micky asked Naz. Micky was just beginning to recognise that the protests were an issue, but he had little idea what it was all about. His lifestyle had been only mildly inconvenienced when traffic was disrupted, although as biker, he zipped round most of the bother.

A few weeks earlier, a gang of around fifty triad thugs had ambushed protesters at Yuen Long MTR and given many of them a severe beating. The police hadn't turned up to restore peace and good order until it was all long over. Two officers had been video'd strolling away from the scene whilst the fight was in progress and several others were filmed chatting amicably to the triad gangs after the incident. Whilst a certain amount of collusion between gangsters and police was a routine part of negotiated policing across Hong Kong, and always had been, this was a different matter. This smacked of the regular Communist party practice of using paid thugs to intimidate people whilst the police deliberately *'looked the other way'* – *'mo ahn tai'* in Cantonese; I didn't see nothing! The police had rapidly lost their name and were now regularly referred to as 'Huk Ging' or 'Black Cops.' A few anti-establishment types had always called them 'Black Cops' thanks to their perceived brutality and corruption, but most citizens respected the police and called them 'Sir.' No more. Ever since Yuen Long, the police were being assailed by chants of *'Huk Say Wooi'* – Black Society or Triads. This insult was being chanted by all ages and Hong Kong wide – it must sting.

Jonny was unequivocal in his view, *'Absolutely they were in on it. That odious Nazi Junius Ho was up there shaking hands with the gangsters before it kicked off, then the cops all mysteriously vanished. There's even footage of them laughing about it with the Triad boys afterwards.'*

Micky was unconvinced, *'Oh come on, they have may have been slow to turn up, but they were probably too busy with all the other shit the rioters are pulling. The vandalism is getting out of hand.'*

'A bit slow? Two of them were there but wandered off. It took an hour for any to turn up. Proper collusion. Paid for and orchestrated by the

Communists, probably through their little gauleiter. He is a proper rabble-rouser that Junius.'

'Paranoia. Mr Ho was just meeting constituents.' Ranald was backing up Micky. He knew Junius from the Club.

'Supposition.' Micky was equally glad to have a pro-establishment ally in Ranald.

'Constituents? That's not his patch, fact! Well, probable fact.' Jonny laughed at his own non sequiter. *'Come on, this is how communist parties have always worked, pay a few agent provocateurs to start the trouble, threaten the locals, deny it had anything to do with them and then come in and save the day whilst increasing security and oppression to stop it happening again and to 'protect' the innocent people. Classic Mao.'*

'True.' Naz was quick to back his ideological compadre up; just as Ran and Micky tag-teamed them back.

'The cops are losing it man,' Naz waded in, *'I got stuck in Pret the other day, opposite the Immigration place, tons of tear gas, people legging it and some riot cop up on the bridge suddenly hurled a bin, one of those big orange bins, down on the people running.'*

'Bollocks!'

'Straight up! It bounced on the road right outside. Another one of them was banging out rounds from his shotgun.'

'What did you do?'

'I finished my coffee and read the paper. Waited for the tear gas to go and carried calmly on old boy.' The lads laughed together. Drinks were supped. A second passed.

'I have to say...' mused Naz with his characteristic aplomb, *'those bomb reports are a bit suspect too. Would any terrorist really be that inept to*

leave kit out in the open in a school or mark his stash with loads of pro-democracy posters, if they were really pro-democracy. Stinks of a false flag operation to me, a set-up.'

Micky was more trusting of the Government, *'I am not so sure Naz. This is how Northern Ireland started, trouble on the streets, petrol bombs and then the nail bombs started coming.'* Micky's obscure Irish heritage made him think he knew a lot about The Troubles. Naz never put him right. Instead, Naz stayed with the point on the 'so-called bombs.'

'Well let's see, if in a few months some terrorists are in court, with links to ISIS or Abu Sayaf or something – like the CIA...' he laughed sharply, and all joined in *'...then I'll believe we have native bomb makers in Hong Kong. But I bet they find a few more dodgy caches and then it all goes quiet. My instinct tells me this is PLA spies planting stuff and messing with the local rozzers.'*

'Yeah right, your instincts honed from years of selling dodgy motors and snake oil.' Micky grinned at him provocatively.

'Don't forget the carpets.' Cut in Jonny.

'We never forget the carpets...' joined in Ran, *'...finest Afghan rugs my friend, twenty shekels a bushel, super number one bargain, my friend, my friend, lookee, lookee!'* Delivered in an appalling simulacrum of a Pakistani – Bengali – Indian-ish accent; appalling in a way only a posh, English educated, Chinese man can do appalling.

Naz drew himself up to his full, seated height, looked down imperiously through his shapely hill-tribesman's nose, and enunciated, in the plumiest of Oxford professorial accents,

'I am a thought leader in a world leading, blue ribboned, multiple platinum rated management consultancy firm that instructs inept property investors – like you Micky - and clueless, avaricious bankers - like you Ran the Damp Man – how to run their business and not fuck everything up. I do not sell carpets, rugs, lino or any other variety of

floor-based coverings.'

His impression, replete with the most pretentious sniffs, head-tilts and nose wrinkles, brought big smiles all round and actual applause. Naz underlined his performance with,

'And despite your impression Ranaldo, I am certainly not Welsh.'

They all laughed again and jeered at Ranald. Their inane chatter was interrupted by a perky, vaguely Canadian voice coming over the pub PA,

'Wahey Ladies and Gentlemen, welcome to the pub quiz, you should all have your answer sheets, a quick reminder of the rules...'

Two hours, three pints, five quiz rounds and a creditable 3rd place (two bottles of red wine) later, the boys were joined by James, squeezing up to the table with a generous arse on a tiny stool. James had endured another long day. With the arrival of their police friend, Naz's inner imp immediately leapt into play,

'So Jonboy, when do we need to mobilise the faithful for another crack at Legco?'

'Blimey, were you two involved with storming Legco too?' asked Ranald with a jolt.

'No, we were supposed to go with the students to do the Lantau Tomorrow Hearing thing.' replied Jonny. With Jonny not wanting to wind James up, Naz added further explanation,

''cept the whole thing got cancelled because the bloody 'violent mobsters' invaded and trashed the place.'

'Not my students Inspector. We are the peaceful ones, the greenies.' Jonny followed up instantly. James smiled and ignored the incorrect rank, they did it on purpose, every time. James just wanted to sit for a bit and enjoy his ale.

Ranald was very interested, seeing as he, Micky and Naz were all working to promote the venture Jonny was agitating against.

'So, what's happening now?' Ran asked earnestly. Jonny shrugged,

'Don't know. Delayed. Postponed. Who knows? Legco are all skiving, taking an extra 6-weeks' summer holiday because they don't know what else to do and have no idea how to run the country, city, essayar, whatever this place is called these days. Still a colony – just different overlords. I told them the unelected wasters they can come to my School and use the hall, but they didn't seem keen.'

The idea of the politicians trying to conduct their business in a modest local school, where they were universally despised made everyone ponder for a moment alone then laugh to themselves, together. Then Jonny realised that he and Naz were supposed to be winding James up and he wasn't playing his assigned role,

'Fuckwits. It was a Police setup anyway. A trap, boys!' Jonny leant forward with passion, Naz nodded vigorously, both looked for a reaction from James. Naz continued the tag-team assault, smirking a-glance at James the entire time,

'Too right, Mr Locke. What police force on Earth would abandon their Houses of Parliament? Can you imagine the Met running away from a bunch of students with umbrellas? Proper setup, orders from Beijing. Unless Asia's Finest are scaredy cats.' Naz grinned slyly at James; James smiled back shaking his head, he wasn't going to bite. It had been another long day.

'Hang on, there was that mystery gas.' Micky was swift to defend any assault on the police, loyal to their mate James. Jonny was inevitably swift to attack,

'Yeah right, deployed by students wearing bandanas and paper masks whilst the Popo all had S10 respirators designed to resist Russian Nerve Gas? I don't think so Micky my man. James knows the dastardly truth.'

James gave Jonny the same tolerant, amused smile he had given Naz and mimed a zip across his lips – he wasn't going to give any insider information away on this one.

Ranald took a typically mature and considered line, *'Michael Tien said it was restraint, the police were being cautious and gentle, gentlemen.'* Jonny gave a typically reactionary response,

'Oh fuckin' really? One minute they are using pump-action pepper spray against a man sat meekly on a wall, they're firing 'undreds of rounds of tear gas down range and inta tha shops, and the next it's all 'softly, softly?' I don't think so Ran. Popo are hard core these days, tough guys.' Jonny turned to look at James and asked loudly,

'James, you are strangely quiet on this one my friend. Were you at the gig or otherwise detained?'

James laughed out loud, *'I was on school crossing duty that day my friend, there's this rough school over in Kowloon, radical English teacher works there, leading loyal patriotic teenagers astray, code name Locksley, thinks he's Robin Hood...'* Jonny roared with laughter back, knowing full well that James and his PTU background would have known everything about the Legco incident and enjoying the reference to himself, Jonny Locke as Robin of Locksley, a flattering joke. He flicked up his hoody top with a whisper *'The hooded man! I'm watching you Sheriff!'* making James and Naz crack up. Brought up on different TV, Ranald and Micky didn't have a clue about the joke. Naz waved his hand at James,

'He won't know or won't tell. The sword of Beijing is held over his neck like all the others – do you want your pension James, or do you want to go to prison as a traitor Inspector Gweilo? Zink of ze children.'

'Anyway, it wouldn't have helped.' Stated Micky with complete confidence.

'What wouldn't?' Jonny asked. The conversation was, as with most pub

banter, meandering. Micky was back to pondering the Lantau project.

'Your Legco complaint thing. It's a completely done deal. Beijing wants the artificial islands; the Government want the money; it will happen. They have already started sharing out the property deals and doing the engineering studies. I know for a fact that the big developers have already sorted out their war chests.'

Ranald backed Micky up, *'I have heard that too. The banks are all on-board, the finance is already being put in place. They are going to build this thing whatever the cost. This is development boys; this is glorious capitalism and progress.'* Ranald couldn't help letting a little pride slip into his voice, whilst not quite ready to reveal his total complicity in the project to his eco-warrior friend.

'Yep, there won't be a harbour in twenty years, we will have paved it over. With gold!' Micky said this half in jest and half as if it was a concrete plan. Jonny looked visibly hurt,

'But what about the environment?' Micky pulled a face like he had just smelt rotting cabbage; Micky had little time for the environmental hippy brigade. He thought it soft-headed to worry about climate change when there was progress to get on with. It was all left-wing hyperbole anyway – fake news.

'The dolphins are almost gone and don't make us much money anyway. Nobody cares. The Chinese will make robot dolphins that can sing Disney princess tunes.'

Jonny was indignant. He changed tack to argue on financial terms, he knew Micky and Ran thought money a more convincing rationale than dolphins, *'What about the cost? That's all of Hong Kong's money? It'll be like that Kai Tak Ferry Terminal white elephant. Or that stupid bridge.'*

Naz raised a cautionary finger, *'That stupid bridge is a symbol of connection to the Motherland comrade, which coincidently could move 400 armoured cars into town in less than an hour! You should know what that bridge is for, soldier boy. Do not criticise the Party, minion.'* Naz took a deep breath as he inhabited his patriotic hero of the nation persona,

'Indeed. Lantau Tomorrow is a glorious vision of today. Resistance is futile. Meddling in the internal affairs of China is despicable and insults the feelings of 1.4 billion patriots. We strongly condemn your incorrect thinking and sternly warn you to kowtow.'

Jonny was beginning to seethe. They may have been being sarcastic, ironic and provocative, but he felt there were all speaking a truth that was inevitable. Nobody could resist the mighty combination of the money mandarins and the Communist Party.

'The fucking billionaires will win again.'

'They always win. They own the world.' Naz agreed, James nodded. Micky and Ranald looked a bit uncomfortable; they came from families of considerable wealth themselves.

'Well, we need the housing.' Ranald knew the PR script. Jonny knew the counter,

'That's a crock. A big lie. The big Hong Kong lie. The tycoons manipulate the price of land to get rich and then fool the people that we need development like this for their own good when there is plenty of brownfield land and defunct industrial space to be developed.'

'True.' Micky spoke up, his specialist area after all. *'There is plenty of land in Hong Kong. Loads of reasons to redevelop industrial and brownfield sites. But none of those reasons maximise profit. They are messy and time-consuming and difficult. Filling in the harbour is easier and keeps the whole industry rich.'*

'So, we're doomed then?'

'Absolutely. But it doesn't mean you shouldn't try Jonboy! Keeps you off the extradition barricades and getting tear gassed by James' and his

ninjas!'

'There's always hope.' Chimed in Ranald.

'Chin up old chap, you might save the world in the end.' James had a poke too. *'If we don't jail you first...'*

Jonny glowered and leant back in his chair,

'We are going to try. And if any of you fuckers' firms are involved in this then you better watch out.' He directed his threat at Micky and Ran. He hadn't considered Naz.

'No, no, my friend.' Naz raised a conspiratorial eyebrow and squeezed Jonny's wrist in solidarity. *'If any of you are involved, and you don't feed us information and help us sabotage the whole fucking rotten, crooked enterprise, then we'll hunt you down, tie you to a chair, nail your hands to the table with a 6-inch spike, pour petrol all over you, and then quietly smoke cigarettes. Gitanes.'*

Jonny was impressed - Gitanes were strong fags. Ran and Micky looked slightly uncomfortable – they were of course heavily involved in the LTV project and were now being exposed as *'evil corporate planet vandals'* in the eyes of their earnest friend. They were also wondering if Jonny was really becoming an extremist, he was pretty anti-establishment and rabidly anti-police lately, less for their rozzer mate James of course. And what was Naz up to? He was working with them on the LTV plan, he was the comms guru. Was he backing up Jonny to even up the sides, a true neutral friend, or just playing devil's advocate as usual? Naz just smiled, completely reconciled to the double game he intended to play and, relishing the friction, he fixed Jonny with an equally steely eye and added,

'Talking of smoking cigarettes? Have you quit smoking yet Jonboy, you dirty raucher?'

'Don't wanna live forever mate. Last packet bruv, last packet. Tempted,

Nick-o-Teen?' and up he got to go out to the street for a fag, Naz in tow.

Back in Black

Twenty-four hours later, James was wondering if perhaps the AC/DC – Metallica – Public Enemy retro-mix that had become popular with his unit since he introduced it, was not the right psyche-up music to play on the way to a job. Details weren't all completely clear in his mind, but the magnitude of the social media clips of his unit smashing the shit out of some terrified, screaming teenagers cowering on a stopped MTR train at Prince Edward was starkly obvious. Fenton had watched various versions non-stop for the last 15 minutes and was mouth-opened catatonic. Chewy and Fei were considerably subdued, there was no cheeky banter or macho bluster as they held their positions around the Prince Edward station.

For the third time, Inspector Fenton Wong looked at James in disbelief,

'What the fuck were they thinking boss? The move down the platform was nice, quick, surgical, shock and speed but then why the fuck did they have to go back and batter the kids, when someone is filming? Didn't they see people filming? Fuckwits.'

James was trying to work out what the impact would be. Firstly, he was extraordinarily relieved that it wasn't him in direct command down there on the platform; then he was furious that it wasn't him in direct command down on the platform as he would have done things very differently. He had detached young Inspector Tang and grizzled Sergeant Tam - Team TT or T2 as they were inevitably nicknamed. Their mission was to respond to a request for help in securing the station and mopping up the cockroaches who had fled down there. The rioters had run in panic when the Raptor squads had achieved surprise by emerging at full tilt from various side entrances to slam the youths down to the floor and arrest them. Working in snatch teams of four, the Raptors were brutally effective. It had started well.

The protesters were stunned. Everyone had become accustomed to the predictable police SOP of forming a baseline, raising flags – blue, orange, red then black, fire tear gas, advance, try and arrest the slowest, all very regular and by the book. It was James who had been pressing for a change of tactics, a change of pace. They had been losing a steady stream of casualties, nothing serious but the twists and sprains were wearing down their manpower. The protesters were getting more brazen, more violent. The thrown plastic water bottles of June had become bricks and petrol bombs by July. Now three months in and the bricks and Molotovs were routine and few hard-core rioters were being taken out. The gloves may have supposedly been off from the start, but not enough of the ringleaders and tough guys were being caught and jailed. The ponderous police charges were catching only the slow, the scared and the confused. He, and most of his young officers knew that what they really needed was to focus on the ringleaders, the fit, fast and brave ones; the ones that would make good Raptors if things had been different.

The breakthrough came when he managed to have a cup of tea with Assistant Commissioner Tang at an after-action review. How his nephew, Inspector Tang, was getting on under James' wing was the ice breaker. Truth was Teeny-Tang was a liability, but James wasn't naïve enough to say that. A group of senior officers were meeting to review what had happened at Tai Koo on the 11th and whether their tactics needed adjustment. Firing tear gas into the Kwai Fong MTR station, and causing a panicked stampede down an escalator, with widespread footage of officers battering people tumbling down the sharp, metal steps made for uncomfortable viewing. Worse perhaps was the video capture of an officer planting sticks in a young man's backpack to ensure that any conviction 'stuck' when he eventually came to court months later. Planting evidence or enhancing criminal culpability to ensure the right man was convicted was routine since the year dot but relied on the covert application of such techniques. The fact that everyone now had a mobile phone, and that police officers were not always the most situationally aware in their stress induced, riot helmeted, reflective goggled tunnel vision, made this harder to get away with.

Running battles down escalators and tear gassing people in tunnels was equally not a good image for the world's press. Prince Edward had shown the same weakness to being filmed. Beijing would be displeased. Consequently, James had a willing audience to pitch his 'precision strike' ideas to. There was considerable advantage to using the regular riot cops to fix the attention of the rioters, and critically the press observer mob, whilst the real killing stroke was being prepared elsewhere - maskirovka. Using surprise raids by Raptors that were over before the press could get there to see anything other than subdued, arrested miscreants being lined up ready for the vans, was an easy sell. Information was as important as action in the digital age. The Assistant Commissioner was convinced and gave quick, decisive direction that in future we would use the regular riot squads to prepare the battlefield, shape the enemy and fix their focus. The Raptors' intelligence assets (blokes with injuries), would dominate the high ground, integrate with airborne assets, and identify high priority targets. Small, fast, Raptor squads, protected by a screen of riot cops, would strike like lightning to neutralise and remove high value insurgents. We were moving from defensive, trench warfare to Blitzkrieg – Auftragstaktik, shock trooper time - Ausgezeichnet! James was chuffed to be off the leash and out the front, the main effort and not the reserve.

Naturally it meant that the Raptors had to move fast and act decisively. If they were to be fast, they had to use overwhelming force, apply it ruthlessly and get any 'messy business' done instantly, before they were observed, or the enemy could escape. This was the message hammered into the boys last week then, preparing them for the new era. Morale soared, this is what they wanted to do, no more pussy footing around on the shackled back foot. Now they would be laying traps, enticing the rats in, then swiftly slaughtering them. Well not slaughter literally, arresting; legally, using appropriate, proportionate and minimum force, of course. Whilst the boys were excited and fired up, the likes of James and Fenton were more concerned with the eternal challenge of running an effective surveillance and targeting system, finding the enemy then making sure the right target was taken out with minimal collateral damage. This was as challenging on the streets of Hong Kong as in any complex counter-insurgency campaign.

The first rehearsals last week, small scale, had gone well. Really well. It was also necessary to keep the press away; special press liaison teams were formed to do that with nice, blue vests and lots of mine-tape. Unnoticed by the press, unreported or captured on social media, the first five Raptor missions had succeeded in stunning a few hard-core 'fighters' who suddenly found themselves with their jaw bones grinding against tarmac and then being bundled like dazed and tasered livestock into vans and whisked down to the cells. Not a single clip appeared on social media to witness it – minimum force was assured.

With a beating, an arrest rap and the career implications evident, wolves were being turned into sheep once more. More importantly, the shock-Raptors had had a chance to practise their integration with other elements of the force, the intelligence, electronic eavesdroppers, undercover lurkers and the choppers overhead. James had also made sure he was working with a smart local commander, Inspector Tong, an ex-riot squad leader who had been in training with Fenton and had served with James when they were both young bucks chasing smugglers and I.I.'s over the hills of the border area.

Today though was a bigger affair. The classic battlefield that was Mongkok and Prince Edward. He had done his first riots here five years' ago and had been back a few times lately, so he knew the streets and alleys as well as any copper. But there were a lot of units here, a lot of commanders and a lot of egos. All of whom were watching and, with the schadenfreude of competitive career officers, not entirely delighted that the Raptors were the primus inter pares on their turf. The earlier snatch raids and surprise assaults had gone well in terms of arrests. The rioters had lived up to expectations and been given space and time to rip up pavements, vandalise the MTR, spray walls, set fires, smash windows and generally condemn and disgrace themselves for the cameras. They had then scattered and were totally routed when the hammer blow fell. It was all going so well. *'Streicholz und Benzinkanister,'* denkt James. CGTN were perfectly placed to capture the 'nasty truth of the illegal riots' for the TV.

Then a handful of blokes, black-clad ninja death-commando Raptor blokes, had gone in hard and fast exactly as they were trained to do. Clearing the rats from the sewers. Sadly, some whining, wailing civvy rat-brat had got his terrified face all over the news whilst a few of his pathetically, cringing girlfriends cowered in the doorway, positively inviting a smack for screaming like the prey they were. They were probably all brave and shouting vile abuse at his stout-hearted and long-suffering colleagues not ten minutes before; chucking bricks, smashing glass, spraying shitty slogans on the walls. Yet now, they were victims. How was that right? How could all their good work, his boys' hard work, their bright ideas, these heroes of the elite forces, suddenly be in the wrong?

Chacha Chain of Schools

Jonny wandered down the gentle hill from where he worked at the Pentecostal Fraternal Association Liang Ming Woo College of the Precious Blood, or 'The Woo School' as he called it for short. Working at 'Woo' made it sound a bit Kung Fu and a bit Scooby Doo, certainly cooler than all that other waffle. It had been an interesting first week back to school. The collective secondary school students of Hong Kong had let it be known that they were joining the 'CENSORED *of our times'* and planning *'actions.' 'Actions'* scared teachers; *'words'* or *'reflections'* or *'wonderings'* were fine – but *'actions*?' This was a huge worry for those of a theoretical persuasion.

Leaflets had been printed (KK's artwork was evident), social media was alight, the students were mobilizing. The Police were contacting schools and asking to be informed of any concerns and how many students were not at school etc. They didn't quite demand **'the names and addresses of the ring leaders'** but the inference, the expectation and the looming threat of 'white terror' was lurking deep in their carefully crafted messaging. Reports were to be filed, information passed up to the Education Bureau, teachers were going to be found responsible and Principals held accountable. Some 'hang 'em high' blues were even suggesting putting cameras in classrooms – unthinkable! Surely?

There had been major panic and considerable consternation amongst the Woo School's teachers as the leadership teams war-gamed 1001 unlikely scenarios and came up with outlandishly complicated plans for what they should do about it. The Government and Education Bureau had made 'strong pronouncements' and given 'stern warnings' that *'children were not to be corrupted by politics and should focus purely on their studies.'* Various veiled, and not so veiled, threats were made against Principals who didn't control their school and allowed *'disloyal, unsuitable'* teachers to *'mislead'* students. Teachers were warned not to take sides, to be neutral, only to talk about their academic studies or risk being *'strongly condemned'*. The collective middle-aged academic leadership of Hong Kong was having a very peculiar crisis, compounded by a mystifying mis-appreciation of what it was all about.

In the event, on the big morning of D Day, as the police started out on their 'visibility patrols,' thousands and thousands of impeccably smart young boys and girls turned out to form human chains all across Hong Kong. They hadn't darkened their clothes; they stood proudly in their bright white, pure uniforms. The enforcement machine's cogs ground to a halt as they glowered behind their visors at thirteen-year-old girls holding hands. Up from Pentecostal and Government Schools, by Woo, the chain ran up and down Perth and Dunbar streets, away up the alley and across to Sheung Shui running through the streets of Homantin's school zone, joining Heep Yan, La Salle, YWCA, St Teresa's, away to Pui Ching and down Waterloo Road past Wah Yan to the schools of Yau Ma Tei and Mong Kok. Jonny smiled as boys and girls stood next to each other held either ends of exercise books or pencil cases, too shy to hold hands with a member of the opposite ~~sex~~ gender. Wild revolutionaries these youths, the teachers and Government were right to panic!

The nearby International school's teachers turned out en-masse to 'keep their students safe and make sure they weren't intimidated.' Jonny smiled some more. Good people but how could such a beautiful demonstration of sweet school kids be scary? The international school kids didn't turn out though. They smiled and were as polite as they had been bred to be, but these were the future elite, the sons and daughters of bankers and government officials, too focused on getting to an Ivy League university and comfortably assured of their privileged place in society to get bothered by local affairs. The private schools were aloof from politics.

Then, five minutes before lessons started, ten thousand teenagers gently said goodbye to their *'radical comrades'* and stepped off smartly to first lesson. They had made their point with poise and grace, and now were going to study, for their future, which the Government was quite clearly incapable of preparing for them as nobody could afford a flat and most had to live with their mum until at least their thirties. Their *'rebellious action'* had utterly outclassed their elders' panicky behaviour. Following behind the last kids as they went in through the gates, Jonny looked a-glance at his colleague, Ivy the Chinese teacher from the Mainland. She was trying to remain dignified, but she had tears rolling down her cheeks. *'I am so proud of them. It's so important. They don't understand how important this is, but we Chinese do.'* Jonny was determined not to show any weakness, but inside he was filled with mawkish admiration for a generation that made his own look brutish, shallow and cruel. He felt a little ashamed just for being an adult.

The only real drama for the adults that week had come when his Principal had removed the notes and messages on the School's 'Lennon Wall.' The act was provocative for sure, probably motivated by a combination of a desire to show patriotic control, strong discipline and loyalty to the Bureau, the Government and the Motherland. Loyalty to the cause of Correct Education itself. The School had recently started singing the National Anthem in assemblies and a few of the bulled-boots Boys Brigade types competed for the honour of raising the national flag (China, not Hong Kong) every morning. Then again, maybe the Principal just thought the Lennon Wall made the place look untidy, which it did a bit. Anyhow, a forty strong group of masked alumni had swiftly arrived at the School gates and demanded, politely but firmly, an explanation from the Principal.

'I can see how cultural revolutions start.' thought Jonny as he watched the Principal, standing stock still, hands resting on an umbrella handle, planted firmly into the ground between his legs. The umbrella seemed to act as an anchor that, if removed, would see him spin away up into the air like a burning, candle lantern. Ironic that the umbrella was the symbol of the Democratic youths, not their dictatorial elders. The Principal's usual arrogance and confidence were manifestly missing. He was as stubborn as ever, but clearly intimidated by the protesting crowd, all of whom knew what it was like to be cowed and scolded by him from when they were students – but not now. They were bigger, tougher and angrier now. He was the one who couldn't meet a gaze eye-to-eye, he was the one now experiencing what it was to be glared at and berated by one in power. He was getting the education today.

At the end of an unremarkable day, as he strolled downhill, Jonny let the events of the week drift and settle through his mind. He wasn't aware of it, but his lips moved as he talked to himself – another crazy gweilo. The mixture of daydreaming and reflecting was part of his subconscious de-stressing routine, tidying up to achieve the eternal sunshine of the spotless mind; a process about to be lubricated and polished up with a liberal application of ale, scoff and his old mate's company on their 'last Friday of the month' appointment. Actually, it was the first Friday of the month today as summer holidays had caused a postponement, but the fact that the boys had managed to keep their routine going for so many years was impressive. *'Once a month is not asking too much for a beer with my mates darling'* negotiations with other halves had prevailed. Jonny no longer had another half. He was already going into the alley by Cheong Ming building when he suddenly came back to consciousness in the present.

The roast chestnut man was under the Moko bridge, vigorously shoveling his coals to billow the sweet, fragrant smoke up into the air which then drifted right the way up to Peace and Victory avenues, even overpowering the sooty, stench of diesel from Kowloon's filthy buses. He wondered whether the chestnut smell was why the homeless girl had staked out her pitch there, as opposed to any other underpass. She was there today, carefully opening a rice box, laid on a tablecloth of a plastic bag, sitting cross legged on her quilts and blankets bed. At first, he didn't understand why, if you could go live on a quiet, wooded slope or out in the hills, why she would have chosen to squat in a castrophonous underpass in one of the busiest, noisiest and stressful streets in town; the buses, the ambulances, the constant bip-bip-bip of the crossing signal. Then, as he passed by every day, he sometimes noticed various people stop and give her food and a little acknowledgement. She got fed and wasn't invisible. He always wanted to stop and talk to her himself, but she never returned his gaze, and maybe she spoke no English, and what exactly could he say? So, he cared inside but did nothing. Every day. He knew that he was failing, but the lights had changed, and he had somewhere to go so he better hurry across McPherson as this was a really slow crossing.

To avoid the crowds and the noise, he dog-legged left as usual, slipped into the alleyway by the exchange booth and cut across Hak Po through the expensive cars, double parked, for their turn in the cheap garages that inhabited this street. Hong Kong always clustered things. He had passed through an area where every second shop was a pet shop, now he was in the car area, next the trainers and tat, before crossing over Nathan Road to a world of bathroom fitters, tools and hardware outlets. He stopped by the back wall of the new building, the flashy looking 'Beacon' (hotel or apartments, he had no idea, they all looked the same), and took a lean by the hanging rattrap where one could stare up at higgledy-piggledy cascade of washing lines. He got his mobile out of his pocket and then had to bend down and retrieve his lock-knife that came out with the phone and landed in the stinky, white-gunky stained gutter. What was that white shit? Washing machine effluent?

He pocketed his knife, wiped his fingers on his bum-pockets and thought about a Telegram but then decided, sod it, let's do it the old-fashioned way, and made Nazeem's telephone ring. He had no idea but Naz had set the 'Pinball' ring tone for Jonny and the boys; reminded him of old times and good pubs.

'Alright mucker, you downstairs?'

'There in five'

'Right O, I shall be down in a sec, just doing my lippy.'

Good thought Jonny, time for a crafty smoke before he gets down here, and he leant back against the new building wall and wondered just who was purportedly offering sex on the number graffitied on the wall and why someone else was looking to rent out an apartment by advertising with a sticky note in a Mongkok back alley? 92288808 was the number to call for a rental of $8800; 92263203 sold something else and he couldn't read the characters but for $3800 he could get a 90ft 2 bed on the 6th floor (no lift) or pay an extra $700 for 150 square foot in Shum Shui Po on the 7ft floor – again 'no lift'. That would get a bit tiresome, no matter how fit you fancied getting. That is a lot of money for a space the size of a London garage he thought; and the neighbours were likely to be a little rough round the edges and noisy at night. They might be workers at the Fruit Market, the legendary Goh Laan, who started shift at 4 in the morning and really were not going to give a toss how much noise they made. Hong Kong people are immune to noise. For Jonny, it was torture. The whine of an electric alarm clock or far away air-con bothered him.

Next to the real estate adverts were some new black-painted protest stencils; a gas mask and an umbrella each with the word 'resist' through them were new, as was *'Respect Existence or Expect Resistance'.* He liked that. He took a photo to show KK. Perhaps he could weave that into a lesson as well. Another stencil had reversed and embedded the word 'love' into R*evol*ution. Should he do a lesson on slogans? That would be cool, the kids would love it. It would of course be a bit revolutionary; he might be deemed a 'deviant' and get purged. He would, at the minimum, be *'strongly condemned'* and *'sternly warned'* by the Principal and perhaps reported to the Education Bureau. Maybe even have his visa cancelled and deported like that bloke from the FCC. Fired – chau yau yue like fried squid. If the 'System' found about it, of course. The kids wouldn't grass him up, but a parent might. Worth a ponder, could be a great lesson…

And that was time up, cigarette done, time to meet the Sherazi boy and head for the RV – Mr Wong's. Or rather, as Google Maps has it *'Ching Chong Cock n Ball Dungeon'* – one of the greatest jokes ever snuck into a map database ever.

Dungeons and Dragons

The *'Ching Chong Cock n Ball Dungeon'* was far from being the S&M club that Google Maps suggested it might be. In fact, everyone called it *'Mr Wong's'* and it was a cheap daai-paai-dong that served endless plates of trashy, cliched but tasty and filling Cantonese dishes. All the 'gweilos' favourite rubbish dishes were there; you didn't get a menu or order, you were just told to sit down by one of the bolshy staff who then hurled, dumped or abandoned dishes of woo-lo yuk (sweet and sour pork), chaau faahn (egg fried rice), chicken chow mein, chop suey and, the really quite spectacular, deep-fried and peppery calamari – chau yau yue. Even better than you got at the Hong Kong Garden in Peckham.

Nobody really knew why the place had the kinky themed name on Google maps, or why it was colloquially *'Mr Wong's'* as the red, Chinese letters above the door announced it as *'Recreation Restaurant,'* but no gweilo could ever read that. There was a stall next door, by the swirling, spiral walkway, where an ostentatiously smart eighty-year-old man sold bottles of strange, ancient Chinese herbal concoctions under the shop sign of a caricatured, pillbox hatted, cue-haired, white socked and black-slippered, sneezing Hong Kong legend called Old Master Q – he was invented by a Mr Wong. Perhaps the author owned the place? Maybe that was it? Nobody really knew. That was the charm.

'Ah, the Local. The boys are going to love it here.'

Jonny and Naz grinned at each other in anticipation of their mates' reaction. This was their 'hood. James of the Force might have been a Pukka Army Officer's son but as a Hong Kong cop he knew all the dives and alleyways and relished the seedy side of town; it was where he hunted after all. James was going to be comfy here, but the other two were from the swanky stratosphere of society: Ranald the banker from an auspiciously, stinking rich dynasty of tycoons and Micky Two-Dads, a future Taipan from old Hong Kong money whose property empire included many of the buildings they had just walked past to get here.

They may pretend to be 'down to earth' and thought their own back-packing japes were fabulously authentic but, in reality, were used to somewhere a trifle plusher; and they were going to be terrified of catching something un-gentlemanly. Micky though would be quite excited by the close proximity of Portland Street and its seedy delights, for probably no more than $500 for an hour, where there was a far higher chance of catching something un-gentlemanly.

James arrived first, was welcomed by the manager as if he owned the place (which one of Naz's uncles secretly did, or at least the block that ran along this side of the market on Shantung Street) and slid effortlessly into a chair.

'Good choice.'

His level of comfort and totally 'non-plussed' insouciance left Jonny a little deflated. However, a phone call from Ranald, stood with Micky on the street outside, cheered them right up.

'I am at the bloody address you sent, but all there is, is some shitty butchers, some grubby freezer shop, two dogs pissing, and a whole street load of crap! And what the ...'

Micky had got distracted from looking for the restaurant and was watching a middle-aged woman in leggings and a purple puffer jacket (it was 28 degrees with 90% humidity), intently staring at, and then intermittently shaking a large, clear plastic bag full of rubbish, mostly plastic bottles, lying by the roadside. Is she looking for something or just mental? There was a lot of mental around these days; he saw two tramps shagging last time he walked through Mongkok, right against the MTR wall. Nobody batted an eyelid. If he did catch the MTR with the proles, then inevitably somebody would be talking to themselves. He was more an Uber man himself, or roaring about on his big, butch bike. The self-talkers would not be like loud, obnoxious, Bluetooth man having a 'business' conversation and trying to show off to everyone that he had a job. The quietly nuts were normally an introverted, conservative, respectable looking type, one that could be found regularly in church, soundlessly mouthing the words of the inner monologue in their head with no idea that their imaginary conversation was being played out all over their face. Quietly and respectfully mental rather than the raving, shouting type of mental one found under a bridge in London or Glasgow.

Micky waved at Ranald to get his attention. The posh boys were definitely in the right place, stood next to the rubbish pile and the various baskets, trays, polystyrene boxes, crates and containers that keep a fresh food logistic chain going. A blue, flaky rusted truck was blocking their view of Mr Wong's – although they wouldn't have dreamed of walking in there even if they could see it. Ranald could read Chinese of course, but the sign said, *'Recreation Restaurant,'* not *'Mr Wong's.'* They had already walked round the entire, filthy block in consternation. The block was configured around a very stinky council refuse centre, and they found nothing but shopkeepers hosing down their pavements, idling vans and chunky goldy-looking chained, triad boys smoking cigarettes and looking at their phones.

On the far side, the Canton Road market was packing up. This was Canton Road, Mongkok; not Canton Road, Tsim Sha Tsui. Different world, mate. This was a proper Old Canton Road with a seventy-five-year-old stall holder doing a bit of eye-burningly bright soldering on his knees on the pavement, next to a sixty-eight-year-old lady stacking polystyrene chests up five high and obscuring the graffiti tag 'Hiding Myself'. If the artist had actually meant for that to happen, they were indeed an inspired street artist. A rather less inspired artist had sprayed 'Fuck the PoPo' in English nearby. The two, tailored, coiffed, city boys were feeling distinctly out-of-place. They'd loosened their ties.

'I'll go get 'em' said Naz and glided smoothly through the carnage of waiters balancing dishes on forearms, passed six shouting Slovakian mature students and a table of nervous looking clean-cut Americans who might have gone a bit too edgy to assimilate everything with quite the gusto that the robust Slovaks were demonstrating. Naz appeared

like a genie in front of Ranald and Micky and almost made Ranald drop his phone in shock.

'Follow me gentlemen.' his soft, Oxford educated tones seemed perfectly matched to his composure and their discomfort,

'Welcome to my ghetto!'

Naz had sized up their discomfort in a heartbeat and was enjoying their irritation hugely. They were visibly annoyed by poverty. They were far too rich to feel anything else.

'Where did you pop out from? You're like fucking Mr Benn you are!' Micky accused.

'You mean the Shopkeeper.'

'What?'

'The Shopkeeper appears. When Mr Benn needs him.'

'The only thing you'd sell is carpets.' Micky spread his hands, palms up and wobbled his head, Ran joined in grinning.

'Magic ones Sir?'

Naz either embraced or ignored the traditionally, casual racism depending on his mood. He led them round the rusty truck and into the maelstrom of 'Wong's Recreational Cock n Ball Dungeon', to be greeted by a boisterous roar of welcome from James and Jonny.

'Yeeay! Didn't get mugged then? Have a seat and I'll have our man bring the wine list. Until that arrives, we are mostly going to be drinking 'Pirates' beer – it is a fine ale, Ahr Harr!'

'Piece of eight m hearties! Eighty dollars all you can eat – and drink!'

'This place is ghastly.' opined Ranald, Micky hovered, unwilling to park his expensive strides on a sticky, grubby, plastic stool.

OriOccidental Origins

They did the obligatory quick round robin of everybody's summer holidays: Ranald – The Shangri La in Bali, just 4 days, very busy; Micky – the Hamptons with an old Cornell chum and a yacht in St Lucia, 3 weeks; Naz – Canada, mountain biking, rafting and horse riding for 4 weeks; Jonny – 4 weeks working at a summer school for under-privileged kids in Shum Shui Po plus 3 days camping in Sai Kung. James complained that he had been working overtime the entire summer due to the protests – they collectively expressed zero sympathy and decided James should have to buy double rounds on account of profiteering from The Revolution.

There then followed a brief prediction for the Rugby World Cup, each sticking to their own traditional teams with Ranald getting the traditional barrage of abuse for being 'faux Scottish.' Other than his dad, he was quite possibly the only Chinese man in Hong Kong who would choose to support Scotland for rugby (as opposed to New Zealand or Australia who generally win, in the same way Manchester United, Liverpool or Barcelona are quite so popular for football). Ranald, as suggested by the fact that he was given the gweilo friendly moniker 'Ranald,' was the son of a Scotland obsessed father, Wallace Chen. Ranald's Chinese names were Tsu Wen, a subtle nod to the famous financier T.V Soong – daddy Wallace thought things through you know. As one may gather from 'Wallace', Ran's dad was in turn the son of a financier whose great friendship with a distinguished police officer called Duncan William MacIntosh in the forties and fifties had led to him calling his son after the legendary Scottish hero William Wallace (Duncan or William would have been too obvious, and too sycophantic a tribute to his colleague).

Grandfather Chen's friendship with Duncan MacIntosh had been based on mutual respect, working together to 'clean up' a lot of Hong Kong after the war. His efforts were helped immeasurably by the prestige of Grandfather Chen's wartime resistance exploits with the East River Column fighting the Japanese. This courage, and a sharp mind, had seen Grandfather Chen build up a vast fortune and business empire with a close affinity to the British establishment. He was aided in his entrepreneurship by Party Pioneer Notable and Mayor Great Grandfather Chen over the border and Loyal Comrade Customs Official Great Uncle Chen on the border. Being friends with the ruling British and the soon-to-be all-powerful Communists was a most auspicious alignment of connections for a business enterprise.

Wallace eventually became a patron of the Police Pipes and Drums Band and so Ranald was duly sent off to St Andrew's University to continue the family tradition of being honorary Scots. Consequently, Ranald felt a great sense of entitlement to wear a MacIntosh tartan kilt for dinner nights and he was a stalwart of Hong Kong Scottish Rugby Club – admired and feted there, for his family history as well as the sponsorship money he bestowed at regular intervals. He was a proud Scot and would burr his 'r's' and throw in 'wee blethers and bahoochies' to conversation, insisting on the distinction between 'smirr' and 'dreichy' with conviction. The rest of the lads naturally found this hilarious. By contrast, Jonny 'English' was born on a council estate in Peckham. He had no idea who his great grandfather had been.

Mr Wong's Manifesto

Naz seized upon a pause to kindly shift the focus from Ranald's heritage, and avoid the next inevitable topic which was his own (A Canadian-Pakistani from a 160-year Hong Kong dynasty begun by an enterprising Punjabi Havildar in 1860). After sport, holidays and property prices, there was no way anyone could meet in Hong Kong and not discuss the latest protest developments so Naz started off, from a carefully sited, heavily sand-bagged, neutrally provocative position.

'Anyone get arrested or fired over the summer then?'

Micky leant back and wafted his hands, *'Woooh. I'm not saying anything. Radio silence. Look at Cathay, people getting fired for their Facebook comments and private opinions. Don't tell 'em your name Pike!'*

Naz took up the thread, *'The Cathay Chairman resigned – apparently he was told by the Chinese to give a list of all 'anti-China' staff; he gave them a list with one name on it – his own.'*

'Good lad.' Jonny and James admired the integrity. Micky wasn't impressed,

'Yeah, but unemployed good lad. Nobody can say anything now or you get fired. Keep your head down and your mouth shut until it all blows over.'

'True boys, don't put anything on Facebook. You don't look right; you'll be up against the wall!' Naz warned.

Jonny added, *'Yep, schools are the same. Teachers are being warned to say nothing. How can we say nothing? It's worrying all the kids and they wanna talk about it.'*

Jonny continued indignantly, *'Sod all that keeping your head down. Self-censorship is where it starts. That's why everyone started wearing masks because they are terrified of being disappeared sometime in the future. Even the cops all wear masks. I ain't wearing a mask,'*

He puffed himself up with a smile and purposefully false bravado *'I'll fight the fuckin' lot of 'em! You'll never take me alive copper!'* He grinned at James and raised his fists in jest. James laughed and pointed in faux-sternity,

'Your fighting days are well over, fat boy!'

All laughed and looked at their own bellies, then there was an almost audible sigh of despair. It's tough getting to 40; closing on 50 is tragically deflating – or rather inflating when it comes to waistlines. Ranald blurted out what was on everyone's mind.

'So, what do we think about Prince Edward? Did they really kill anyone? I think it's probably exaggerated nonsense.'

The mood sobered. Everybody paused. Nobody was going to shoot from the hip on this one. This was important. This was a pivotal moment in the Hong Kong protests, for sure. More importantly for them, their friend James commanded in the Police Tactical Unit, one of whose squads had carried out the 'suppression operation' in the MTR station just ten minutes' walk from where they caroused. The week before, on the 31st August 2019, Raptors had been filmed moving fast and furious through a static MTR train, smashing the heads and bodies of young people there, youngsters who seemingly were offering no resistance or fighting back. There had been some trouble out on the streets earlier, but the footage captured a rout, and the police mopped up brutally. Already the figures '831' were being graffitied all over town, joining the '721' accusations of police collusion with Triad thuggery at Yuen Long back in July. James and his team had been dwelling on the after-action review ever since.

Micky was first into the ring, *'The rumours are ridiculous; nobody was killed, and no bodies were dumped.'* He nodded vigorously at James, expecting a pat on the back for defending his friend.

Naz started with the conspiracy theory, *'Then why did they move the wounded by train to other stations? Where is the CCTV? Why did the filth not allow the medics in?'*

Jonny conspired further, *'And why did they have to beat the kids up so savagely in the first place? Those Raptors were out of control, they all think they're terminators.'* He looked at James, hoping for something in return, not goading with any real spite or malice, just hoping for a rational explanation and the other side of the story.

Micky held his ground, *'You didn't see what happened before. You only see the edited bits from the left-wing fake news sites.'*

Jonny decided that James was going to keep shtum and focused on Micky, his traditional opponent, *'So? What could have happened before that, that college kids deserved a full-on, fucking beating when they're sat screaming and scared on the MTR?'*

Micky was resolute, *'They could have been beating up other people, throwing bricks at the cops, burning shops. They are smashing up stuff for no reason. They've got patrol bombs – would you want a petrol bomb thrown at you?'*

'Actually, I have had quite a few petrol bombs thrown at me.' Jonny played his Army card which normally gave him in a distinct advantage in any discussion involving violence.

'But that doesn't matter. It is a policeman's job to remain calm, de-escalate situations, only apply minimum force. Those boys were well out of control. There were no molotovs down at that tube station.'

'I hope they weren't your lot.' Naz looked at James. They all silently hoped but doubted that. James said nothing, just looked calm and interested as to what their take on it was. The Force had not yet put out an explanation that anybody believed. Whatever the truth was, he had little to add.

Jonny, as ever, contrarywised, *'I hope they were your lads so you can smash 'em a month's wages, put 'em on Christmas guard duty and give 'em a ballistic bollocking. The officers need to get a grip of their fuckin' boys, they are getting totally out of order and it will massively backfire in the long run. Already most people have turned against the Popo. You can't police without consent and the cops are not above the law themselves.'* Jonny was at pains not to direct his comments straight at James and shifted to Micky with his eyes halfway through his tirade.

Ranald was equally resolute, *'You can't let hooligans get away with smashing the place up and stopping decent people getting to work. Look at the chaos they caused disrupting traffic and up the airport. Business will pay the price. Hong Kong's reputation will suffer. Capital will leave, investment fall and confidence collapse. We need a secure and stable city or the very people rioting will lose their jobs. Then where will they be? It's self-destruction.'*

'Exactly.' agreed Micky, *'The police need to go in hard. Sort out the ring leaders, arrest the yobs and make sure people behave themselves. We can't let them get away with all this vandalism. Did you see the bricks torn up down the road back there? The barriers are gone, the traffic lights are smashed, traffic is a nightmare.'*

'We burn, you burn with us.' Jonny was defiant. Micky was dismissive,

'Nihilistic bollox.'

'Hunger Games bollox.' Jonny replied, as an English teacher, correct referencing was important to him. Jonny was set firm,

'Still never an excuse to batter people. It will make things worse. The searches and arrests breed bitter resentment. If you unfairly arrest a 15-year-old, they will hate the police for the rest of their lives. Your principles and sense of fairness are acute as a teenager. I know, I have to teach the little monsters!'

'Absolutely matey. And every police abuse is on social media and the

more you see, the angrier you get.' Naz was calm but pointed.

Ranald continued to defend the police and the silent James, *'But you don't see the twenty good cops doing the right thing, you just always see the one or two having a shit day and losing it.'*

Naz was firm in dismissing Ranald's plea, *'Doesn't matter. That is always going to be the way. Good cops aren't news. Normal is boring. We will always only see the extremists and so we will all think that everyone is an extremist. Same but in reverse for the China press.'*

James silently communicated agreement with Naz, then looked at Ranald with gratitude, but still said nothing. Jonny realised that his police mate was uncomfortable, had probably had a shit week, and really didn't want to have this conversation right now. He felt bad and put his hand softly on James' arm in apology. It was accepted with a nod. Naz tried to rebuild the bridge,

'That is exactly what has happened here, and in the States and UK. There is no intelligent middle ground anymore. Everyone is a bubble of their own prejudice. Distorted mainstream media owned by prejudiced tycoons and rabid, unregulated social media echo chambers.'

'Except us, the Bohemian intelligentsia, of course. I still put up with you even though you are fascist, right-wing, banking toff Ran! Monetarily rich, morally bankrupt!' Jonny grinned.

'Thank you, Trotsky! It's nice that you and comrade Nazanista haven't put me and Micky up against the wall just yet.'

Micky laughed,

'Although they are trying to fuckin' poison us bringing us to this dump, Damps!'

Eastern Heretics

'I love that place.' Said Jonny to Ranald as they left.

'I have to admit, it certainly ticks the value for money box, and the food wasn't entirely ghastly.'

Micky's head appeared between them, his arms resting heavily on their shoulders, *'Indeed, indeed but can we pleeease now go somewhere I don't feel that I need to shower afterwards?'*

'You sure Micky?' asked James, one eyebrow arched, *'Behold to my left,'* he had spun around and was walking backwards, *'The delights of Portland Street, where one is expected to shower both before, during and afterwards!'* and he waved his arm down towards the shabby but colourful road that, between metal shops and work clothing outfitters, had a fabulously seedy offering of 'foot' massages amid pink and red lights.

'Ah. In for a penny, in for a pound then hey?'

'You'll need a bit more than a pound Micky, be generous son, you can afford it!'

'Grubby men. I shall wait for you in TAP.' Jonny wasn't playing that game.

Jonny wasn't one for the brothels; he had been there as a youth, done that, got the t-shirt, an itchy but minor STD and wasn't ever going back. He had also developed morals and a conscience over a lifetime of seeing the nasty exploitation all across the world. Several worthy attempts to change his mates' behaviour had been met with a wall of male incredulity that seemed as if their birthright was being challenged. Which it was. The oldest profession had to be respected, the 'gentlemen' insisted.

'TAP for me too. Double tap, boom boom.' Naz was equally unimpressed with such behaviour, for similar moral reasons, a little dash of his wider family's faith-based puritanism and the fact that he was secretly gay. Deeply, secretly gay. He wasn't even quite sure himself and he was way beyond forty. For such an incredibly bright man, he couldn't understand how he couldn't understand his own basic desires. They fuck you up your mum and dad apparently. Your Imam doesn't help a great deal either.

Thus, three boisterous roister-doisterers went South, like nervous teenage boys they once were, to explore the shady doors and dodgy staircases of backstreets Mongkok. The two noble abstainers walked to the MTR, intending to go under Nathan Road but the entry by Jollibee was metal shuttered and stained black by fires. The underpass was closed for repair following some extensive vandalism that the 'Empty R' had been subjected to. The MTR company was now labelled an instrument of state oppression thanks to its practice of closing down stations to restrict protest movements and its complicit Omerta on the Yuen Long and Prince Edward beatings.

That left Naz and Jonny briefly scoffing and scowling at the riot cops loitering on Nathan Road trying to look invincible, before the two of them headed off to a hipster bar a few blocks away. The trendy craft-beer joint had calmed down after the usual 6-9 o'clock cramming and they got themselves a couple of stools up against the window, looking out onto Hak Po Street and its dark array of diverse denizens. They chose each other's beer, a *'Fuck Art, The Heathens Are Coming'* for Jonny to honour his squaddie past, and an *'Eastern Heretic'* for Naz for being a rubbish Muslim.

'Cheers!'

'So, how's the consultancy gig going?' Jonny was never entirely sure what Naz actually did. Naz normally liked to keep it that way. Naz had plenty of dark secrets that came from a bright place.

'It's OK. I am on a construction slash government job. ELM or Lantau Tomorrow Vision it's called. We are doing the comms brief as well as the scheduling.'

'Fuck off! Really? That bat-shit plan to pour trillions of dollars into the harbor and waste all of Hong Kong's money on posh flats for Mainlanders, destroying the environment and bringing us all completely under Beijing's control at one evil stroke? You are Satan.'

'Oh, you've heard of it? Most people haven't a clue.'

'Heard if it, mate I've protested against it. Been on a march, written letters, I even went to Legco for the public consultation farce.' It had been discussed the month before, but the boys' liberally lubricated pub banter went in one ear and out the other. Besides, Naz had spoken against the project on that occasion, despite working hand-in-glove with Ranald and Micky to promote it. Consequently, Naz knew all the arguments for and against in great detail. Professionally he remained beautifully balanced atop the fence so that he could design the messaging to influence, persuade and convince any designated targeted audience of reception. Personally, he thought it another tycoon inspired swindle that meshed nicely with the politician's ulterior motives. Naz feigned ignorance and asked Jonny about the Legco consultations,

'How was that? Did you feel heard?'

'We each had three minutes, a big clock ticking down to keep you under pressure, and all the social workers and greens and university people said it was an awful idea whilst all the construction industry patsys said it was a great idea. Some of them had clearly been paid to be there, one bloke barely spoke Cantonese and read from a script. Farce. Didn't matter what we said. The 'Committee' sat on the other side read their emails and the China Daily and then one of the chubby farts said something arrogant and pre-prepared about us not understanding serious matters then off they fucked for tea and cigars. Waste of time.'

Naz knew that Legco consultations were simply box-ticking

smokescreens designed to demonstrate that the people had been consulted and politicians listened and reflected. One of the charades of Hong Kong's pseudo-democracy. Naz had no mood this evening to string Jonny along with any of his carefully crafted PR lines-to-take,

'Yep. It's going ahead whatever. Beijing wants it, it will happen. Like that pointless bridge poised like a noose around Hong Kong's throat. Can bring a lot of limousines or tanks across that bridge depending on whether it's a business day or a patriotic day.'

'So, you don't agree with it either?' Jonny respected Nazeem's intellect and ability to remain non-partisan and objective on most issues. Nazeem was in an honest mood,

'No. Nobody does. They tried to sell it first as a money-making scheme. We wrote briefs on how much profit land sales would make for the government. Then everyone got a bit moral because of the 'housing crisis.' Now of course, everyone with half-a-brain – which is a tiny minority - knows the housing crisis is manufactured between the big developers and the Government; there is enough land, it is just hoarded by the billionaires. So, the main angle now is to pretend it is about 'houses for the common people' and then lots of 'smart, tekky greenwash' to make like we are Singapore and shut the hippies up.'

'I'm a hippy. I don't want to shut up. So, if you think it's bollocks, why are you doing it?'

'It is my job. Pays the mortgage mate.'

'You sell out. And you ain't got a mortgage, you own half of Kowloon Tong.'

'Less than 2 per cent in reality. Anyway, thanks for that, big, white, English teacher earning twice what a local earns and doing half the hours.'

'Ow. Harsh but fair. Brown millionaire plays the colonial guilt card and

trumps white chav! I'm sure I do the hours though. You want to see my marking pile mate!'

A shiny penny finally dropped in Jonny's head. *'We talked about the LTV at the pub quiz – you didn't say anything about working on it then.'*

'Didn't seem the right time. And you threatened to set us on fire. Psycho boy!'

'That was you! That was definitely you!'

'Oh yeah. But you would have actually done it. At least aided and abetted a known felon.'

They both thought for a second, Jonny having been involuntarily distracted by a lot of leg revealed from a very short skirt passing by on the street outside. Gone grey, but still just a boy.

'Chicks are great!' he grinned. Naz laughed.

'You are far too fat, old and ugly and I thought the whole hashtag metoo thing was all the rage with you right-on teachers.'

'Yeah. I feel the guilt, but I can't help but notice a pretty girl mate. Rude not to. At least I am not like those creatures back there on Portland street being despicable.'

'True. They will justify it as supporting the local economy and the inevitable price of capitalism.' Naz paused and visibly changed his face as he shifted thoughts and gear.

'They could be worse though, they could be working on LTV too...'

Jonny gave a physical little twitch, raised his eyebrows and dropped his jaw a little. Naz didn't need to elaborate; Jonny got it. Micky and Ran – dark side. No shock there, they were his mates but the establishment after all. Naz looked thoughtful then switched tack, sharply,

'Mate, I think I'm lost. Wasting my life. None of us know how much time

we have left, and I just think that I am wasting it. I used to do meaningful stuff, now I am peddling lies I don't believe in. Philosophy on a cereal box is what I do. I am part of the great Satan. How did that happen?'

'I know what you mean Naz. The Army was often shit, hard work and, let's be honest, most every op we did was a failure in the long run, but at least we tried. It meant something. Most of the time. Now, I am being restricted in what I teach more-and-more every day. They might as well replace us teachers with robots. Maybe they'd produce more data for the grown-ups to mis-interpret – the Principal would love it. Data, data, data, results, results, results and a prescriptive, dull, curriculum to brainwash the little marching patriots. The more they say creative and innovative, the more they mean conservative and prescribed. It is soul destroying. The kids are dying inside. They are too bright to believe the lies, too scared to rebel.'

Naz considered the comment on operational failures that Jonny had been involved in,

'Maybe Ireland and the Balkans worked out – maybe not yet. I don't know what you lot were doing in Iraq.'

'Not our call mate, the Yanks and Blair are to blame for that. Afghanistan was worth a punt. Didn't work because we fucked off too early, but it was getting somewhere before the politicians killed it. Kids were going to school at least. Taliban would've stopped that by now. Back to the middle ages. Normal service resumed.'

Naz was silent. Was now the time to reveal to Jonny that he was also in Afghanistan? He half-thought that Jonny knew. Of all of them, Jonny was the one that Naz confided in and spoke about such things in a way he never did with the others, the 'civvies' he had been at school with. Not even James the cop. Too many years of being a spook held his tongue, although he desperately wanted to confide in his friend, to tell him what he had seen and done, to share the intense experience, reduce the stress. How many times have they told us that it's good to talk, to deal with PTSD, to look after your mental health? Unless you were MI6 apparently. Then you had to stew in your own secret little mind-prison. How very Sherlock. So, he made another choice. The opposite choice. Dry your eyes time.

'The 'Stahn. Bore off soldier boy! You oppressed my Taliban brothers, infidel! Now my brothers and sisters are free!' He used his full-on comedy Pashtun accent to deliver it.

Jonny shot back with what he could remember of Pashto, *'Waderega!'* (Stop*!)*

Naz came back, *'Tersha!' (*Move!)

'Chup sha! Aaram sha!' (Quiet! Calm down.)

'Delta raasha! (Come here!)

'Wasla dee paramzaka kegda. Khaberay meh kawah.' (Put your weapons down. Stop talking). Naz was deliberately not hiding his fluency.

'Wah, I can't remember any. What was 'wait here?'

'Delta woesah.'

'Don't move?'

'Harahkat ma cowa.' Then Naz added *'Wadarega Yah da-well-um.'*

'Oh yeah! Stop or I fire. Tashakor'

'Manana, Ha kala rashay.'

Jonny pursed his lips, Naz was very comfortable in Pashto. Naz was very comfortable talking about weapons, tactics, crowd control, tech, international politics, and fit as ten men. He also used words and terminology that were military. There was no way that he had really spent the late nineties and noughties working for a *'multinational import/export firm, wheeling and dealing, ducking and diving, swerving and skiving...'* as he had always told any of them when they had met up in London or Hong Kong.

In the Nineties, Jonny had bumped into Naz in Thessaloniki, just south of Kosovo, where Jonny was working and Naz said he was on holiday, alone, to visit Alexander the Great's tomb – who goes on holiday there, and alone? Again, they had crossed paths in a pizzeria in Cheltenham. Naz was sat with a bunch of people who looked like IT geeks, not international wheeler dealers. His fellow diners were white folk whereas Naz's business network was supposedly entirely south Asian, mostly Muslim or at least Indian or Sri Lankan. These pasty-looking dudes were clearly not Naz's usual crowd.

But the memory that now flashed up front and centre of Jonny's brain was that day in Helmand, driving through the Bari Gul Bazaar, bouncing along in the turret of his Ridgeback armoured wagon. The Bazaar was actually a little village, just to the west of the Green Zone and twenty minutes out from Forward Operating Base Pimon – manfully named after the mongoose in a Disney cartoon. The Bazaar was allegedly a notorious Taliban trading post and Jonny's unit had driven a small, 20-wagon combat logistic patrol straight through the middle of it under a blanket of surveillance assets to see what reaction they provoked.

It was early days in their tour and the patrol were on their way home to Camp Bastion having done all their deliveries. They were nervous, but excited, at the thought of a confrontation on the way back – they hadn't fired a shot or hit an IED yet (that would change) so were still pretty gung-ho. In the event, nothing kinetic happened. A DROPS truck got bogged in for a bit about 5kms later, but nothing untoward or interesting happened and they got in for de-kitting and showers with no dramas. The ISTAR assets though, unseen up in the sky, made some very illuminating observations of motorbike trails and intercepted comms that provided a couple of start points that led to arrests and cache finds a month or so later.

One thing about that little diversion had bugged Jonny. He was in Whiskey 1, lead Ridgeback, and as he traversed his turret about, eying up all the shady, turbaned characters glaring in disbelief that they would have the effrontery to drive through 'their territory', one Talib stared straight into his eyes, wide-eyed and open mouthed. He held his gaze for just a second, then tugged his black scarf over his nose and mouth, but his eyes never left him, and he swore the Talib grinned. He could have sworn that he was looking at an astonished, bearded Naz. Then he laughed to himself, blamed it on tiredness, and went back to looking for ground-sign and IEDs whilst tracking the motorbikes that had started zipping around the countryside. He had dismissed it consciously as ridiculous; but sub-consciously that memory was carved sharply into his brain. And right now, in a tiny bar in Mongkok, he knew.

'I didn't know you spoke Pashto. I thought you just did Punjabi and Urdu?'

'Urdu and French of course, I'm quite the windswept and interesting, international man of mystery and adventure old boy.'

'Yeah, but not Pashto.'

'They are all related. We're neighbours. I have business contacts, for carpets.'

They looked at each other.

'You were in Afghan, weren't you?'

'Yes.'

'And you never fucking said. Ten years. Never a word.'

'No.'

'You're a fucking sneaky-beaky wanker, aren't you?'

'I was. So now I am Ex-spook. A has-been, used-to-be, faded ghost boy,

like you gweilo.'

'I fucking saw you, didn't I? Helmand. Barry Ghoul's Bazaar. Fuck! You never said.'

'Secrets mate, you know the score.'

'How long you been out?'

'7 years.'

'Wow. Same as me. I knew you weren't never no fucking carpet salesman!'

'More weapons, explosives and comms kit to be honest. Although my main business front was renewables, solar or wind farms mainly, then we siphoned off the cash for the dodgy gear.'

'You fucker.'

'Well. That's not the worst thing. I nearly shot you once.'

'What?!'

And with this revelation, Naz suddenly felt a whole lot better. Confession was good for the soul after all. Two hours later, the brothers were joined deep in blood and politics.

'We are agreed. We are going into politics Naz. My brains, my good looks, and your money, we'll be irresistible. You're the talent, me the consiglieri.'

'Si, Baroni. We'll be ourselves. What we believe in now. Agenda priorities - Environment, Lantau Tomorrow and Housing. Fight for equity but avoid the protest stuff, be the middlemen and bring everyone back together. Avoid trade and finance, too dull. Be green, be wellbeing, be windswept and be cool. Don't argue with the Empire, no tweaking the tail of the tiger and nothing too socialist lefty either Jonboy! I know what you are like. Try and keep your mouth under control. Middle ground.'

'We need a bit of left hand down, Naz. It'll keep you honest. Your time has come my Arabian Prince. You saw what happened when they water cannoned the mosque. Brown is cool. And you speak perfect Cantonese. The Chinese are stuck; too stubborn; too much face to lose; too entrenched in their camps. They need a peacemaker. Brown is the new....'

'Black? Pink?'

'Yeah. Except I don't think Hong Kong is ready for pink; they don't really get the gay thing here. You aren't gay, are you?'

'Ha ha! Not yet.' Another secret thought Naz. If I keep this one for another ten years, I'll be dead before I can ever relax. Still, one big secret revealed is enough for one night, a gentleman must retain his mystery.

'Now, seriously, if we have any skeletons in the cupboard, we need to bury them and not mark the graves. And swear we were both playing darts. In the woods. With three bears and no, we never saw Red Riding Hood.' Jonny and Naz grinned at each other.

'Got any bodies buried Jonno?'

Jonny smiled sideways. Then didn't.

'A few. No hurts cuz. Hard as nails.' They bumped fists. *'Secrets.'*

Chapter 4 – Say Lah

Nodding Dogs

'Alright Jonno.'

James arrived within 45 seconds of Jonny; the policeman and the ex-soldier were always the ones to hit the start line on schedule; or rather five minutes before just to be sure. Jonny had been concentrating on his phone, checking out a Campus News capture of a large number of fully kitted-up riot cops hitting, pepper spraying and violently arresting a single youth outside City Hall. The boy had a pale blue canvas bag on one of those two-wheeled shopping trolleys in his hand and was being buffeted and battered. He didn't have a chance to get a single punch in, or even block one, before he was on the concrete, armoured knees and batons subduing him decisively. The police were brutally efficient. Training was working.

Jonny had just been watching another clip, Be Water Facebook, where six or seven riot cops stood on a pedestrian bridge, seemingly dropping bricks and debris over the parapet onto the road below. He thought about asking James about it, but decided it wasn't a great way to start the evening with his police buddy. Tactfully, he put his phone away. Not before letting James catch a glimpse of what was on the screen of course. Jonny noted how James' eyes had that thousand-yard stare vibe,

'Hey J. Man, you look knackered pal. Tough week? Been livin' under a

bridge?'

'Tough life mate. Life's shit and then you die eh?'

'S'about it mucker; that is just about it. Whatcha 'aving?'

'Whatcha got there? Gweilo?'

'Nah, Moonzen. New in. S'alright.'

'Same for me then. Same, same but different.'

Jonny turned his attention to wave at the barmaid who spotted him instantly, beamed broadly and oozed towards him to take his order, all inviting curves and theatrical lashes as a saucy barmaid should be in an old-school Wanchai boozer like Churchill's. Gina knew the boys and had a thing for Micky – their tallest and blondest – but Jonny was always the polite and respectful one. Jonny called her 'Ma'am.' Micky called her 'Gorgeous' or 'Princess.' James slung his heavy day-sack on a hook below the bar and wriggled his stool to mark out a little larger territory for his elbows.

The place was rowdy, this short 50-metre stretch of Lockhart Road between the Sports Bar and Coyote's was the most raucous little patch of Wanchai at happy hour. HK$40 a pint compared to the usual HK$80 had retained the loyalty of Lockhart's traditional crowd: predominantly white, tattooed, burly, beer bellied, rough around the edges and tough in the middles. It was the closest thing to the Corporals' Mess that Hong Kong offered, and so Jonny felt at home there. He could converse in his natural, profane vernacular without fear of embarrassing eavesdroppers. Nobody gave a toss around here as long as you didn't spill their pint or gob off during the pub quiz.

James, despite his more refined upbringing, found nowhere else so calming. In amongst the shouting, swearing bovver boys, all bantering about football, rugby, booze and birds, he was just another white face. Unlike at work where he was often the only white face, and always an officer, a boss, with expectations, responsibilities and a reputation. This was the one little corner of Hong Kong where he could get drunk, swear, cadge a fag, have a minor scrap and nobody would know or care. The police generally let the white hooligans get on with it as long as their ignorance and violence didn't spill out and affect the civilized Chinese society that tolerated them, for business reasons, in their city. There were rarely cops around who might recognise James –the few other gweilo officers left in the Force were less alehouse and more supper parties and cappuccinos nowadays. Things were more professional without beer.

The bar was boisterous. Swearing and arguing, loudly and ridiculously, were a core part of the culture with disagreement and dissent considered compulsory for a colourful discussion. The rest of the crew had yet to arrive, so no need for the volume and posturing to get turned up just yet. The rest would be somewhere between 15 and 45 minutes late because they were slack, inconsiderate, useless civvies. Accordingly, the uniformed boys had time for a grown-up chat. A quiet and thoughtful force field settled over them, oblivious to the riotous banter all around them.

'What's up then buddy? Beat up the wrong 16-year-old again?'

James rolled his eyes, his head gently following the motion up and back down again and snorted in faux exasperation and smiled warmly. He may have taken offence at that from anyone else, but they had been mates for 20 years, and Jonny knew what it was like to be covered in sweat, weighed down with kit, a radio net in one ear, people shouting in the other and yet another decision to make, order to give, action to take. He was a fellow traveler who understood that living on the edge of constant violence and being ever in command took a mental toll. James gave his mate a sideways glance, and in the intense concern of Jonny's eyes, he felt the psychic hug and support that was being given – with abuse, naturally. Eavesdropping outsiders on their conversation would think them dark, obnoxious and cruel. Nobody was listening, and if they were, nobody would understand the true concern and care in play.

'*Man up, Pansy*.' Jonny said and gave James a little elbow dig to the shoulder aiming to make him spill his beer.

'*Wanker*.' James mimed a back-handed chop to Jonny's nose, close enough to make him flinch and grin.

'*Mate*,' James began, '*It's been fucking months. I am knackered. We are all knackered. But it's the being hated; deeply, bitterly hated that is doing my head in. A 10-year-old called me a Nazi the other day.*'

'*It's the blond hair mate. And all the black kit. To be honest, you do look like a bit of a Nazi.*' Jonny switched to his 'allo 'allo German accent '*Tallest and blondest, macht schell, achtung wo ist mein tear gas?*'

'*Hey ze var is over. That's just racist nowadays.*'

'*Yeah, but you're white, and blond, so that's ok. And they always win on penalties so we can be mean to Germans. And Scousers. And Gingers. As long as we say Auburn.*'

'*True. True. I just don't think I can keep doing it anymore. I haven't seen my kids for weeks. They are getting shit at school for being 'piglets', you know we got doxed don't you?*'

'*Yeah, saw you on the internet. It's out of order. I don't mind fighting the cops, and a lot of your lot deserve a slap, but bringing the wives and kids into it is bang out of order.*'

'*It is just so nasty. And the brass are fucking useless.*'

'*Well, the pointless puppet Government have put you out there as the punching bags and now you are the scapegoats.*'

'*It's not just the Government, it's our own commanders. Everything has changed. We were doing OK, Asia's finest and all that, but the last couple of years, since Occupy, there's been this pressure.*'

'*White terror?*'

'Sort of, but not terror, just a sort of presence, a pressure, like the eye of Sauron out there and you never know if one day it is going to turn on you. And when it does, you're fucked.'

'Crush your bodies and shatter your bones sort of thing?'

'Exactly. Well no. It's insidious, not obvious. Maybe not Beijing but the Mainland, the Special Rep, the PLA and that bloke in Guangzhou. They are the ones giving the orders and our bosses are doing exactly as they are told. Or they fall over themselves trying to be the most loyal and patriotic and tough guy. They are like fucking Nazis, 'just following orders, your honour.' I don't want to be a Nazi, Jon mate.'

'We guessed you were all muzzled when the Legco thing happened. No police force on earth would have abandoned their Houses of Parliament, so it was obvious you had been told to vanish.'

'You may be reading too much into that. There is always the good, old-fashioned cock-up Jonny boy! Anyway, I can't say anything about that. I don't know the score to be honest. But, yep, my unit were told to go for scoff then head off to TST. It is one thing standing up for what you believe in, being professional, but when you know you are being manipulated, that's hard. Too hard. A lot of the protesters deserve a slap, but then every five minutes some fucking numb nuts pepper sprays an old lady or batters a random 18-year-old kid with glasses and asthma. It might make the bosses feel like tough guys in their air-conditioned offices, but it makes us look like proper cunts!'

'You do look like cunts to be honest mate. I know that there are still good cops doing what they should, but that ain't news, so we don't see the good cops. But what has really killed you, is that nothing ever happens to the bad cops. The bullies are above the law. We hate that. You aren't 'our' police anymore, you are 'their' PLA. The people hate you, you know. Fucking hate you. It's not good.'

'I know. I am beginning to hate me too.'

'Mate! Be strong. Dry your eyes princess. You're alright. Bit posh, shit at football, but not an utter shithead. Unlike Chen Chen here!'

Jonny had just seen Ranald weaving his way through the mob towards them, all corporate suited, man-bagged, slack tied and 20 minutes late. Micky loomed up tall behind him, a huge, playful grin on his face. Time for compassion and honesty was over. James took the cue, spun around and raised his watch hand,

'What was it, an option on the Footsie, hostile takeover of an orphanage, exhausted counting your gold bars?'

Ranald boomed back *'I'm only five-ish minutes late! Fashionably late mes amis.'*

'And I am positively early for me!' laughed Micky.

'True, true blue – did you get the day wrong, were you thinking it's Thursday?'

Jonny turned back in close to James as Ranald and Micky shifted their attention to getting their beers, Micky demanding his obligatory kiss on the cheek from Gina the barmaid.

'The thing is mate, it's the justice being seen to be done thing. If it was us, when somebody fucked up they would be in front of the CO, three week's pay or ROP's or whatever and night guard at Christmas. They would be smashed, quickly and openly. Nothing ever happens to your lot.'

'It does, we have procedures and complaints are investigated...'

'But we never see it. You never admit it. Those PR robots, that twat Vasco Williams and his 'kicking a yellow object' bullshit, the speccy bland one, handsome plastic-PR cop. No credibility. We can all see the videos, everyone knows when a copper is out of order, but it's always say nothing, deny everything, make counter accusations. It's embarrassing, I'm embarrassed for you and I ain't even a copper.'

Jonny wanted to be supportive, but the PR spin aggravated him. James could see that, although he was guaranteed understanding as a friend, Jonny had completely lost respect for the police, for James' profession and for the cause he had been proud to serve for 25 years. It was a cause that he was having doubts about continuing to serve. What he needed right now was some good news, some positive feedback. It wasn't going to come from Jonny, but Micky and Ranald had arrived and would change the mood.

At least the Prince Edward MTR incident hadn't come up again. The boys all knew it was James' unit; they all knew he was on duty that night, but none of them really wanted to know if he was involved in that rampage. That knowledge would have threatened even their bonds of friendship. They must never know what he said or did that night, the words he used, that may have caused some of his lads to behave as they did, that may have unleashed the situation he couldn't control. He wasn't even sure how culpable he was himself anymore, things were complicated. He was tired.

Micky and Ran were back, pints in hand.

'Soooo, the Irish smashed the Jocks then, the English are having easy matches and the Welsh are destined for glory!' Micky played the ball James was hoping for, the Rugby World Cup conversation, James took the lifeline,

'What? On the basis of beating Georgia, where even is that? Let's see how they do against the Aussies next week!'

'That'll be a test.' Micky agreed.

Ranald had zero interest in rugby but felt he had to say something out of politeness,

'The All Blacks are going to win it, so why worry?'

'I don't know, England are looking good...' Jonny felt obliged to stand up

for his mother country,

'They are...' chimed in James *'but they have to get past Wales or Australia...'*

'How about South Africa?' Naz made everyone jump as he had mysteriously materialised beside James' shoulder.

'How does he do that?' thought Jonny who prided himself on being alert to things, 'You can tell that bloke used to be a spy.' he thought. Then asked himself for the thousandth time how he hadn't worked that out years' ago. Naz must be a good spy.

'Nah!' Most everyone joined in dismissing the South Africans, Micky was the self-declared expert on all matter's rugby,

'I mean tough as ever, but they aren't world champs this time around. Too pedestrian. Anyway, aren't you supposed to support Canada Naz?'

'Yeah right. Maybe for the ice hockey I'll come over all Canuck ay?' chuckled Naz. *'For Rugby, I'm a Saffa – a Bokke!'*

'A Focker!' put in Ranald super sharp,

'Nah that's James, he's a proper Nazi! Ask any school kid.' Jonny grinned at James who retorted loudly and with a huge laugh,

'Fuck off! Did you even go to school, what do you teach, skiving?'

Normal banter was resumed. Tension erased. James continued,

'What's the plan then men?'

Jonny was bandmaster this week, *'Pints, Jojo's for a curry then The Wanch.'* Micky was uninspired,

'Ugh! The Wanch? That noisy, sticky little cupboard? Can't we go to tottytastic Amazonia?' Jonny was not to be put off,

'The Wanch is a classic, an iconic rock venue my man. Besides, Big Baz is playing.'

'Bloody 'ell. Stairway and Rock the Casbah?'

'How did you know?'

'Same old, same old, same, same but different my friend.'

Nods, sucking of teeth, grins, *'Cheers Boys, good to see you!'* glasses raised in salute,

'Up your bum!'

Retail Micky Take

Micky was not having a great day. Bright and early into Pacific Coffee, his eye on one of the rarely empty comfy, red armchairs. He had collected his grandé latté and turned around to find a stout taai-taai had swooped in and seized the prime real-estate with a bustle of bags, dispatching her docile looking husband off to the counter. There were no South China Morning Posts left in the reading rack, just a China Daily and, despite being no literati, he wasn't crass enough to resort to reading that bombastic, propaganda rag.

Having met his accountant / PA / keeper-on-the-straight-and-narrow May in the coffee shop (she declined a drink and sipped hot water from her flask), he had spent the entire morning - three exhausting hours - meeting various clients and landlords around the Shatin area. The diligent May had gotten Micky to each rendezvous exactly ten minutes late each time and then frantically taken notes as he bluffed and blustered, cajoled and stone-walled his way through a series of increasingly infuriating appointments. Under direct and uncompromising orders from Big John, he had given out eviction notices and final warnings. Dirty work and an emotionally draining experience that his tough talking boss never actually did himself. Micky wasn't as cut up about this as May secretly felt inside; he was merely following orders and being ruthless was an essential requirement for a mover and shaker. May was no pushover, but she had more empathy for those who had to work for a living, as opposed to those born lucky enough to bluff for a career.

The protests were having a significant effect on business. Footfall had collapsed in the malls and shopkeepers were struggling. Bars and restaurants were deserted, and fear had risen to a new level now that businesses were being classified as either 'Yellow' or 'Blue'. Boycotts, vandalising, even burning 'Blue' businesses had become a protester tactic that made things even tougher. It was manifestly unfair thought Micky, and he was chuntering to May about the violent, ignorant vandals and rioters as they walked through the swanky and untouched IFC Mall. Micky was feeling far more relaxed and upbeat now he was back from the 'dark side' of dirty Kowloon and the barbarous New Territories; now he was safely on 'The Island' again.

'Absolutely terrible.' agreed May. *'The waiters and shop-girls aren't blue or yellow, they just want to do their job, get paid and sleep. They don't deserve that abuse.'*

'I wasn't thinking about that.' admitted Micky, *'It's more that if they don't make money, they can't pay the rent and the landlords don't get paid and so we don't get paid. The bloody landlords refuse to lower their rents for the shops, but they wail and whinge to us to reduce management fees. No shame.'*

'Well, Mr Cavendish, we have refused to lower rents on our properties too.'

'Yes, but we can't reduce our rents or where would it stop? Everybody would want a discount and that way lies ruin dear May. Besides, Mr McEwan forbids it - we are to hold the line, weather the storm and stay strong.' Micky unconsciously slipped into a slightly sarcastic version of his boss' Scottish accent for the latter part of his statement.

'Mr Cavendish, I don't think that is the right way to go. Then everyone will suffer. People are losing their jobs; nobody can afford a flat. The rents have to come down or Hong Kong will die.'

'We burn, you burn with us?' Micky repeated the oft heard protester phrase that he had picked up from Jonny. He continued holding forth, oblivious to having adopted the tone of tall, white privileged colonial schoolmaster that May was enduring like nails down a blackboard,

'We're a business, not a charity May. Don't hold out much hope for a bonus this year sweetheart. Thankfully I've already paid for Verbier at Easter or KK would be preaching prudence at me. I don't understand that woman – her dad's a gazillionaire and we are hardly broke and yet

she's always complaining about how much we spend.'

May said nothing and looked away. The unfathomable wealth of a dynasty like the Tangs, from which Micky's wife came, was a source of wonder and horror for regular Hong Kongers. May's mum lived in a council flat, she herself rented a shoebox and her lone, lonely daughter went to a local state school. Despite her husband being a highly qualified (if mind-numbingly boring) engineer, and her own steady white-collar job, they still earned less in a month between them than Micky did in a week; a week in which May worked about 55 hours and Micky spent about 40 hours nominally at work but mostly chatting, socializing and scanning the property pages.

'Still, May May, we can't save the world. To business. What the Dickens should I buy my wife for her birthday?'

'Well, Mr Cavendish, what does she like?'

'I don't know. Nice stuff. Lady stuff. Can't you pick something for me?'

'Well, Mr Cavendish, what does she need?'

'Nothing. She's rich. Jewelry? Clothes? Shoes? A bag? New phone?'

'Do you know her size?'

'Erm, about your size-ish. Maybe a bit thinner. But nowhere near as cute May May.'

Micky's eyes roamed all over May, sizing her up, comparing, initially purely for the scientific purpose of ascertaining whether his wife was taller, slimmer or trimmer. It didn't take more than a second though before his quantitative analysis of May's figure started to move towards a qualitative appreciation of her curvier bust and wider hips. He knew May had noticed and gave his best, impish grin. He was convinced that May had a thing for him, he was tall and very handsome after all whilst May was somewhat plain, but somehow sexy.

May did have a thing for him at first, he was tall and toned as men should be, but she had soon judged him as vain and conceited with absolutely no head for mathematical figures and a despicable interest in female figures. Typical spoilt, idiot gweilo. He was a bit of a letch, a 'harm sup yan' but he got away with it because he was rich and good looking so most of the office girls flirted, fluttered and fantasised away tractably. This irritated May hugely and she despised them even more than him. On the occasion that he had given her a bit of a cheeky squeeze, she had reacted with silent, eye-watering fury and he had got the message. He was actually shocked at the virulence of her negative reaction – that hadn't happened to a good-looking princeling like him before. At least, he got the message. For about a month each time, after which his unconquerable belief in his own irresistibility returned and he had another lascivious try to cheekily seduce her. It had become a bit of a joke for him, convinced that one day she would relent and serve him with erotic abandon.

It was never very funny for her because she was indeed lonely, frustrated and desperate to escape her own passionless marriage. She wanted a 'Micky' to escape what she saw as the doomed city of Hong Kong and give her a new life of leisure and privilege, to settle her daughter at a fine private school, riding horses, playing hockey and going sailing like Micky's kids did. Maybe she could afford a second child? May didn't want this Micky though. She thought him a 'mo liu do' – another empty suit. Now, she was having to select a present for his perfect, have everything, society wife because even after 12 years of marriage, three kids, and hundreds of romantic weekends and couples' spa-breaks, he had no idea what his wife actually liked, needed or wanted. May pointed at an Aigle shop full of high-end chic, adventure gear.

'Isn't she into hiking these days?'

'Oh yeah! Great idea, she is always disappearing off to the hills lately; mid-life crisis, she'll be marathon running next. Let's start there, then Lululemon. I'll treat you to something sporty too for helping me out. You

should get more exercise; you work too hard.'

Micky grinned at May, imagining her puffing and clumping away in a Zumba class. May headed swiftly into the store so he couldn't see her puffed up cheeks and pouty irritation. She wasn't that fat, she thought.

Twenty minutes later, May was scurrying behind Micky touting four large paper bags of gifts for Mrs Perfectly-Spoilt Cavendish-Tang. They were heading for Tag Heuer or Tiffany's as Micky thought they needed a little, last something or his kids would think he hadn't tried hard enough. Micky paused and gazed into Sixty-Eight, a lingerie store. May shuddered. She knew what he was thinking. He was about to suggest going in there and then, once inside, he would 'jokingly' ask her to model something, but he wouldn't really be joking he would really want her to. Actually, Micky wasn't thinking that at all; there was no way on earth he would ever be brave enough to buy lingerie and as KK had stopped sleeping with him a year ago there was no point. Rather, he was distracted by the poster of a blonde who reminded him of the Russian girl that had entertained him in Portland Street after Mr Wong's and made him feel all Rasputin again. He was wondering if he had the courage to go back and find her.

Something changed in the air. There was a murmuration of drama. They were suddenly conscious that the mood of the Mall had shifted and belatedly noticed that there were a lot of masked youths about. 'Oh, Good Lord,' thought Micky, 'one of those irksome walk-about slowly shopping protests. Here, on the Island. Dreadful.' He glowered at the baseball caps and black, surgical masks of the young rebels. A few shop shutters were starting to come down. May was instantly nervous, she didn't like the Government, but she was frightened of any disorder and terrified of violence. She didn't mean to, but instinctively closed-in tight to Micky's side, glancing about skittishly.

A squad of menacing riot police, helmets on, batons drawn, were barreling along the shop frontages towards them, staring down the youngsters from behind their black, mirrored goggles and shaded visors.

A single youth, black shorts, black leggings, black backpack, dark blue cap and black hoodie was 10 metres in front of May and Micky. Unlike most, he hadn't altered his path and stepped aside to avoid the police wedge. Even from behind, Micky could sense his defiance, his head up high, his shoulders square and rolling, a swagger in his step. May hadn't even noticed him; she was transfixed by the police and the pepper spray canisters and batons in their hands. Micky wasn't going to stand aside either, he had every right to stroll confidently upon his way, these police johnnies served citizens like him, he had nothing to fear and expected the officers to defer to him, nod respectfully as they passed, and he would wish them a 'Good Afternoon' in return.

May forcefully grabbed Micky's arm, her nails digging in deep, and pulled him off to the side. Surprised, he didn't resist but was not distracted enough to miss the sight of the lead police officer suddenly adjust his trajectory to smash into the confident youth and propel him hard up against an emergency exit door. A second and third cop immediately homed in on the lad splayed up against the door, number 2 delivering a burst of pepper spray to the face, number 3 a swift baton strike to the collar bone. As the proud boy slipped down onto his butt, the emergency door swung open to tumble him backwards. The cops simply turned away and carried on walking.

'Wah! Did you see that? Why they hit him?'

'He probably deserved it May. He was probably gobbing off earlier. We don't want this place turning into Shatin. Remember last month when they roamed all over Shatin causing trouble, costing our tenants money? The cops need to show 'em who's boss.'

'But he didn't do anything.'

'Nothing we saw. But it's like 'yellow object.' It looks like the police were just beating somebody up, but we don't know what the yobbo was doing before. They have always done something. They always deserve it. The police don't beat up just anyone, do they? They didn't bother us, did

they? This is Central, we can't tolerate the riffraff here or the place will be like one big council estate. They can keep their grubby, little protests elsewhere.'

May didn't want to argue. *'We should go now.'* She really wanted to just get home, get to safety.

'No, no, if we are quick, we'll be fine. Let's get that watch, then I'll treat you to high tea at Lane Crawford.' He took her arm and steered her away.

'*What a brave, kind boss I am*.' thought Micky and he smiled at the top of May's head. May looked down at the shopping bags she carried. '*What a bastard!*' she thought.

Unseen, a quiet, masked-up, black-clad protester with a daysack half-full of leaflets watched them from behind the coatracks. *'So that's one his girlfriends*.' KK said to herself. *'Bit fat.'*

Looking Sharp

It's the noise that gets to you. The infernal cacophonic noise everywhere, everywhere in Hong Kong. This barbers is cool. It is why he went in. Shiny and new. Black and white tiles, chequered like a two-tone riot of ska music with brassy highlights of bright, sparkling stainless steel on the chair stems, the mirror rails and the glinting, glistening scissors. Clean and sheen, crisp and sharp white shaving brush hairs and translucent gels lined up on the smooth, black, marble counter; implements and tools with lots of silver and gleam – precision and style. The staff wear matching black uniforms, baggy but gathered, sleek and loose, neat Japanese samurai chic fashion, their haircuts as sharp as their scissors, skinhead short and floppy long, spiky-gelled all at once.

This place is spotless. It is order and purpose and focus. If only it was on mute. But it isn't. It is a fucking headfuck sound of a murder noise just like the street outside. A tablet is in front of him. The News. Distinctive intro music for Pearl News – derderder – derderderder...der. Cantonese version. Government approved. At the next seat, 87 short, sharp centimetres away is the next tablet. Soap opera. Ching Dynasty drama. The other side of him, another channel for his neighbor, a neighbor sat so close he could break his nose with one reverse strike and barely shift in his seat; his video tablet is set to something different as well. Another soap. Modern. Korean. Dubbed. The actors look like perfect, plastic, doll-people. Great haircuts. The aircon ticks and thrums. The hair-sucker brushing thing hoovers and gurgles. Right next to the tablet in front of him, literally actually touching it, is a small, red radio, volume equal to the tablet, tinny music blaring. Right next to it, right next to it, is another radio, playing another load of noise. And nobody else notices. They just talk away. Volume 10 gah laaah, gah laah, gah fuckin' laaaaaaaaaaaaaaaaah!

Breathe. Calm the demons. Smother the triggers. Control. Relax. Don't hate them. They are but humans. They know no different and they have no choice. They are not woke. They are the sheep; you are the snow leopard, and you are Zen. This is their place. You don't belong here, you are the outsider, the visitor and the guest so you must accept their world, conform, comply, obey. And you need a haircut son.

His dead, expired barnet is coming off with the trimmer, the little lumps and clusters of unwanted, dry hair dropping onto the well-fitted, neat, nylon poncho; a swish little tissue paper choker around your neck to keep the itchy, messy, debris away that tumbles from your cleansed scalp. More grey than brown now, more white than grey in fact. It is coming off and you are feeling clean, purified, prophetic.

The barber shows him the mirror. The haircut is good, short, smart and respectable. It is the same haircut he has had since he was twenty-five.

'*OK?*' The barber asks, moving the mirror around from side to back, back and sides. She has done a good job, swift and neat in execution, sharp lines and a clean finish.

The correct answer is '*Yes, that's great, thank you, mmgoi.*' He looks. It is the right haircut. Short back and sides, longer on top. Respectable. Presentable. Suitable. It is the right haircut and he knows the right answer. But not today.

'*Take the rest.*' He motions with his hand above and across his head. '*Skin-cut sides. All off. Stripe on top.*' His gold tooth flashed in the mirror as he grinned.

'*Ho fing? Alloff? No! Too much short for you. No handsome!*' and I just spent ten minutes with the scissors making it look really good you chiizing gweilo, she is thinking.

'*Whole thing. Like this short.*' he pinches his fingers for emphasis. '*All over less the very top.*'

'*Duk. M leng.*' Shrug. Eye roll. Tiny huff. '*Skin cut. Hol fing laah. Ho chun.*'

Jonny felt the need to be cleansed.

Duckin' and Divin'

Out onto the street. The crowded street. The number 16 bus passes close by the dirty, black kerb, right up behind the grubby old 13D, the throb of its diesel engine deep and incessant, the fumes invisible but right there, right up his nose and sooty-smeared all along the side of the bus. Choking streets, corrupted lungs. He wants to go forward, but an old couple are right there, doddering. A man in a suit and tie (it's 30 degrees, idiot) is pushing past. Three fat, heavily branded Mainland tourists have stopped dead in front and are looking bemused and immovable; the apologetic jewelry shop girl is holding out a flyer for pointless, gawdy trinkets. He moves three steps, a slow-moving, stick-thin young woman is texting and wavering in front of him, teetery-clippy-cloppy-needly heels wobbling, her fake eyelashes so long he can see them from behind. He moves to overtake and a man in a stained white vest is bearing down on him with a shin-cutting, four wheeled flat trolley full of flat cardboard flatpack scything a path through the throng. Step right, almost into the bus-stop post, edge round it, back behind skinny zombie, phone, pretty, pretty thin girl. Four more metres gained, the crossing beacon ticktocks then speeds up to clickerclickerclickertak as the green man flashes his incessant orders to move, move now, but a minibus is stuck in the way, its engine revving, the fumes visible, a taxi right up its bumper, driver smoking a filthy fag and hitting his horn as an ambulance crawls past the T-junction, flashing and blaring but hardly moving through the snarled, angry traffic jam.

That's when the tough guy bumps him. A hard, deliberate shoulder to shoulder contact. Chewing a toothpick. Red baseball cap, silver letters. Tight white vest. Working-class gangster muscles displayed to maximum effect, bulky gold chain, jade beaded Buddhist wristband and rock-hard tattoos. A micro-second of eye contact to pass the message 'This is my neighbourhood white boy, stand aside.' Gone. Moved on. Nothing doing. He did it on purpose.

The correct response is no response. Ignore. Keep going. Don't even look back. But not today. Today is the day to notice exactly what he looks like, how he moves, where he is heading. Today is the day to abandon the crossing. Turn left. Next left into the alley. Past the alley barbers, skirt side-shouldered alongside the vintage chairs, step over the white stained, milky, spunky, stinking running water-trail and slip around the four, gaping roach-ridden trash bags insolently rotting in the gutter. Blank the graffiti, ignore what is down the side snicket, do not notice the rat-trap cage, just get to the next junction. Be sharp. Focus on drawing the blade. Don't cut yourself. Don't show it. Have it ready. Squeeze past the key-cutter's tiny display board and switchback left, back onto the main street. Time to prove something to the world. Time to kick back hard enough. This is my fucking neighbourhood too.

And the traffic-light man guardian is red. The cars are moving, the people are crushing, waiting for the crossing, the ticktocktick blind guide is ticktockticking. The tough guy is 4 metres away, looking the other way, looking at his phone, flexing his vest. Everyone takes the chance to check their phone. All eyes are on phones. He's rehearsed this strike a thousand times on a thousand commutes. Just like a prison shank this needs to be. Fast, flowing, flawless. Up behind and beside the target, barely any movement, the least flex possible, a precision strike, a sorcerer's sleight, with just enough force to puncture swiftly, to get into that kidney area. In, out. Don't stop walking. Don't look. Move on. Alley. My alley. Blade vanishes. Magician quick. Turn left. Keep walking. Don't look back. Drift right. Get on the next bus. Whatever bus. Get on. Blend in. Disappear. Breathe deep. Breathe slow. Polluted air. Don't breathe too much.

The lights change, the traffic-light man guardian goes icon green, clickerclickerclickertak, eyes off phones, the crowd surges across, instinctively separating into two-human-wide columns that pass through and beside the two-human-wide columns crossing the other way. All but one human. One tough guy alpha-human. One big-man gangster geezer. One wolf who doesn't understand why he is hitting the floor with an indescribable pain shooting through his right side and his phone has hit the tarmac and the screen will probably be shattered and his throat is full of bitter, iron spit and his right knee has given way and he is tumbling and people are looking at him and he has no idea what is happening and he is gasping and he is on the floor now. A big-man gangster geezer who now looks like a small, confused puddle of seeping blood. Ex-wolf. Little, stuck sheep. Blaaaerh. Slaughterhouse. Who?

Nobody there, the nothing man, the you-are-in-my-way man, the you-don't-belong-here man has already gone past the exchange counter, down the alley, turned right, he's up on the bus and the Octopus card reader has beeped and that's all good, and a quick look down shows not even the tiniest splash of blood on the wrist, just a dab on the hand and a wipe and that's all good, and the blade is still out and in the pocket and a bit slimy and stabby if you move too much but that's not bad and if you scooch into that little space for wheelchairs and face the wall then nobody will notice you, adjust your position and gently close the blade, just in your pocket and now that's all good. So, look relaxed, look natural, slow your pulse down, try and stop sweating, breathe, don't stress about it, just a bit of justice delivered, think about something else, for your own well-being, inner peace Po. Still sweating, face your head to the aircon vent. Don't catch anyone's eye. Wow I'm sweating. Get your old Vietnamese red star cap on your head. Don't push. Be invisible. Breathe slower. Good man. Control. Become Zen. Become water. Become nothing. You are nothing. You are a gentle grazer. Baaaah, baaaah white sheep.

Argyle and Nathan

'Sir, HQ want us to go down to QE2, there's been a stabbing'.

'One of ours?'

'M hai laah. Some yoof. Maybe cockroach, maybe triad.'

'For fuck's sake, where is Sid? Can't they see we are on litter patrol? Not our fucking job to do follow-ups is it? We're here to do the fighting, not chit-chats with gat tjats.'

'HQ wah Sid tai mong, they've jumped a gang of villains in a shed up Homantin. Proper criminals for once. They even had a car chase.'

'Wow! Actual car chase? Over thirty and everything? C.I.D. got out the aircon for once? Just like proper plod. About time. I am still not interested in Triad stabbings though. Sooner they all kill each other the better. Chavs.'

James H-J was leaning against the wall of the MTR stairs at Argyle and Nathan, the back of his helmet resting against the big, black, painted 'O' of 'Fuck the Popo' sprayed on the wall behind him. It was hot. It was always hot. His squad had come down to secure the area and had been expecting some aggro from the protesters but, apart from a few shifty youths and the usual press vultures, the black shirts were keeping their distance today. Today was a normal day. Nobody knew when it was going to be a riot day. James had been looking at the piles of square bricks that had been torn up from the pavement and scattered along the roadsides ready to block the road or hurl at him and his mates. The roaches didn't tend to be so aggressive when his team turned up; everyone knew the Raptors didn't fuck about and could move faster than the usual plod in their pukey green jumpsuits. Plod reminded him of Ghostbusters in those saggy outfits; not sleek and cool like a Raptor's gear. Life takers and heart breakers, his boys. He could see his reflection in the bus windows. He looked ally. He felt like shit. Still, duty calls,

'Alright, get Fei and one of his boys to come with me then tell George to get us a motor. One with aircon.'

'On it Boss! Tramp on chips.' Fenton grinned. How was he always so perky? James fixed eyes on his second-in-command, mustered his best US Navy Submarine Captain voice and stated,

'Spec Wong Son, you have the con. I am gone.'

'Aye Aye, Herr Capitan Wong Seung!' the young officer chirped back, saluting with a boing and smiling under the black facemask. 'Cocky fucker' James thought as he strode off, good cocky though.

Across the junction, on the bus, Jonny was staring at the police staking out all four corners of Nathan and Argyle. His serenity was disturbed. Traffic was still moving despite the haphazard efforts of a couple of cops directing traffic with hardly any of the talent that a couple of bus drivers had shown the previous evening. He had been trapped on the bus for 13 minutes now; ever since he had slipped onto it. He was no longer in psycho mode.

'Fucking pointless dog-shit cops.' he muttered under his breath. Then he took a frozen startled stop-breath as the unmistakable sharp, white nose of James H-J appeared striding across the road with two of his henchmen hanging onto his coattails. The bus was just about to move when one of the cops raised his baton and started shouting at the taxi in front of his bus. *'Shit! Maybe I have been i.deed. That treacherous fucker James has picked me out on CCTV. So fast?'* He looked around, he was stood right at the front, where he always stood in the space for wheelchairs.

'Driver! Open the door!'

'Cannot! Dahng danhg!'

'Hoi Mun. Open the fucking door, I want to get off'

'Cannot! M'hai nido. Yiu dahng.'

20 metres away, James' car had arrived from Prince Edward Police Station and he was trying to cram his tall frame into the passenger seat, baton, torch, pepper spray and assorted hard-man-tools jangling on his batman utility belt getting caught in the gap between seat and door and digging into his arse. Sergeant Fei and a sidekick were similarly trying to stuff themselves and their weapons and kit into the back seat; Fei's shotgun made a hole in the roof fabric as he shoved himself inside – he hoped the driver hadn't noticed. After briefly slamming the door onto his shotgun butt, the car moved off towards Queen Elizabeth's Hospital, passing a stalled line of buses – James took his stinking helmet off and smiled as he noticed some punter was wearing one of those touristy Vietnamese army caps like they all got in Hoi An that time. Happier days. The car had aircon.

Jonny was oblivious to all of this minor keystone cops' kerfuffle; his juvenile nihilism and rage had slunk moodily away to be replaced with a teenage fear of getting caught and a now feverish determination to de-bus. Just as he contemplated putting his blade to the driver's throat, he noticed the police car with James' blond stuck-up helmet hair inside, passing swiftly by the window on the other side of the road. He exhaled deeply then his brain clicked back in – no way they could be that fast. Hang on, they will work backwards. The bus has a camera on it; the MTR has cameras everywhere; the street junctions have cameras; he needs to get off the grid. First thing; mobile phone off. Best option – taxi or minibus. For now, just be cool. Still dripping with sweat. Focus. Be cool. I am cool.

Getting off by the street market refuse centre, he saw new graffiti in Chinese characters 'CENSORED of our times' indeed he thought; he had just crossed a pretty sharp red-line for no better reason than dysfunctional fury. He wasn't supporting The Revolution, he was lashing out at anyone in his way. He'd had enough. This wasn't like putting a few rounds down range from the gympy at the bottom of the Loy Mandeh Wadi; this wasn't a focused application of extreme violence in order pacify Her Majesty's mortal enemies; this was a petulant stabbing of a grubby street punk. Felt liberating though. He fucking deserved it; you just knew he fucking deserved it. Maybe there'll be a next time, maybe aim high and take out a copper; plenty of them deserve it too. But to have the opportunity he needed to switch on, make sure there was no way a connection could be made to him, find an off-grid route home and just pray there was no CCTV on that zebra crossing, or it had been smashed up. Could he slip back across the line and resume normal jogging or was this his new destiny. Assassin. Or nutter?

He headed straight into the press of the market, past the fruit and veg stalls, along the refuse department's wall with its bold tags of *'Hiding Myself 2017'* and 'Survive Rough Times' still unmolested by the protest graffiti - prescient street art and predictive collective mental illness advice. He scooted across in front of a scratched, white van-truck and along the sopping wet frontage of the butchers with its cuts of fresh pork hanging on hooks and nails, the trails and rivulets of water heading down to the gutter streaked with swirling, oily traces of pig blood. There was an actual pig's face, the whole face, looking straight at him with empty eye sockets and the black fur still on. They probably sold the eyes separately. Trying to keep his trainers dry past the fish stall being hosed down by a gnarled woman in short, yellow wellies, white-ish apron tied round her bulging curves; not treading in the balsa-wood and sopping cardboard mush alongside the curb; down and left to where the cardboard grannies and the plastic-pilers turn their trash into string-secured pallet sized cubes ready to be trucked up to the recycling factories in the New Territories. Merge with the mob, get lost in the maze Alice, vanish into the street-filth. Be street filth.

Alley to Work

Just as Jonny always did, Naz preferred the alley to the human-choked, fume filled bus noise of the main drag of Argyle Street. He had never dared walk this way when he attended the posh school up the hill, but now he figured that, like Samuel L as the meanest motherfucker in the valley, or the alley, he need fear no evil. This route was the real city to him, one of the places in-between, a literal rat-run. He strolled, alert but relaxed, you show no fear in the city. It was a bit stinky at sections, there is the occasional rattus rattus dancing along a utility pipe, or an undulation of them rifling through a trash-bag of rotting food, but it is safe enough and like Mongkok itself, smartening up year by year. No junkies these days, barely a mugger, trash vanishes most days. If it's a romp of otters and a murder of crows, what's a pack of rats called?

The snicket gave him peace to think and it beat enduring the throngs of pushy people. Paradoxically the 'dirty alley' was considerably less toxic with ten times fewer PM 2.5 particles than the bus diesel choked smog of the main street. Scientifically, the dirty alley was the clean air choice. It was quiet, just Naz's padded footsteps and the occasional drip from leaky, overhead aircons, drying laundry and stuttering water whooshing through wall-mounted utility pipes. Quiet didn't happen much in this neighbourhood. It was a wondrous thing made possible only by ugliness and disdain.

Mongkok is a legendary urban district, the name means 'Busy Corner' (Wong Gok) and it is one of the most densely populated places on Earth. No space in Hong Kong is wasted and certainly not here. The alleyway took Naz from the clean, safe sanctuary of the Homantin School / Residential Zone, past the smart, trendy new apartment blocks, to the air-conditioned Retail-zoned malls of Langham Place - a polished, ergonomically engineered miracle Place that integrated 21st Century Mall with a Mass Transit Railway Station and Urban Lifestyle Apartments' solutions. That led onto the light-industrial zone. There is no classic Art Deco design or air-conditioned glassy-steel polish in the alleyway though. It isn't zoned. No marketing or consultancy gig for him down here. That's why he liked it.

Unlike the 'blue riband, high value projects' that filled his workday, the alleyway isn't consciously designed, it has just happened, it just is, but it forms a vital part of street life. At the mouth of one cut-through is a daai-paai-dong noodle stall where time-pressed workers wolf down huge clay bowls of noodles. Another alley exit emerges onto a press of small children, perched on tiny stools, clustered boisterously around their collapsible homework table clinging to the end of their mother's market stall. The entire market has to be built and collapsed every single day; the stalls, the stock, everything. The Government enforces urban discipline firmly. The traders work hard to survive below the poverty line, kept soundly in their place by iron-willed officials with large hats and armbands, to the satisfaction of a harmonious society. Plebs know their place; prosperity is assured.

In the middle of the alley sits a classic hidden gem of Hong Kong – a sliding, iron shuttered hairdressers that Jonny pretends he uses but Naz doesn't believe him. Huge vintage barbers' chairs stick out into the ginnel and the seasoned master styles, trims and shaves his customers under strip lighting against a wall of mirrors and cluttered paraphernalia: an old cutthroat strop razor flashes alongside German electric shavers, Japanese scissors and Chinese hairdryers. It is the only place people talk in the alley. The customers are Men.

Naz passes by poverty stricken cardboard grannies, collecting their trash to eke out life for another week. The 'dirty smokers' lurk in the twitten-alley, pariahs on the edge of society, dumping their butts into the gutter and adding to the filth. Shop and stall workers dump leaky bags of trash, which mysteriously disappear sometime in the early hours. Grannies and Grandpas don't retire in Hong Kong – they survive and work shifts. HK$37/hour. A Big Mac Meal. Yesterday, Naz passed a young man burning paper ghost money and a cardboard car in a red tin, offerings and respects for a deceased parent who needs such things in the afterlife.

Naz was lucky today, his first appointment was in Mongkok, up in the Argyle Centre for a concept meeting with a new client in the private education business; easy stuff so plenty of time for one of those big, clay bowls of noodles that Ah Sheung dished up for him to slurp and slop down, sat on a tiny, plastic stool, pushed up against the plank-wide counter facing into the steamy interior of the street kitchen. He was a regular there, a minor celebrity, his easy Cantonese made him 'one of their own, who had made it.'

He was doubly popular because where he supped noodles was where the Pakistani and Bengali boys parked up their wagons and swapped loads, puffed on woodbines and had a break. Naz's natural charm and communication skills meant he was as comfortable swapping bawdy tales and banter with the street lads in Urdu and Punjabi as he was going to have to be all Oxford-Englishly smooth and corporate up in some bland, swanky office in about 20 minutes time. Naz waved and greeted the lorry lads,

'Salam Aleikum brothers. So, what's up boys? Been tear gassed lately?'

Naz smiled widely as he waved his greetings and received a round robin of nodding heads, hands waved near hearts and mumbled *'Waleikium salaams'* in reply. The lads took a moment from loading scrap and rubble onto their tail-lift truck.

'We know when to scarper from the tear-gas Tommies. Not a bad thing these protests, the rozzer dogs are all too knackered beating up college kids to come give us their usual shit.'

'Damn right! I haven't had a parking ticket all month man! Street racism is declining; it's a scandal! Praise be…'

'The Triad boys are getting braver though, you wanna watch your wallet jingle-boy,' the lorry lads laughed and nodded, giving Naz concerned glances and caringly raised eyebrows.

'I think I'll be alright. My dad's Bruce Lee.' Naz joked back.

'Serious bruv. Gotta stabbing just by there, yesterday.' The lad waved his arm to indicate past Naz, back down the alley towards the railway.

'Triad boy got shanked.'

'Turf war starting?' Naz asked.

'Nah, I tell you that white bloke did it!' This statement from the small van driver made them all hoot and howl in derision.

'As if some old, white guy is gonna get involved in Tong business!' They all mocked the driver with ridiculous faces. Naz was interested though.

'What white guy?'

The painfully thin van driver came closer to Naz, low voiced, pointing and gesticulating with his tendon sharp, blotchy forearms and veined hands, voice full of drama,

'I was sat where you were, on that exact stool, when I looked up and saw him, saw his face like dark murder and saw the knife tucked up back in his hand like this,' he mimed the position of a hand trying to conceal a knife by turning the wrist in close and up to the flank like hiding a fag from a teacher. One of the others gave him a small, modicum of support,

'Yeah, that guy is down here often, about five-ish he goes past, he has a look you know, a don't fuck with me look, walks with a swagger, like George Bush. Army cap.'

'Ha ha! Yeah, I know that guy, struts like a duck!' and he did a little waddle, a good impression of a Londoner who 'bowls' down a street on the estate thought Naz. The only white man he had ever seen prowl a Hong Kong alley was Jonny. He laughed. It was definitely a Jonny walk. Curiouser and curiouser.

'Yeah, he's pretty old like, like you Mo!' one of the younger lads laughed at Naz. As far as they were concerned, Naz was Mo, he enjoyed the

occasional alias when in rougher climes.

The youngster continued, *'He still ain't no gangbanger boy though! He's a one of them NETs, that's the only thing the white folk round here do. He won't have done it, white-privilege teacher-boy, that were gang business. Tong shanking.'*

Naz handed his empty bowl through the little glass window and gave a little wave to the trash-truck boys as he walked away. He crossed diagonally though the traffic and then paused at the corner of the next alley and typed a Telegram into his phone.

'If you ever need to be somewhere else, there's always mine.'

PMQ OP

Micky drew up his Norton Commando 961 Café Racer Mark II by the Shing Wong steps, parking up next to where Jonny always abandoned his battered old blue and white Vespa. The Vespa was there now, probably broken down again thought Micky. He thought to himself how their bikes reflected their characters; his big, sleek, powerful Norton versus Jonny's shabby, chavvy mod scooter. He had to admit that Naz's gleaming BSA A65 Lightning made him jealous though, it didn't have no poke, but it was so vintage Honkers; simple, spartan but cool and modestly classy. The kind of bike that demanded a slender, cheong-saam wearing girlfriend on the back and some natty 1940's fighter pilot goggles. James, of course, had a Harley Droptail Slim, what else would a Terminator Cop ride? He wasn't meeting any of the bikers though, he was meeting Ranald who was normally delivered in either his Tesla or one of those bulky, black Gangster looking MPVs with Mainland plates, complete with bullfrog-necked chauffeur toting a bulky, beaded, Buddhist bracelet on his wrist and a toothpick hanging out the side of his mouth. The momentary thought of the urbane Ranald on a motorbike made him smile; he'd get oil on his Gucci loafers.

PMQ, the restored heritage site on Staunton Street, was indeed an excellent choice of venue. Police Married Quarters – now gentrified and converted from prosaic housing for Government forces to hipster boutiques for the glory of commerce. The new China. It was mid-October and summer's stickiness was waning; the open, breezily windowed buildings were chic and comfortable with no need for aircon. The air felt bright and clear, a perfect day yet to be rusted. Micky found the trendy little coffee shop Ranald had suggested easily enough and found his friend approaching from the other direction, browsing intently at the unique artist's creations in the boutique windows down the corridor, absent mindedly fiddling with his cufflinks. Micky oozed up on his shoulder like a stalking tiger and made him jump,

'You'll never fit into it my friend, but the colour sets off your eyes wonderfully!'

Startled at first, Ranald drew a deep breath and laughed with huge warmth as he recognised his buddy, and not a mugger. Not that Ranald had ever been mugged. He did worry though. Ranald composed himself,

'I don't know,' he drawled, smoothing down his silver-grey Armani suit jacket, *'I am quite trim for a man my age.'*

'Indeed, most impressive for a gout-ridden man in his seventies. Is it the bollock cancer keeps you skinny?'

The two friends laughed and shook hands warmly in greeting. Ranald drew his friend forward and gesticulated at the bohemian, hand-made trinkets in the window.

'This is good gear though; most of it is made in little workshops at the back and in the corridor. You should get something for KK, she'd love this stuff. Artsy like her.'

'Oh, I should think she found this place years' ago. Looking for something for Eva?'

Eva wasn't artsy. Eva was Designer. Blingy. The boys knew each other's wives well, a variety of barbeques, dinner parties and cocktail events, often sharing a table at the same charity ball, had meant they were well acquainted. Micky's wife KK Tang was from a legendarily wealthy Hong Kong dynasty and was, on the surface, the epitome of a Tatler savvy society lady. Head Girl at Chinese International School then radical art student at St Martin's College when she first met the tall, blond, teenage dream that was Micky Cavendish at the Hong Kong Stadium. Micky was all confidence and bluster having brought a few of his chums over from Cornell to experience the ex-pat carnival of carnage that was the Rugby Sevens.

Micky's American friends were having the time of their lives and their impressive protein-enhanced physiques were ensconced in tiny Disney princess costumes - Micky was Tinkerbell, Brad was Pocahontas and Charlie was a buxom-pecced Snow White. Their silky fancy-dress stretched taut over bulging muscles had turned every red-blooded girls' head in the beer-soaked bear-pit of the South Stand. KK had brought over two yuppie friends from London and had taken advantage of Daddy Tang disappearing for an urgent meeting by swiftly escaping from the plush, corporate box that her father owned in order to go 'rough it' and experience the real Sevens. A few jugs of lager, a taxi to Lan Kwai Fong and several rooftop Mojitos later and KK had experienced her first act of rebellion and succumbed to the man she would marry 5 years' later. He was a reasonably sensible, but somewhat modest, investment from her family's perspective. He was a big, strong boy from hers.

Another 21 years of ski chalets, jungle treks, lagoon dives and tantric spas had passed by. Three photogenic children had been magnificently sired, elegantly birthed and were now being wonderfully raised by Nanny, two helpers and a driver who had recently taught the two eldest how to fire a catapult and gamble at Mah Johng. KK chose the Nanny. Sinead, the second child, was devilish sharp at gambling. KK was endlessly involved with worthy causes, which she genuinely cared deeply about, but she was also so desperately sick and guilt-ridden at all the wealth, privilege and deeply, shallow expectations and affectations that she had fought an epic battle against a gin and marijuana habit for years. Her art, though fine, had failed to take the world by storm.

Nobody in their sanctimonious social circle of the rich and privileged had noticed her vices. They were all too busy with work and social engagements and holidays and being successful whilst KK was far too shrewd an operator to let anyone know anything about her that she didn't want them to know. Just as they all shrouded their own miseries with polished charm and pizazz, KK was an accomplished dissembler. KK felt the guilt of subterfuge but loved the self-destructive thrill her hidden vices of nihilistic escapism gave her. She had been looking for adventure and a bad boy all those years ago at the Rugby Sevens but found the wrong one. She had found a spoilt young man playing a bad boy. She relished the fact that some of her family were mildly scandalised by her shacking up with a white chap from a merely, mildly wealthy, Mid-Levels level family, but nobody could deny he was a handsome brute. He was indeed devastatingly handsome, but he wasn't quite the wild escape KK really yearned for. It had taken her six years to realise, and fifteen more to stray. A random encounter in a good cause café had led to her meeting her true, wild boy, but in a small-town like Hong Kong, three degrees of separation were guaranteed. One degree of separation was her bad luck. Her husband and her lover were drinking buddies and she was in too deep by the time she realised.

Ranald's introduction to his wife couldn't have been more different. At the age of 36, and still shamefully single, Ranald Chen was introduced to chartered management accountant, Eva Szeto (35) after church service. Once Ranald's mother had cajoled a deeply reluctant Ranald and his father to join her for worship instead of playing golf, they 'accidently' bumped into the Happy Valley Szetos, Mrs Szeto and Mrs Chen having become firm friends over the last six months at the Stables and Spa they both frequented. Naturally, the matriarchs never breathed a word of their 'arrangement' but Ranald's father Wallace clocked it instantly, rolled his eyes and then admired the shapely calf of both generations of the Szeto ladies; decent choice. Eva's father was not present; he had run off with a Filipino helper to run a Dive Resort in Puerto Galera a decade earlier, leaving most of his money behind, a small price he willingly paid for freedom. He had never been spoken of in polite circles again.

Eva Szeto was tall, slim, conservatively and painstakingly well-dressed and knew how to smile perfectly. Ranald was tall, slim, a sharp dresser himself but had no idea how to smile or talk to girls and bumbled and stuttered his way through the most awkward ten minutes of conversation of his entire life as if Hugh Grant had possessed his very soul. He was utterly smitten, adorable in his clumsiness and Eva's ice-cool management accountant's brain quickly calculated that he would make a shrewd investment. She was very fond of Notting Hill and Love Actually and Ranald actually said actually a lot. He had a higgledy piggledy hot-potch of British accented charm, sveltely wrapped in a silky, high-class, ethnically Chinese changshan. With her DGS colours and Hong Kong Under 16 squash champion medal on her window sill, she was swift to invite Ranald down to Football Club for a fiercely sweaty squash match the next Wednesday evening, that she let him win by a slither.

They were married within a year, Reception at the Hong Kong Club, and Hamish the young princeling was delivered 9.5 months later to secure the deal. Eva was back at work within 3 months, terribly brave girl that she was, and Ranald had dutifully paraded at church, christenings and charity galas ever since. The Nanny brought up the child. Ranald found the Nanny, Eva approved her employment. Ranald had been the one to make every sports day and Christmas concert as young Hamish Chen displayed an aptitude for choir, the violin and middle distance running before he had reached the age of 9. Eva bestowed approval, when deserved, sparingly.

Ranald was exactly the husband Eva required him to be, he met all the criteria and complied with her explicit policy direction with no aberrations. Accordingly, he was rewarded with sex once a month, again in compliance with her athletic but tightly scripted directions, derived from Cosmopolitan to achieve fulfilling orgasms. For her, naturally – his were guaranteed. Men were basic creatures. She had no idea that Ranald was in fact, a trifle complicated. He had been secretly in love with Micky Cavendish since he was 7 and their Valet / Driver had been selected more for his rakish, good looks than his driving or polishing skills. Nanny liked sensitive men too. Eva hadn't ever noticed his sideways glances at other women, he wouldn't dare, and she certainly had no comprehension that he also occasionally glanced the other way at attractive men. She was too busy smiling entrancingly at them herself and flashing off her latest Tiffany accessory.

Outside the boutique, Ranald dismissed Micky's suggestion that he might get something for Eva,

'I think Eva has enough of everything. I was actually looking for something cool for Hamish, he's ten next week.'

'Woah. Almost ready for big school. I trust he'll be joining the mighty green machine of Crozier House?' Micky retained a boyish enthusiasm for his School House and always made Sports Day to present prizes as a generous alumni.

'No, Micky,' Ranald said exasperatedly, *'he shall be true blue like his father, a rowdy Rowellian.'* Ranald was the least rowdy man in Hong Kong, if not Asia. In truth he couldn't care less who won the competitions, but appearances and social conventions had to be maintained. Micky continued, oblivious to Ran's ambivalence,

'Dreadful. They tried to put my eldest in Nightingale cos KK did the forms and didn't know the right answer to the key question. I had a word with the Admissions lady, Nazzy's kid sister, who saw us right.'

Micky and Ranald had met ostensibly for a 'key head-to-head' about the LTV Finance Package but, seeing as their sidekicks had it all comfortably in-hand and they only invented the drama of tough negotiations to build up their corporate go-getter image, they were taking the opportunity for a good old-fashioned natter. They turned back towards the coffee shop Ranald had recommended and ordered a couple of flat whites, and a spinach salad with caramelized walnuts, cranberries and blue cheese served with home baked olive sour dough bread. They took a pew, a high stool each, up against the windowsill on a little balcony at the back that looked across the broad courtyard, five stories up, to the charmingly restored South Block opposite.

'Family all good?' asked Ranald.

Micky was a proud dad, 3 kids (Conor 12, Sinead 10 and Ruari 7), little mop haired tearaways, all lithe-limbs and scratched faces who had taken to rugby, skiing and sailing with the same hurtling athleticism as their father, combined with a creative streak of subversion, guile and mischief inherited from their mother. Good kids.

'Awesome little monsters as feisty ever! Conor has just made scrum-half; Sinead has decided she is going to be a rioter for Halloween – or freedom fighter as she calls it! I am going to dress Rauiri up as a riot cop to keep her in hand! Bit worried about Ruairi though, keeps wanting to play kissball. It's James' fault, his Charlie is a cracking little footy player. Charlie has been teaching Ruairi keepy-uppies, so now the boy thinks he's Ronaldo.'

Ranald couldn't resist playing the heritage card himself for once, riffing on Micky's legendary, if somewhat mythical, Irish ancestry, *'George Best surely? Or that one other decent Irish player, who was that, there was one in the last century, an Irishman who could play football, Liam ......nah it's gone.'*

'Ha ha! Well in that case Ran my man, here's one for you. A Scotsman walks into a bar.'

Micky stopped. Faux dumb.

'And?' Ranald said.

'That's it. Pub's empty. The Englishman, Irishman and Welshman are all

still in Japan at the World Cup.'

Ranald couldn't help but smile for a micro-second. Then sternly didn't. Micky roared with laughter, slapped him on the shoulder and decided to change the subject.

'Did you hear about that bomb at the weekend? It is turning into Northern Ireland here.'

'It's not that bad! But, yeah, and that copper that got stabbed in the neck.'

'It's not good for business my friend. Needs controlling and a lot of locking up doing. See the cops have shot a couple of people.'

Ranald nodded. Everyone knew live rounds had finally been used. *'Deservedly though, that one in Yuen Long, they were chucking petrol bombs and battering that plain clothes lad.'*

'True, and the first one at Tsuen Wan, those yobbos were piling into his mate on the ground and the cops were outnumbered, I don't blame that cop for shooting and the yobbo hasn't died, has he?' Neither Micky nor Ranald were opposed to the need to crack down. Ranald said what they both thought,

'That one was fair enough, although Jonny will bore you about how they got themselves into that situation. If the rioters want to play rough, then they are going to get hurt. The Hong Kong Police don't muck about and the kids are stupid if they want to start a fight with that lot. Better keep it peaceful kids.' Ranald did the warning-finger mime; Micky finger-pistol shot him back. Ranald did the childhood shot-in-the-heart impression and made Micky laugh, remembering how they'd played at school. Micky chuckled and followed up with another old saying of theirs,

'Don't bring a knife to a gun fight Ranald. And how are our subversive hippy brethren? Have you seen Jonno, or the long-lost Baz and Jenkins?'

'Nah, but they should be out for the next drinking sesh. Monkers again I think.'

'Oh good lord, edgy Mongkok. Better get your jabs. If there isn't a riot on. Why do they pick there? I swear it is just to wind us up. Locke... and Naz. He's complicit, that man.' Micky had a sudden mind-flash of the Russian girl from Portland Street,

'Then again, there are certain parts of Mongkok that a chap can enjoy Ran.' Micky raised his voice and did an 'Only Fools and Horses' cockney impression; entirely lost on Ran. Micky couldn't do Cockney, but persisted,

'The young ladies of the Portland persuasion are always keen for a rubby-dubby.'

They grinned like naughty schoolboys remembering their last foray into Mongkok when Jonny and Naz had dragged them to Mr Wong's, but not joined them 'for desserts.' Ranald looked reflective and carried on,

'How come Naz isn't married yet? The women he 'as 'ad on 'is arm. I'm sure he pays for them you know?'

'You reckon? Escorts? Nah, he's a good-looking boy our Nazza. Remember that one he brought to your Christmas Ball at KCC? Waah Aiyaaah! That was some dress.'

'She was smart too; and loaded. I talked to her and got a poke in the ribs from Eva. All those girls, never seem to see them twice though. Surely one of them would've taken 'im in.'

Micky answered, *'You would have thought so; maybe it's the curry farts. What about Jonny? You never see 'im with a woman. Reckon he's a secret whoopsy?'*

'Michael! That is homophobic language and quite inappropriate.'

Ranald did his best schoolteacher impression, effortlessly hiding the fact that he truly thought his friend's casual disdain a little troubling; after all Micky was a beautiful man and Ran wished he was better than that, as sophisticated and open minded as he was handsome.

'Bore off Ran!'

Micky laughed whole-heartedly. Even after forty years, he remained completely oblivious to even the idea of Ranald not being as straight as he was and, although he knew his friend admired him, that was entirely natural because he was better at games, taller and considerably blonder. Ranald was thinking,

'You know what? Let's not do Mongkok again. It's Halloween, we should do Lankers like the old days. When we were young, dude.' Micky looked keen,

'Good call. I'll speak to the gang. And let's start somewhere civilised, somewhere Jonny should be barred from. I shall pick a suitable establishment.'

Ranald busied himself tidying up the debris of their lunch; he was always considerate of the staff and took the tray back to the counter himself. Micky thought that weak. Whilst Ranald did the waiter's job, Micky allowed his gaze to traverse languidly across the void to the corridor balconies opposite. They were just 100 metres down from Jonny's bijou top-floor flat on the terrace that stank of dog piss so, despite being spookily coincidental, it wasn't actually terribly weird or surprising to see that Jonny himself was sat with his back to the sky with his arm around a woman to his left. Recognising Jonny still made Micky jump though. It was a weird coincidence to have just mentioned Jonny and then seen him, but the real surprise Micky felt was that somebody had actually finally seen Jonny with one of his elusive, never mentioned, women.

Micky had really assumed that Jonny's girlfriend was particularly fat, ugly or offensive and he loved her too much to risk introducing her to his judgmentally boisterous friends with their immaculately tailored and toned wives. Jonny kept his mates and his love life separate. The bloke was always a bit Schizo, Micky thought. This woman looked attractive though, even from behind, he could just sense that she was cute and lively. The couple were sat right at the end of the building, where there were no shops or cafes, just some artists' studios and comfy window sofas.

'Ah ha! A first sighting of the mysterious, rare-plumed Jonny's bird.'

None of the gang really thought for a second Jonny was gay, despite the enigmatically vague love life about which he never spoke. He never had introduced his girlfriends and he avoided their wives with whom he had nothing in common. Jonny was never properly 'one of us' thought Micky, he hadn't been at school with them, he had no real money, and he couldn't quite remember how or when he had joined the group - probably Nazeem's idea. The woman was making him laugh, a lot. Jonny was clearly relaxed, enjoying her company and he pulled her in close as she rested her head on his shoulder, black, ponytail swaying. Micky still couldn't quite see her as she was half obscured by a pillar, slunk low in her seat and wearing a black baseball cap and a black hoody. Must be one of the protester chicks – very Jonny to hook up with a rebel. The way she tilted her head when she spoke seemed really familiar though. Really familiar.

Ranald returned, *'Come on mate, back to the grindstone.'*

'Right oh.' Micky looked down at his phone as it beeped, another impossible deadline had just been set by Big John. *'Oh, Bollocks! Does it never stop?'*

He stood up. Micky didn't want to keep watching or mention that he had seen Jonny in any case. He followed Ranald out.

Chapter 5 – Guts and Drive

Uptown Top Skanking

Ranald and his sidekick Quant Emily, plus a young buck from their office called Alexandre who fancied Emily, had met up with Micky's team on the roof of the swanky and pretentious Treva Bar overlooking Chater Garden for cocktails and nibbles. Naz arrived five minutes later with an impossibly sleek French girl called Katell on his arm, complete with Halloween fascinator and Dia del Morte makeup. Ranald quickly judged her as another one they would never see again and went back to teasing Alexandre in order to undermine his chances with Emily; not because he fancied Emily or Alexandre, just for fun.

Micky had started out loud and was getting louder with every sip of his martinis. He was already two drinks ahead of everybody else. At one point, his assistant May had to call his name twice just to get his eyes out of Katell's cleavage which Naz had noticed but didn't care about, as he was enjoying the look of haughty disdain on his date's face that was making her nose look more poetically French with every cringy micro-second.

Finance Charles and Plans Sophie had taken a spot leaning on the balcony and were quietly chatting so Naz decided to extract his date from Micky's gaze, took her gently by the elbow and steered her towards their more refined company. Sophie was midway through explaining her thoughts on how the relative architectural styles of the Bank of China and HSBC reflected their corporate cultures when the familiar braying voice of their boss made her pause and stiffen. Charles tensed, inhaled deeply and closed his eyes, unwilling to turn around and acknowledge that the evening had just gone from pleasant and relaxed to 'time to go.'

'Micky! What are you doing here you scoundrel?'

Big John didn't wait for an answer, *'Aah and Ran right? How's it hanging? Ha hah! And who is this? Emily? Great to meet you Emily and Alexandre, great suit Alex, looking sharp, and there's a couple of familiar faces...'* His Johnship gesticulated grandly towards the balcony where Quant Emily and Finance Charles had been trying to blend into the bamboo planters.

Big John was in triumphant mood; a couple of premium properties had been acquired at bargain prices as their owners had gone bankrupt and the last irritating tenants of a block he wanted to convert into sub-divided flats had been evicted. The strong were prospering at the expense of the weak, and John was big and strong. Amidst every crisis there was always an opportunity, for those sharp taloned enough to strike fast. Great week!

Charles and Sophie smiled weakly, then more broadly with relief as John's attention had clearly bounced straight off of them and landed snugly on Katell's bosom, to whom he advanced.

'And Helloooo! We haven't met, hi, I'm John, Director at Hardwell Land. Senior Director.'

'Bon soir, I am Katell and this,' she turned to introduce Naz, but John waved a hand dismissively at him,

'Oh yeah, we've met. Hey Narim, the lady's glass is dry, how about another? And a G&T for me, that'd be great. You can put it on my tab, or better still, Micky's ha ha ha!'

Naz took a step back but didn't move away as he was directed, just passed his own drink to Katell to finish off, tilted his head and watched with interest at what was about to happen.

'Sooooo, Cattle, what do you do here mon Cherie?'

'I work for WWF.'

'Oh great, charity work, NGO, great, great. I'm doing a sponsored run next month, half marathon, training hard, do it every year you know?'

'Vraiment? Formidable, vous devez être un homme incroyable, une légende parmi tous les plus gros caleçons de la prefecture de tête super taille.'

John didn't miss a beat, pretending he understood every word, when actually he had understood 'super.' Sounded like she liked him.

'Well yes, it is a super cause and a formidable effort, but I feel like we just have to give back in the best way we can you know? Inspire others. Inspire futures.' Earnest, head-nodding, sincerity, mirroring lexis as taught on professional development management training.

Naz was stifling his giggles whilst Katell betrayed nothing on her face but rapt attention to the man she was about to play with so deliciously. She breathed in deeply, ensuring her bust was displayed to maximum effect to confuddle Big John and lure him in. She took his elbow and nudged him into the centre of the group. Mimicking his Scots accent with French undertones, she led in with,

'Soooooo. 'aaaardwellllll Lornd. Sounds very prestigeeoooooohs. You must be very superb et clehvert. I am sure you have some awesome, amazing...' she did the Trump thumb and forefinger OK sign for emphasis and Naz had to take a step back to snort and fully enjoy his friend's absurdly French Femme Fatale routine, *'...prohjex. Tell me something inspirashional dahliiing.'*

'Well, yes, I have a lot of irons in the fire, hares running, balls in the air, you know. Lots of great projects.' John was evidently struggling to name one. He had little actual idea what was going on in his company.

'Tell me about a biiig one.' Katell pouted suggestively. Naz mouthed

'LTV' at John from behind Katell's shoulder.

'Yes, yes, LTV, the Lantau Total Vision, amazing project, taking a leading role. Cutting edge. We are going to put in three, or four, massive islands, high speed magno-rail, smart internet you know? Integrated, wireless, networked, smart communities, great stakeholder buy-in, huge deal, biggest ever, Carrie Lam right behind it, Beijing on board, I've been shaping the vision, driving the thought leadership capacity,' his arms were waving, his chest swelling. Sensing that he could go on for some time yet, Katell raised a hand, palm up. He stopped.

'How much?'

'Errrr, how much what?'

'Money. Who pays?'

'Oh 700 billion, maybe a trillion, PFI, part Government funded and of course big, big commitment from us and..'

'How long?'

'To build it? Oh maybe 5 to 10 years' timeframe horizon outlook projection...'

'Why?'

'Well obviously Hong Kong needs more land, we are so short of land, that's why the property is crazy, you know...'

'Not true. It's a lie. It is a youge lie. Waste of money.' Katell's demeanour transformed. Velvet cushion became steel stiletto.

'No, no, we need more land, a lot of it will be for Government housing,' He had begun to detect that he was not as impressive to this lady as he expected to be, he started to feel a little nervous, all eyes were on him.

'What cost?'

'I said, 700 bill plus...'

'Non. Environmental cost?'

'Oh come on! You can't stop progress because some granny in Cheung Chau wants to hug the dolphins. The people need jobs, we need development, progress, how are we going to be the biggest and best city in China, in the world, if we don't invest and develop and grow?'

Katell curled her lip and gave her best *'Pah!'* turned on her heel with such style and panache that all heads followed her as she elegantly stalked towards the door. Naz was there before her, opening it with the gentlest swish and following her to the lift. From over at the balcony, Sophie nudged Charles, and indicated with her eyes where Katell, with the masterful misdirection of her 'Pah' plosively pouted into Johns face, had deftly tilted her glass and emptied the rest of her drink onto his crotch. Charles saw the wet patch at just the same moment Big John felt it.

'Fuck!'

All Hallows Party Popors

Ten minutes later, the group had reassembled in Dr Fern's Gin Emporium down in Landmark's Basement to toast the triumph that was Katell. Micky wasn't sure whether he was going to get the blame or not, but after four martinis he wasn't in the mood to fret,

'Did you get John his G&T Naz?'

'Got it right here mate but he doesn't seem to have joined us. Quelle domage mes enfants!'

Katell laughed, *'Ha ha! He had no idea what I was saying to him in French.'*

'That's fair enough sweetie, we have no idea what you are saying to us in English!'

The group enjoyed their drinks before Naz, taking a call from Jonny, announced that they were late and should have been up in Lan Kwai Fong twenty minutes ago. Finance Charles, Plans Sophie, PA May and Quant Emily made their excuses (*'skool night'*) and disappeared into the MTR whilst the others headed up through the atrium to walk up the hill to Lankers. They were supposed to meet the boys in Havana's and all of them had arranged either an off-site meeting, day's leave or a spurious training course the next day – Halloween had been a legendary night out since they were 15 and so worth a bit of deception where work was concerned.

Jonny was in-place, sofas secured, sipping down a mojito and quoting Maynard Keynes, embellishing a bit of Thoreau with Rousseau, trying to impress a voluptuous red devil (Gina from Churchills') who had called in sick to her bar-job in Wanchai and was sat snugly against him with two saucy angel friends who had also flown their employers' clutches for the night. Gina was hoping Micky would turn up soon – Jonny was incomprehensible, obviously poor and decidedly too short.

The police cordon at the base of Lan Kwai Fong blocking Micky's et als approach to the rendezvous was therefore an unwelcome disruption to Plan Waheyhey. A crowd was gathered and had been remonstrating with the police for some time. Despite all the costumes, jokes and exhortations, the police were clearly not in the party spirit and a few of them were beginning to simmer and steam, faced with the rowdy and defiant part goers. A sea of V for Vendetta masks, with the odd Shrek, Yogi Bear, Spiderman or Xinnie the Pooh, defied the police. Ranald and Naz took a check pace.

Micky wasn't to be put off by this nonsense, not his war this, he needed to get up the hill to the bar and so strode purposefully through the crowd and up to the police line, to face off with the tallest officer he could see, who was still considerably shorter than Micky. He started off nicely-ish.

'You look like you're in charge my good officer. May we please go meet our compadres up in Havana please my good man, Sir, please?'

'No. Go back.'

'Oh, come on chap, we are late as it is.'

'No. Too many people'

Micky looked up the hill, compared to a normal LKF Halloween, things were pretty sparse.

'You're joking, the place is half empty. They neeeeed us up there! Look how fucking dull it is!'

Micky's volume had gone up a notch and his swearing had caught the surrounding police officers' attention. One moved in from his flank and gave his shoulder a poke with his baton. Micky took a step back and squared up. Five cops were now focused on him. The one who poked him pointed with his baton at Micky's teeth and shouted,

'You need to leave this area now!'

'I am going to the bar.'

'No. Go home. Leave the area now!'

'Why?'

'People blocking roads and setting fires.'

'Where? You can't tell me what to do. We pay your fucking wages. What's the problem? You are the ones blocking the roads and where's the fucking fire Popo?' Micky couldn't understand why they were in his way, he wasn't a protester, his taxes paid their wages. Jumped up, little fascists. Martini had provided him an alternative perspective on the police this evening.

'Come on, let's just go.' Ranald took hold of Micky's arm, Naz edged Katell a little further away and back into the crowd.

'Why should we go? Bully boy, black cops.' Micky used the Cantonese for 'black cops' – 'huk ging' which really seemed to annoy them despite his mangled tones. The pokey baton copper shouted back even louder,

'You! Leave now fucking cockroaches.' the pokey cop had switched to Cantonese now. Naz stepped up and raised two palms, speaking Cantonese,

'Calm down'

'Calm down? Are you going or not? Fucking cockroach trash, go!'

Micky wasn't going to let it lie. He hadn't quite understood the shouted Cantonese. Ranald had though and he wasn't being spoken to like that by some ignorant beat copper. He was no rioter.

'Cockroach? Who are you calling a cockroach?'

'You. I say, you do. Now go!'

'Call me a fucking cockroach? I earn more than your Chief.'

Ranald was spitting as he snarled back, Naz wasn't quite sure which of the two of them to restrain, pokey cop seemed apoplectic,

'Leave now! Leave now!'

Katell shouted out in English, *'Don't argue with zese dogs. Zey are crazy. Let's just go.'*

Micky was wondering who he might hit first and how to do so without breaking his hand on a helmet or visor; Ranald was not thinking of violence at all but was absolutely not going to back down; Pokey cop was raging,

'Fucking ridiculous garbage. City wankers think you own the fucking world. We run these streets. Go! Now!'

'Garbage? We make Hong Kong rich, fascist! You embarrass us. You haven't even got a degree dog boy.'

'Noone cares what you earn wanker. Go home and die.'

'I bet you didn't even finish Form 5 did you dog boy! Can you even fucking read or just shout?'

Naz decided he better get back in there and managed to slip forward and move Ranald back from where he was probably going to get a smack in the head or a pepper spraying. Ranald wasn't a fighter. Naz was level voiced, he spoke to Ranald in Cantonese, loud enough for the cops to clearly hear the same message,

'You should calm down. Show respect.'

Naz's measured tone worked. Pokey baton cop, with a colleague's restraining hand on his shoulder, took the cue and went down a level,

'I have a loud voice. Doesn't mean I am not calm.'

'You should respect your own uniform.'

They decided that Naz probably wasn't an off-duty police officer, despite being able to speak Cantonese. He was probably just a low-grade local immigrant. Naz's remark set four of them off again, barking like attack dogs,

'Respect? Who do think you are talking to cockroach bitch? You call me Sir! Police are in charge. You show some fucking respect brown boy.'

'You cockroaches ruin Hong Kong and you tell us to respect? Obey the fucking law. You show respect.'

'You ruin everything, garbage, go home! Get off our streets!'

'Fuck you! Go back home!'

'Fuck you! Pakki!'

The ferocity of the police's abuse and a test spray of a pepper can had seen most of the crowd retreat back twenty paces and Katell was leading Micky away whilst Naz had Ranald firmly by the arm and was quite forcibly propelling him downhill back towards the MTR. Ranald was still shouting,

'You fucking halfwits don't belong in Central. Get back to Yuen Long you Triad fuckers! Go home to Shenzhen you fucking PLA. We work here, we live here, you fuck off back to the dog house, you PLA puppet pigs. There are millions of us, just thirty thousand in your little puppet, Mickey Mouse Army.'

He had hardly calmed down by the time they reached the shut-up cobblers' stalls by the MTR, whereas Micky was back in good spirits.

'Blimey Ranald, thought you were a true-blue police fan!' Micky was laughing. Ranald was not,

'Well, it's fucking Halloween. Can't we have one night off the bloody riots?'

Naz looked at the three of them, *'Right Plan B, I'll get Jonny and the girls to meet us in Mongkok instead.'*

Katell looked askance at him, *'Hang on. Mongkok? Aren't we trying to avoid the riots?'*

'It's Ok, my app has the rozzers up at Prince Edward tonight, we'll be fine over by TAP or Joes, and easier to get home afterwards for me.'

'In these shoes? I don't think so. Another time Cherie.'

She gave Naz a kiss on each cheek then one on the end of his nose before vanishing in a swirl of style and panache into a passing taxi. Naz waved the rest of them down the MTR steps and started to call Jonny. It was only 7, the night was young. Plenty of time for fun yet.

Spilt Chips

Four hours later, having craftily beered, darted and pooled at Joes, Micky toddles out of the Meat Factory kebab shop queue and leans up against a yellow streetlight.

'Not quite a proper London kebab but not bad!' clutching a soft, gooey paper bag containing the essential nourishment a man needs after 6 pints and four martinis on a Thursday Halloween night. Gorgeous Gina, wobbly on her heels, balances herself by firmly hanging onto Micky's manly arm.

'Best chips in Honkers sweetheart, here have some'.

It's not yet midnight Cinderella but having started early, it is time to take the lovely Gina, charmed and romanced with wit and snakebites, back to her place for a squeeze, a massage and maybe, if you play your cards right Tonto... Jonny and Naz are still loitering and bantering outside the Airsoft Military Supplies shop arguing about which is the best assault rifle for looking 'ally. Ranald and the angels are deciding between curry or honey mustard sauce on their chips, or whether to go crazy and try the seaweed?

Micky picks out the pickles and the excessive coleslaw, no one needs that veggie shit, and hurls it backhanded into the gutter. He pays it no mind. But two cops, stood in a thicket of loitering Popo 20 metres away, do notice. A heavy built law enforcer, with a skin-cut and a mohawk, shouts out *'**Hey!*** Helmets off, cooling hot heads after an afternoon battling protesters, the other police look over. Another copper shouts something in Cantonese. Micky has neither heard nor noticed. The Mohawk warrior starts striding towards him; one buddy in close pursuit, a third perks up like a meerkat and beckons numbers 4,5 and 6 with his head.

Micky's eyes are on half on his chips and half on Gina, so he has absolutely no idea why one of these is suddenly knocked out of his hands by Mohawk and the other pushed out of the way by a second cop. As fast as his beer-befuddled senses can react, he steps half-back then juts his head forward half getting out an *'Oi!'* before his chin is forced up and back, two more cops are on either side of him and he is pushed back into an alley. A leg hooks round his and he is hurled to the floor. Gina screams and flaps her hands at their stab-vested backs as they barge past her, passers-by start pointing and raising phones to film. Popo Numbers 4,5 and 6 form a screen and push the phonie-filmers back, batons out, pointing into faces, shouting orders.

As he tumbles, Micky has enough about him to remember to tuck his chin and prevent his head smashing backwards onto the filthy, stained alley concrete as he hits the floor. Whilst not entirely clueless in a ruck, he isn't ready for a smack in the mouth from a gloved hand, stiffened with hard plastic reinforcements, padded on the inside to protect the policeman's hand whilst causing solid damage to the target. A baton comes in fast from the right and Micky gets a wrist between it and his eyes. The other baton that is smacking his knees, left hip and groin he can't see but is beginning to feel. Mohawk is now throttling him with his knee on his neck and considerable pudgy weight on his chest.

Popo Numbers 4 to 6 have blocked off the mouth of the alley so nobody can see what is going on. Micky is still feeling the blows and aware of the savage shouting but remains entirely clueless as to what the noble officers of the law are roaring at him in their special, loud, Canto-fascistii voices – he got a **'Pok Gaai', 'Sek Si'** and a **'Diu Lei Lo Moh'** – he knows the swear words, but he has no idea of Mohawk's rant:

'Fucking gweilos think they rule the world, think they are off limits, not any fucking more, you white trash, stuck up, arrogant pig, cockroach Yankee pig-faced scum, think you can tell us Chinese what to do? No more! China Number One! We have all the money and power now white boy, eat shit, sek si laaaa!'

Then, with sweat pouring into his eyes and spittle drooling from his mouth, Mohawk stopped. The two, shoeshine boy varlets with him also paused. One straightened himself up, twisting his boot as he pressed down on Micky's hand and looked up to check the other cops had formed a screen and prevented the cockroaches and assorted media vermin filming them. Safe. The second copper leant back against the alley wall to draw breath, straighten his kit, thinking about what to do now – surely, they would have to arrest Micky now to justify the battering? That was a Mohawk decision though. That would involve paperwork and there was no time for that nonsense these days with so many deviants to correct and subdue. Crimes were being left unsolved. The Police were under incredible pressure.

At the mouth of the alley, with no real knowledge of what had just happened with Micky, Jonny was nose-to-nose with numbers 4 and 5 after number 4 had pointed his baton and shouted at him once too often. Naz was torn between holding Jonny back and steaming in himself. Ranald was doing his best to physically loom over number 6, looming is tricky when you are 65 kilogrammes, five-foot-seven and wearing glasses. Even at five-foot-three, Number 6 was unperturbed.

'Take off your fucking mask and maybe I'll understand you Bully-Boy!' Jonny was firing up on number 4 who was equally wound up and had decided he was going to smack Jonny in the mouth in two seconds unless he backed off.

Naz was negotiating in his polished, fluent Cantonese with number 5 to put the pepper spray down and Ranald had given up 'looming' and was now trying to stop Gina and the angels swearing at numbers 5 and 6 and getting pepper sprayed for their efforts.

As Mohawk was starting to wonder if arrest was the best course of action despite the paperwork, Micky was beginning to understand what was occurring. He had just been beaten up by a bunch of cops for no discernible reason other than perhaps stepping on the cracks in the pavement, wearing a loud shirt in a built-up area or, at worst, dropping a bit of bio-degradable garnish in the gutter. He hadn't even seen the coppers lurking to be fair.

'Fucking Yank!

Mohawk dribbled out the end of his rant, in English so the stupid, ignorant foreigner could understand it and know that he, Hong Kong's Finest Police Officer was better than the lanky, white moron; he could speak Cantonese, Mandarin and English and was not to be messed with. Beating administered, it was time to either plasti-cuff the 'criminal' and make up some story about him abusing an officer, failing to show ID and resisting arrest – or just get up and walk away. There would be no come-back; there never is, Hong Kong Police rule the streets, and the Government quashes all complaints with the conviction and weight of the monolithic Communist Party looming over all dissent. The Party loomed much more menacingly than Ranald ever could.

Mohawk had just decided that walking away involved a lot less paperwork, sub-consciously removing his weight from Micky's chest and looking up at Varlet 2 to tell him ***'Ngoh Dei Jau'****(We're off)* when his head accelerated rapidly and astonishingly sideways. The shift in weight, the pause in shouting and hitting, was just enough space and leverage for Micky to smash a solid right into Mohawk's jaw, coming from underneath and gaining complete surprise. Varlet 2 watched frozen as Mohawk's jaw dislocated in slow motion and sweat sprayed up into the air.

'Fucking Yank?! I'm fucking Irish!' meant nothing to the cops but served as a rallying cry to Naz and Jonny who were still nose-to-nose with the cordon of numbers 4 to 6 blocking off the alleyway from sight. It seemed that mistaken nationality was one thing in life that really annoyed Mr Cavendish.

Mohawk tumbled and Micky had pushed him off to the left and was surging to his feet. Playing Number Eight since he was about 8 had given him a remarkable ability to explode with power from the horizontal, and he had now registered that his exploded nose and cut forehead streaming blood into his left eye needed some recompense. Fair play had not been observed by the opposition. He had no idea why he had been ‘mugged’ in the first place. Varlet 1 started to turn his attention from the cordon to the roar behind him; Varlet 2 was going backwards in terror when the furious ball of Micky Cavendish-Tang came head first into his goggles and he was tumbling back and sideways all-at-once as Micky’s forearm and elbow hit him with such force that his Darth Vader face protector split, caught between the irresistible force of Micky’s rage, his own skull and his police riot helmet which slammed hard against the solid, immovable object of concrete wall.

Jonny had a clear foot and 10 kilos advantage on number 4 who he had clothes-lined against the left-hand wall for trying to hit him with a baton; Naz had stocky number 5 by the throat and an arm, 6 had already been sent to ground by a forearm smash which was devastatingly effective against a 50kg female officer who two months ago had been a smiling, neighbourhood, Schools’ Liaison Officer. It wasn’t a very Naz-like action to hit a lady, but these were modern times, and she had all the gear and no face (just a mask) so, with blue touchpaper lit, the furious wookie flattened the tiny stormtrooper.

In the Alley, Varlet 1 had his left hand out-stretched with the faintest, fingernail grasp on Micky’s shirt shoulder material. His right baton-arm was raised high behind him, torso twisted to strike, all focus on shattering the back of Micky’s head with his truncheon. He had no idea Jonny was behind him. The cop was at the perfect point of vectored balance and rising momentum to be lifted totally off his feet by Jonny’s base of palm open-fist-strike. Jonny’s hand shot upward, avoiding the riot helmet’s visor and carbon-fibre facemask to connect at the single point of weakness that he had been contemplating for weeks now; how to get past all that armour with only bare hands and not break your fists? Take the head, take it backwards and take it fast. In reality it was normally impossible to get a movie star kung fu shot in like that; except for that one sweet, perfect moment in a Mongkok snicket. Beautiful. Better than Aikido class. Better than stabbing wideboys.

One second before it all erupted, Ranald had been pepper sprayed by number 5 for talking too much and was blinded and out of play. The angels had suffered the same fate and police number's 8, 9 and 10 had arrived from nowhere and had Ranald and the two girls up against the kebab stand counter to cuff them whilst trying to ignore Gina's furious blows to their body armour; Number 8 was struggling to stay on task now that Gina had got her nails into his neck. Help swooped in for Gina with a sudden rush as lithe black-masked, black-lycra, black-shirts had appeared like a storm of furious bat-people and started raining blows from umbrellas and fists into the police. The poor old kebab man was desperately trying to get his sauce bottles out of the way.

Consequently, the chaos of the melee outside meant that inside the alley, things were becoming more composed by comparison. Time and space were taking on different dimensions in the dark of the ginnel. Varlet 2, knocked unconscious and broken nosed by Micky, dropped to the floor like a sack of cement, pepper spray can and baton clattering into the filthy, stinking gutter. Jonny had made sure Varlet 1 had hit the floor after being hit mid-air lineout leap, landing head and shoulders first, conscious but out of play. Which left a compos-mentis Jonny looking at a blooded, half blinded and visibly steaming Micky who had fixed his attention onto the dazed Mohawk who was just getting back to his feet. Two wounded tigers snarled. Jonny was just a shadow on the edge of their arena.

Time was growling and bouncing around Mohawk's head; his senses tilting and tottering, his world spinning but not too drunk to hold on. His heart and nerve and sinew were keeping it together with indignation that some capitalist toff had had the impudence to hit him, a mighty hero of the People's Police Force, serving with loyalty and honour. They were going to pay. He went to shout but his busted jaw suddenly and sharply reminded him that he wasn't at his finest or most irresistibly powerful right now. His brain commanded him to take a leap forward and smash his baton into the face of the second gweilo who had appeared from a wormhole, but his body mis-fired and he took a teeter into the wall, bouncing back again off his left shoulder.

Time in Micky's head was also fuzzy, squashy concept. He knew he was hurt, blood dribbled and flushed warm into his eyes and dropped in fat globulets off his chin. His jaw ached, his head pounded, and his right-hand knuckles were just starting to register as a bit fluid after the solid punch to Mohawk's jaw. He knew that the big, bully boy cop coming to his feet in front of him had attacked him, he knew there were lots of other cops close by, but he wasn't really sure what had happened and why they thought he was an American. He paused to think, and as in uffish thought he stood, instinctively raised his open hands up to face level to signal a stop. Time out.

Time in Jonny's head was almost dead still. It ticked. It tocked. Calm. Slow everything down. Breathe. Don't flap. This is what you've been waiting for; a chance to even the score. His knife reminded him it was there again, pressing into his upper thigh, burning in his pocket. No need precious. The press of police at the alley mouth was embroiled with trying to arrest his other mates and fighting off the youthful blackshirts. Micky was up but clearly battered and maybe concussed. Mohawk was glaring at Micky, coming slowly, very slowly to his feet, his baton hand drawing back to strike. Mohawk was moving forward, his face contorted as if he was trying to shout but the words were being strangled in his throat. Mohawk was a twisted abomination of a grizzly bear. Mohawk was the target. As he reached the vertical, the big cop inexplicably toppled to his left, like a staggering drunk, rebounding off the wall and then moving right just a bit further than his balance would have liked him to. Inhale the weakness. No rush. Speed and focus, precision strike young Jedi. All that riot kit, plus a good bit of bulk and fat, protected Mohawk's body. The target had hard knees, a bony jaw and the balls were nearly impossible to strike cleanly. He didn't have a helmet or face guard on though. Hello nose! Don't break your knuckles; use open-side-fist.

As Mohawk's brain concentrated on registering the rebound from the wall and then the correction for the stumble to the right, a sudden, flashing raised palm from Micky caught his dazed attention. Then something whirled by to his front, half-left, a sweeping forearm advancing block from Jonny that just caught Mohawk's left forearm nicely and spun him ever so slightly squarer on. Neat and square for a hammer blow, which smashed into his nose and broke most of it with an audible crunching and, despite being a burly, heavyset man, the momentum was enough to send him crashing down again with buckling knees, bellowing like a bolt-gunned bull. He ended up face down, broken jaw busting just a little more as it hit the rancid, rat ran concrete and his baton clattered away like a scuttling cockroach. Jonny's war cry stunned him further – *'Pok Gaai lah!'* This foreigner spoke his language.

Exhaling on the strike, Jonny took in a huge recovery breath. Good hit. Man down. Now to disable. He quickly checked his six to make sure he was not going to be interrupted then put his knee on Mohawk's shoulder blade, his left hand dug hard onto the back of the target's right elbow, took firm hold of the wrist – and wrenched. There was a groaning, expulsive *'huuuaarh'* but no real crack. Disappointing. He tried again. Better. Snicker-snack, this time something surely cracked in Mohawk's elbow area. Hard to tell for sure though, he was a beefy, chunky bear of a boy. I wouldn't want to meet him in a dark alley – apart from today like, he grinned inside his head. Today I am the Joker, fatman. Try again, change arms, take the left limb between your legs, roll over backwards and use the hips. The alley wall made Jonny scrunch up a bit but, with a wriggle and a squirm, he got the leverage he needed, and with the left arm held firm by the wrists and forced out by Jonny's groin fulcrum and hip power, something definitely broke. Textbook. That elicited a higher pitched whimpering wail of agony. Calooh, Callay, oh frabjous day! No tap-out for you fugly. Always wanted to do that for real, ever since year 8 judo.

Jonny scowled at the damp, horrible grubby stain on his trouser flank from lying his butt down in the stinking alley to get the lock on. Then he went to pick up the baton as a souvenir, before thinking better of it – fingerprints Dr Watson. Instead, he took Micky by the arm, who was standing open mouthed and bleeding, drooling and dripping away. Jonny led the dazed Micky down the alley to a cross-point, then right down another dirty lane. The rest would have to look after themselves. Mohawk was huffing and whimpering in the slithy alley. Now, should he take Micky to the hospital (Kwong Wa was just across Dundas, metres away, seemed sensible), or should they just disappear and clean themselves up? The latter. Hate fucking A&E queues; full of whinging sickies. Off up the alleys to Fa Yuen then; need to try and hide some of the blood getting into a taxi.

Mop Up Op

By now, the blackshirts had scattered as twenty-four disciplined officers of Green Squad stormed into the street as a formed unit of order restoration and peace enforcement. Ranald and Gina had been arrested. Naz had been pepper sprayed at some point and by the time he could see again, having been helped by two volunteer first aiders, Ranald and Gina were already lying face down in the gutter, cuffed hands behind them, surrounded by cops. No-one was bothering Naz, sat on the floor leaning against the Circle K window, although the old boys in their grubby vests who had come out of the Bookies on Fa Yuen to watch the show were debating him and asking whether he was a terrorist, *'He is a huk-yan and looks like a Muslim and we all know ISIS are over here now working with the protesters, read it in China Daily and The Standard...'* Despite the lingering taste of pepper spray in Nazeem's mouth, their fags stank, cheap Chinese made ones cut with all sorts of poisons and toxins. One stained-vest, pot-bellied tough guy took a toothpick out the corner of his mouth to spit, close enough to Naz to make a point.

'Fuck off, you moronic scum!' He swore at them in fluid Cantonese. Tone perfect. He stood up in case they needed extra persuasion. The good 'ole boys formed a surly, beer-bellied, dirty vested wall of defiance blocking him off from seeing what was happening with Ranald and Gina. With her hands plasti-cuffed tight behind her, Gina was hoicked up by her arms from behind, she didn't weigh too much after all. The plasti-cuffs dug deeper into her wrists, her shoulder joints clicked and tore and her upper right arm muscle instantly bruised and started to swell. Someone shouted something or other into her ear that was probably being read her rights but with a face full of pepper spray scouring her eyeballs and snot pouring down her face from her burning nose, she wasn't really concentrating on the Cantonese and was wailing in Tagalog. The indignity and torture of not being able to clean the irritating, noxious substance out of her face was maddening. She then

did all that she could at this stage, which was to start screaming.

This added a level of stress to the arresting officers which made them treat her even more roughly as they propelled her rapidly towards a white van that had pulled up to take away the captured cockroaches. Having writhed her arm away from him, one male copper grabbed her from behind by the first bit of her that came into range, her shirtfront, tearing her buttons in the process. A second cop, female officer Cheung P. C., kept firm hold of Gina's other arm behind her back but needed more leverage and Gina's hair provided the necessary grip and control of her head by which she could be steered forcefully into the van. It made for strong TV and was all on Stand News and Be Water websites within minutes. Within an hour the 'Sexual assault' narrative was out there in the Yellow Press, as was the 'Devil Slut Shame' story in the Blue Media.

Ranald had a bit of sight in one eye, was aware of the screaming and felt compelled to do something, which was to jam his heels into the roadway and push backwards as he was being led to the wagon. This earned him six rapid blows from a truncheon to his neck and shoulder, but fortunately the sixth blow hit the knuckles of one of the escorting officers who was gripping Ranald's neck from behind and so the beating stopped. At least until they got him in the van.

Ranald, being ethnic Chinese, got none of the hesitation one his white friends might have earned just by being a foreigner who might bring unwanted attention. His protestations in Cantonese didn't stop another close-range peppering as they sat him down in the van and *'My mother's a lawyer you morons'* only got him a laugh and two more slaps and a '**Now fucking behave freedom cunt**.' At which point the pepper spray, lager, adrenalin and panic combination led to an almost inevitably uncontrollable spew of vomit chundering across the van, splashing onto Gina's legs sat opposite and speckling the boots and trousers of the police lady, Cheung P.C., strapping Gina into her seat.

Her buddy P.C. Sze got a few sputters on his toecaps, '**You dirty fucker!**' The problem for P.C. Sze is that there is very little room to swing a punch or a baton in the back of a police van. Nonetheless, if your victim has their hands cuffed behind them and has a seatbelt on, there isn't a lot they can do to avoid anything you can get in. After the ninth Saturday night riot shift in nine weeks, a lot of frustration was built up in police constable 83107 Sze P.C. and it came out in a torrent onto Ranald's head as he sat defenceless in the back of the van. The beating was fast and furious but the limited room to swing meant it wasn't going to be fatal. It was enough to knock him out though before the female officer and the driver, Liu P. T., who had got off his air-conditioned arse for the first time in three hours and ran round to the back to help pull Sze off. 17215 Sgt Wong K. H. noticed P.C. Sze being dragged away from the van and calmed down by two more composed officers. One look in the back of the van, at the snotty, whimpering, half-dressed Gina, a whole sloshing floor of puke and the bloody mess of Ranald Chen sagging unconscious in his seat told Sgt Wong they had a potential PR problem.

Everything else had calmed down a bit, or at least moved up a junction. The Green Squad cordon, (green lumie sticks) with a robust combination of strobe torches, shields, pepper spray to the face and a couple of quick digs and raps to the knuckles has pushed the press scrum and mobile phone brigade back far enough that the back of the van beating remained in darkness. 17215 Sgt Wong K. H. turned to (No Number) Driver Liu P. T., who was looking desperately at him for guidance.

'For fuck' s sake.'

'Jun hai Sarge, what the fuck do we do now?'

'Fuck knows! Right, get that boy to hospital. Not Kwong Wah, take him up to QE2, too many rat-faced press around here'

'What about the tart Sarge?'

'The young lady needs tidying up, keep her in the back of the van and take her to the station afterwards. PC Cheung get a buddy and look after the girl, Liu, grab the Chan Chan brothers to get the casualty to hospital and put that fuckwit Sze in the front seat and don' t let him leave it until you get back to base, ching choh?'

'Crystal, boss, on it!'

'I will come down the hospital as soon as I can get away from here to start the fucking endless paperwork this shit show is gonna cause us.'

Raven's Roost

James H-J was close to his usual haunt, lurking with his ninja death commandos in the alleyway down the back of the construction site hoardings near Changsha Street. The 'lurk' was close enough to be on any bit of Mongkok's stretch of Nathan Road in sixty seconds and come up behind the roaches in order to bowl a few over, smack 'em, cuff 'em and get 'em in the van to meet the arrest quota and keep the stats high. He had half an ear on the radio chatter, and most of his imagination on what could be happening with those two Mainland strumpets who had lingered him a glance as they turned up to start their intentional loitering in-and-around Portland Street. After a few giggles and winks they had sashayed away, all tight clinging fabric and sumptuous curves. Taunting Popo when they were clearly on other tasks was a key part of playing the game.

The radio net reported a fight and a number of arrests down on Dundas by the takeaways. Nothing very interesting at first, but then a report of a seriously hurt police officer and a few others who had taken a bit of a beating before the rioters were sent running. Five minutes later, in amongst the usual chatter, the phrase '**Where did those gweilo pigs go**?' caught his attention. Being a gweilo 'pig' didn't particularly offend him, in UK he would be routinely described as a 'pig' just for being a police officer, whereas here in Hong Kong he was of course a 'dog'. What was more interesting was that it was unusual for gweilos to get mixed up in scuffles in Mongkok; on the Island sure, sometimes in TST, but over here on the 'dark side' there weren't so many.

Then a little cog clicked in his brain that the boys' WhatsApp had reported a shift of venue from Lankers to Monkers. Once again, he had missed the boys' night out thanks to fucking work thanks to the roaches' incessant aggro. Maybe, just maybe, next month's run ashore up in riot-free Sheung Wan, then Ranald's birthday bash on sleepy Lantau, would take him far enough away and out of comms not to be dragged back to another grubby helping of shabby street cleaning. The 'riots' were mostly just waiting around for him, sweatily enmeshed in a low-interest entanglement. He had become bored of earnest youths calling out rude names, badly thrown bricks and desultory petrol bombs.

Nothing much else happening, he began to pay attention. It seemed the gweilos had started a fight and attacked the police – improbable if not impossible but the story had to be straight from the start, radio traffic was logged after all. A Senior Constable called Hong was apparently being loaded into an ambulance having had his arms broken and face smashed in. James knew him, the Prince Edward Copshop bullyboy known as 'atchett 'ong who had a despicable reputation and had been turned down by PTU twice for being 'unstable under pressure'. Interesting, he is a big unit and always hunts with a pack of hyenas; who could have taken him down? James stifled a smirk. About time somebody did.

Perhaps we should wander over the other side of Nathan road and have a look:

'Hello Zero, this is Romeo three zero alpha.... Request we put a screen across Argyle and sweep south....... see if we can pick up any suspects fleeing the scene?'

'Zero, wait······ roger that three-zero-alpha, nothing much else on, take your callsign and clear Argyle down to Dundas, over'

'Copy that, we will do Sai Yeung to Sai Yee, can someone else block off Yim Po Gaai?'

'Roger, there is a mobile callsign at Waterloo and Wylie, another at Moko bridge.'

'Roger out.'

'Excellent,' thought James; *'might even pop past TAP see if the lads are in there, let the boys see me all alleyed up in my ninja gear.'* He grinned,

grew an inch and gave quick orders.

'Right, uncage the colours boys, let's get swinging. Inspector Wong my good man, take Red and Green squads, start at Nelson and sweep down Sai Yeung and Ladies to Soy and hold. I'll take Blue and Gold and do Sneakers and Sai Yee, alles klar?'

'Aye, aye Super. And what are we looking for exactly?'

'Good question, well spotted. We are sweeping up roaches running from Dundas and looking for where they vanish and lurk, so poke your heads in the alleys and tong laus. Oh, and check out any gweilos you see.'

'Gweilos? Surely you are the only white man in this village boss? Interesting.' Inspector Fenton Wong grinned and turned to his squad leaders, James turned to his own trusted sergeants,

'Fei, Chewy – we are hunting white ghosts and black roaches. Fei on Sneakers, Chewy one block over, let's get over there pronto!' And with a whoosh of black combats and dark metal, the Raptors erupted from their alleyway like an unkindness of ravens, terrifying passers-by. Up above, two pneumatically built hookers watching from an upstairs window agreed that they quite fancied the young one and old, blond one, despite his big nose.

She Sells Sanctuary

'No, it's down here.' Micky protested and pushed on Jonny to head right as they hit Nelson Street, hesitating before stepping out of the rat-run into the mass of shoppers and revellers. Jonny held Micky back, firmly by the upper arm,

'You need to get cleaned up a bit before any CCTV picks us up. The bogs in the alley further up here. We need a change of clothes too.'

They crossed the road, heads down, and looked up only as they breached the mouth of the next alleyway to narrowly avoid 4 black-masked youths pegging it in the opposite direction. At the far end of the alley, a glint of light on goggles and a sharp torch beam telegraphed the presence of Raptors working their way towards them from the North.

'Sod that. Follow me!' Micky spun on his heel, took five strides and was in and up some steps with the neon enticement of 'Foot Body Massage' lighting the way. Jonny almost fell over his heels as he followed him up several, rancid flights of steps and rang the bell on a solid door. It opened, a woman shrieked, Micky said,

'It's me Lula.' and she gave another shriek

'Oh, my baby, what has happened?'

'Come on!' Micky physically pulled Jonny inside and pushed the heavy door shut.

'Sanctuary mate.'

Jonny had inadvertently discovered Micky's special place of safety and de-stressification. They also did his back hair here. Lula and Maggie would mother him, tend to him and comfort him. They'd also do a nice ginger tea for Jonny whilst he waited. A foot massage was probably out-of-the-question this evening though.

CC on TV

As Micky was being tenderly administered to, Ranald was lying strapped to a wheeled hospital bed, guarded by two cops, both called Chan. He had been dumped out of the van onto a wheeled stretcher by the A&E door, swiftly seen by a stick-thin, exhausted junior doctor and dispatched post-haste to get a CT scan. A brisk and brusque nurse had checked airway, cleaned a little blood, glowered at the Chan Chan cops who were sneering down at the casualty-slash-rioter-slash-so-called victim and checking out the nurse's generous bosom at the same time.

A porter appeared and was tasked by the nurse as she hurried away from the leering policemen. Ranald was wheeled into a lift and up to the CT Scan area.

'Wait there 10 minutes. Busy.' the CT area gatekeeper told the porter and police escort and shooed them back into an alcove by the lift doors. The doors opened, the porter got in, keen to get away from the police who were now looking down their noses at him for being a hospital skivvy; whilst he turned up his nose at them for stinking of tear gas and body armour odour – a particularly virulent strain of stench.

An unconscious Ranald suddenly puffed out an explosive breath. Then another. The cops jumped. Then Ran groaned and his head moved slightly. Chan 942 and Chan 832 looked at him, felt nothing but disdain for the cockroach and decided to take off their helmets and discuss the nurse's tits.

'Great arse too, wouldn't mind some time on that' Chan 832 opined. Ranald, through his haze, thought they were still in the van and harassing Gina.

'Leave her alone you fuckers! Keung gahn fahn, Suht yan fahn!'

That touched a nerve. The protesters and people in general had been calling the police 'rapists and murderers' for a while now, based on hysterical and, to the police's assertion, fake news on Yellow media.

There were a flood of stories carrying accusations of rapes in police custody and 'so-called suicides' actually being dumped bodies from extra-judicial killings, the 'suicide classification' being used to cover up police excesses. They had got used to being 'Huk Ging – black cops' and 'Huk Say Wooi – triads' since the Yuen Long beatings. Due to the normal low-level corruption and collusion, and a certain amount of local tradition, they couldn't really get too indignant about that. They could take being called Ha Ha Ba Ba bullies – they were, and they enjoyed their power; but they weren't rapists or murderers. That was a red line not to be crossed.

Chan 942 grabbed Ranald by the cheeks, squashing his mouth in and forcing more blood to ooze out between his teeth.

'**You shut your fucking mouth freedom cunt, you hear**?' Chan 832 took his baton out. Chan 942 took a fistful of hospital sheet and rammed it into Ranald's mouth.

'**Just stopping the bleeding, bit of first aid for you.**' as he pushed hard down blocking both airways. Chan 892 laughed at the panic in Ranald's eyes. He was going to take his time and enjoy this wait. '**Bit of direct pressure on the wound for you.**' Chan 832

'**So, assaulting a police officer hey? Serious crime. You don't look so tough now. in fact,**' Chan 832 suddenly swept the blanket aside, pulled Ranald's shirt up and undid his belt before tugging his trousers and pants down.

'**Look at your scared little dick, the nurses aren't going to be impressed by you cockroach prick!**' He then gave him a little swat with his baton on the genitals, then a meatier thwack onto his exposed lower belly. Chan 942 laughed and started giving his face little, sharp slaps.

Ranald was in catatonic horror, his mouth tasted of puke, his eyes were swollen shut, still burning with pepper spray, his head throbbed, he felt almost nothing below the neck. Chan 832 gave him a slap then pulled his trousers halfway up, tugged the blanket back over him and leant back against the wall. Chan 942 did likewise. Then leant forward and gave Ranald's face another little slap and laughed. Chan 832 laughed back. Waited a few seconds for comic effect and then gave a little backhanded slap himself; and that is how the Chans waited until the medics appeared to take Ranald for a scan. Chan and Chan were completely unaware that they were being captured by CCTV the entire time. After months of this mayhem, the medics and security guards had chosen their side. It didn't take more than four hours for the footage to be on the internet. Ranald's humiliation was now out there for public consternation. Blue Media were struggling to explain away this one.

Ghost Hunt PXR

'Well? Recognise any of 'em Boss?'

Loyalty. To the Cause, to The Oath, to The Service. Justice, Truth, Honour, Duty. Loyalty to the Boss – usually a tyrant if they are the type 'who values loyalty above all else.' Loyalty is a sacred pre-requisite of disciplined service, to your subordinates and colleagues. Indisputable. But how do your best mates rank against everything else you stand for?

It was the Loyalty virus, with a massive backwash of integrity, that was clogging and cracking and tilting every neural cog and shift-sparking synapse in his head. His mental software had analysed the image, recognised the patterns, accessed the memory and identified the two men loitering and joking by the airsoft weapons shop; the other two who had passed by with three girls a second earlier were equally familiar. Now Loyalty was pinballing round his head like a wrecking ball bearing, giving him a strashing, changging, bodoinging migraine.

'Not sure...'

He tried to remain inscrutable, poker faced, ice cool. It wasn't convincing. Even the most flat-footed detective could detect the blush on his neck, the slight tic of his right eye, pensive lip and microscopically unusual tone and tempo of his two simple words *'Not sure...'*

He was lying, and it wasn't missed, for Inspector Fenton Wong was absolutely no flat foot. In fact, he was one of the sharpest little twinkle-toed, iron fisted young officers of his generation. And he knew with certainty, though he had yet to reach Holmesian heights of deduction, that his boss was lying. This was a bit of shock to be honest. His Boss was a good boss, one of the best in the force with a reputation for incorruptibility and honour that was a bright, shining rarity in an organisation that had been going steadily backward as the Mainland's influence and practices strengthened their insidious grip. So why lie? Only one reason made sense – the same reason that commanded his respect for Superintendent James Heaviside-Jones, the great, bright, white chief of his Tactical Unit. Loyalty.

'Should I lie? Can I lie? I don't think I can physically lie...' The cerebral torment in James' head was now physically prevalent in his harsh breathing, his frustration visible in every furrow and crease of his face as shock gave way to indecision and flew swiftly to anger. Why was he having to make this fucking decision? He had to make enough shitty decisions every day, tactical orders, management calls, leadership pronouncements. Endless and constant demands on him to make decisions, take risks, give orders. This one though, this one, this one was a fucking shit sandwich of indescribable proportions. Why the fuck are his mates getting involved in street violence? Have they got political – or were they just monumentally pissed?

He looked at his loyal sidekick and protégé and he knew that he knew that he knew. There were no 'unknown unknowns' in the tiny viewing room; no secrets between two men who lived in each other's pockets and worked, thought, investigated and operated together as one of the best leadership teams in The Firm.

'Picture's too blurred. Seem familiar but can't quite remember why, where. Maybe from rugby....'

'Difficult to say hey Boss?'

'Yep'

'Shit. That's proper shit. No leads, there is just this footage Boss.'

'Hmm.'

Silence. More silence. No eye-contact. Inspector Wong wondered if today was the day he would finally need to bend the rules. In his head, he had already chosen his preferred course of action - forget what he knew he knew but couldn't prove and didn't want to. Who would know?

'So, what do you want to do?' Fenton shifted the onus back to James.

'It ain't our investigation Fenton, they just asked me because I'm white and so are two of these geezers. This is Kowloon West work not PTU business, I'm not doing their fucking job for them. I want nothing to do with it. They're on their own and the Prince Edward shop can go fuck themselves too – they didn't exactly look after us the other month. Their thug deserved a kicking; he's had it coming for months.'

'Roger that. I'll tell 'em you don't recognise any of them.'

'Good, good, yeah good call. Cheers Fenton.'

Blimey, thought Inspector Wong, he never calls me Fenton – this is going to be a tricky, few weeks. As if things need to get any trickier!

Chapter 6 – Almost the Last Hill

Remembrance Day

Micky was no longer listening to Plans Sophie going through version 7.4 of the Lantau Tomorrow Vision finance plan. He was wondering if he should do another Thought Leadership video-blog on Linked-in. Big John was doing them regularly now, mostly on Servant Leadership and Team Wellbeing, all without a trace of irony. It was great for profile. Micky's team had met Ranald's people downstairs in the Bank of China's coffee shop at Plans Sophie's suggestion. It was possibly the world's poshest Pacific Coffee with expensive, executive furniture, all traditional Chinese sculpted deep curves and polished wood. To get rich is glorious. Plans Sophie felt and thought much better when away from their 54th floor headquarters and the overbearing presence of Big John and the myriad of corporately cloned apparatchiks, lackeys and sharp-suited shoe-shine men. Plans Sophie and Finance Charles were sat with their backs to the ornate semi-circular archway; PA May was sat next to Micky, leant forward intently; a bruised Ranald and a perky Quant Emily were beside him, relaxed and confident.

They had a really taut package planned now and this was the last session they would need before presenting to directors, board members and uber-executives for approval and signing. The big boys would sign. They had had enough cosy chats in their cloistered clubs to know, from the horse's mouth, that the Special Representative and very highest echelons of power were behind this. Chief Flunky Carrie Lam had hung her hat on it very publicly in her recent Chief Executive's Policy Address. The 'Vision' would be built, the tycoons and politicians would all get rich, and it was Micky's responsibility to dot the 'eyes' and cross the 'tees' and make sure everything added up, pieces were placed, ducks were rowed and shits were socked for his firm's role in the enrichment plan.

Alles was indeed in Ordnung and Micky could finally, after months of days-into-nights, actually enjoy his pink salt vanilla latte. Ranald, still bandaged and tender, sipped his chai tea with satisfaction; he lived for this corporate planning porn, but Micky really wasn't that interested. Micky dipped his spoon into the froth and licked it off, careful not to disrupt the artistic flourish of a triple heart that the barista had created on top. He suddenly noticed how clear Plans Sophie's skin was, how her lips described an impeccably crafted cupid's bow. He realised he hadn't thought about women for ages, certainly not his wife. Gina didn't count; she was just for fun. What had his wife been up to lately? Exhausted with The Help and the kids he supposed, or all that hiking she had taken to. The discussion wound up, there was a pause and the others looked up together and turned to him for approval. He had no idea what they had proposed. He beamed.

'Splendid stuff Team! We're there aren't we? It's been hard, but we are ready for final sign-off. Here's to Wednesday's meeting – and Friday's beers!'

Ten minutes later, all took their leave with hugs and handshakes like old friends and headed back towards their offices across Chater Garden. Micky touched May gently on her upper arm with a single finger,

'You go on back. I'm going to take a little stroll. Clear my head.' May recoiled slightly to the touch but tried not to show it. Be calm she told herself, be patient.

'You OK Mr Cavendish? Want me to send a car?'

'I am OK May May, I am just fine. I want to think about a few things is all. I'll get an Über back over later on.'

'So, no car?'

'No. No car.'

Micky came out of the building, scaled the steps alongside the waterfall and came up to the podium level by the reflecting pool. Two elongated bronze heads were set in the shallow pond, one male, one female, both distorted and stretched but still beautiful; sorrowful as they faced each other but seemingly looking straight through and past one another.

He climbed a few more steps and crossed the bridge over the highway, into the welcome haven of the rock garden with its lush greenery and another trickling waterfall. He felt calm descend upon him as he meandered again and entered the precinct of St John's Cathedral. He paused by the memorial on the right. There were a number of fresh poppy wreaths laid at the base; oh yes, this was actually Remembrance Day. The Sunday beforehand, the uniformed coterie of Hong Kong had held their ceremonies. Maybe for the last time – it wasn't a Motherland Occasion. Micky had attended service as he had done since he was a small boy stood alongside his father by The Cenotaph. The others went too, Ranald, James and their fathers were always there near the front; Jonny and Naz, at the back. The Lone Piper and the Last Post still moved him, but he never wept like the older ones did. He'd never been to war. It always amazed him where all these old, white people came from and how the stiffest of pukka-Sahib Brits lost their composure and let tears roll down their cheeks, washing away their dignity and losing face in his eyes.

He noted that old Chinese soldiers never wept, and he remembered Ranald always being proud to tell his friends about his family's history of resistance to the Japanese. Ranald still never did deals with the Japanese; it took a lot of cunning to get out of it sometimes, but he always avoided it. Micky dealt with whoever had the money to play with and thought Ran's prejudice hopelessly 1940's. Micky had never thought about The War or the cultural dynamic much before. There was a school trip to Stanley and vague memories of some atrocity having taken place, but he couldn't recall the details. His old school had some ghost stories from when the Japanese had occupied and used it for a hospital, a bit of torture and an officers' brothel.

There was a lone grave there in the precinct; Private R D Maxwell, Hong Kong Volunteer Defence Corps, 23rd of December 1941, 22 years' old. One grave in an Asian cathedral. A Westerner's. No mention of the Lais, Lees and Leungs of the East River Column. No mention of the millions of Chinese that fought and died expelling the Japanese, only for the British to come swanning back in again. His faux-Irish antipathy towards the dastardly British began to rise; but it was an affectation and deep down he knew it. He hadn't been oppressed in West Belfast or Derry, he wouldn't know the difference between the Falls Road and the Shankhill if his life depended on it. He had grown up with a rugby club, swimming pool and exotic holidays and the first time he had seen a petrol bomb in real life was looking down on Admiralty from the balcony of Sevva where he had been sipping cocktails with overseas investor chums whilst the locals were rioting. They laughed heartily when he quipped about laying on the street entertainment especially for their business trip. They had all assumed he was an American. National identity was a PR image for Micky.

He hadn't come to the Cathedral for history or culture though; his reasons were a little less intellectual. He had managed, with considerable guile, to put a little bit of spyware on his wife's phone. Actually, it was Ranald's cunning to be fair. Ranald had been tracking his wife and son for over a year and mentioned it to Micky over tea at the Hong Kong Club one afternoon. Ranald used the software to avoid Eva catching him misbehaving; Micky was using it to follow KK. Micky was impressed with his Bond-like skills in getting hold of her phone before she locked it when she came in from hiking one evening. She dumped her kit and dashed off for a shower, leaving her mobile on the bedside. He had been tracking her for a week now; nothing strange really, but today she was right nearby, and he was intrigued. She hadn't joined the choir as far as he knew, and she didn't believe in God either. Why was she at the Cathedral?

Micky stepped across the narrow path under the eaves of the entrance. There was a broad notice board – Castaways the charity shop; maybe she was donating or meditating? There were several adverts for Peace, Stillness and Prayer taking place in the Lady Chapel. She had changed a lot lately, there was something different, but had she really turned to God? She went to church as occasion demanded but had no faith, she went to respect her mother's conviction and polite society's expectations. A large, faded brass plaque caught his eye and informed him that the chime had been presented in 1953 in honour of Her Majesty Queen Elizabeth II by the Hong Kong and Shanghai Banking Corporation – the majesty of Church, Power and Money in perfect harmony and good order as the world should be. Except now, God was dead, The Party preached the holy path to righteousness and the Chairman's PLA were the irresistible power. The money however, the money was a constant – the immutable real power behind all of history's thrones.

The doors into the chapel were light wood with glass windows so he could peer in before he gently opened them and stepped through. The cool, the special church cool of stone and tile and serenity embraced him and welcomed him in. There were four people, three ladies and one gentle man, all sat apart, alone and in contemplation. A fifth figure was down the front, to the right, looking up at the faded, decaying military and police flags that hung there, reminders to the sacrifices of previous generations. There were a few Union Jacks up near the eaves, perhaps the last refuge where the old colonial masters' flags were allowed to fly. Probably only safe because Communists were allergic to Christianity and so unlikely to ever realise that the imperialists' relics were still being held sacred somewhere nefarious like the House of Christ. Hail Mary, full of grace, blessed art thou for honour and dignity, and standing up to the brutality of the godless, thought Micky.

None of these people in church were his wife though. He checked his phone, the app wasn't that accurate to be honest, but she had to be close. He walked a circuit of the church; rather quaint, bijou for a Cathedral, but bereft of his spouse. He had better check Castaways the charity shop then. As he re-emerged into the portico, he saw an arrow for the shop to his left, but another sign caught his eye - 'The Labyrinth' and 'The Nest Coffee Shop.' Seemed possible, he turned right and followed the edge of the Cathedral wall. A small information board informed him that the Japanese had used the place as a social club during the War – irreverent bastards, perhaps Ranald was right to hold on to the old prejudices. Must have missed out on some really good deals though.

He looked down a few broad, stone steps at the bright white counter in a small glass box that housed The Nest coffee shop. A woman had her back to the window, fussing with the shelves whilst a young lady looked straight at him, broad forehead outwardly displaying her Downs' Syndrome, huge smile and kind eyes revealing her inner beauty. Micky couldn't help but smile back and return the little wave she gave. Then the counter girl's smile dropped away as she noticed the tall, blond man's reaction to something he had noticed off to his right.

Six tables were spaced out next to the cloistered arched walkway that bordered a square patio. A dark haired, slim and precise looking woman of about forty was sat at one of the tables in the open, her laptop before her. Micky noticed her first, nice looking, very presentable, great calves. Not KK. At one of the other tables to the side, nestled into The Nest's cloister sat two other people. He couldn't see anything but a slight shoulder of the one with her back to him, concealed by a brick pillar. Black ponytail, black cap on the table. The one facing him was Jonny. PMQ clicked. A beggar with his queen. Micky almost cried out in surprise and greeting, then something in his mind borke and held his normally blurtful tongue.

Forgot to Brake?

Jonny was enraptured. There was no other word so appropriate for the location. He was totally beguiled as he listened to the gospel, the amusing light-hearted gospel of joy that the person sat opposite him was sharing. She was his world. His salvation. His face was lit up, touched by a pure and holy light. Her hat, a plain, black baseball cap lay on the table. Micky could just see her right hand, waving about as she spoke with animation and then her sinful, slender hand lay a gentle palm upon Jonny's wrist. As she profaned with her worthiest touch, Jonny smoothly covered her hand with his own, not at all roughly. He looked nowhere else but into her eyes as Micky's eyes burned holes into the back of her head.

'Now tell me the truth, how does your hand feel right now?'

She looked down, her nostrils flared, her lips skittered to a slight smile.

'Alive.'

Jonny hadn't felt himself being watched, his sixth sense was overwhelmed by all his others; he didn't look up and see Micky turn and stalk away. The girl behind the counter did, she crossed herself. It felt as she had just seen the devil pass by. She wouldn't tell anyone though, they wouldn't believe her; the devil was short, dark and red, not tall and blond.

Jonny had not seen Micky as he had never seen KK's husband, although he knew he existed and was a suit. In two years, KK had never let him see a picture of her husband, her kids or even her parents. To him, she was 'Kay,' just K. She had remained an enigma and, knowing how she wanted to keep it that way, he had been true to his promise and kept himself in willful bliss. He knew by now that she was rich, she talked about her nameless kids with great love, complained about her anonymous husband with perfectly balanced bitterness, and shared the trials and tribulations of her wider, enigmatic family. Poised, she never gave quite enough for him to join the final dots; none of her family had names, just the usual Chinese denotations – older brother, mooi mooi, lo goong, eldest, mother-in-law etc. He had learnt enough Cantonese to recognise the hierarchical connotations now, which initially he had assumed were their nicknames.

Whilst Jonny knew no details of Kay's husband, the opposite wasn't true at all. She knew all about him, inspected his phone and his photos regularly and was incisively aware of his newest friends and oldest lovers. She was acutely conscious that he was one of her husband's wide circle of drinking buddies but had no intention of ever clouding their relationship with that inconvenient truth. She discovered it early and resolved to bury the issue instantly and ruthlessly. They ate lunch often at their first meeting place where they planned secret adventures all across Hong Kong, exploring the hidden trails, hills, temples and back streets with an insatiable desire to discover, experience and enjoy every last moment of their stolen hours together.

She had met him in a homespun Homantin café staffed by a charming bunch of special needs waiters and cooks. Special Educational Needs was her charity work of choice, yet another area the Government was proving hopelessly inept at providing for, and so she brought her time, patronage and fund-raising skills to a number of SEN schools in the area. None of her own kids were 'special' but she loved the experience of working with people who were different and challenging. She would often pop into the café for lunch between appointments and when Jonny walked through the door one day, classically framed by sunlight beaming in through the windows, she noticed.

Actually, everyone noticed because all the employees looked up and waved and called out a greeting. Carmen came from round the back to beam one of her charming smiles. Phil heard the hubbub from the back of kitchen and came out for a grin and a wave. Jonny was obviously a regular, and a popular one, and he simultaneously puffed-up with pleasure and shied with humility. He ordered a cheeseburger and coffee in halting Cantonese, had his order repeated back to him by the lad on the till in a questioning voice, said it again, had it repeated, said it again, had it repeated, paid his $55 and got a little number on a bendy-wire stand with a porcelain base.

He looked up and realised with visible dismay that there were no empty tables. His choices were to join the big ten-person table that had an unruly bunch of six teenage schoolboys on it, sit with the old couple on a four-man table that had two spare seats, or ask KK if the spare seat opposite her was free – a move that he would love to have the courage for, and in his imagination, he had the style for, but in reality, would be unthinkably presumptuous and a surefire recipe for misread intent. He would unnerve her and have to spend the entire time awkwardly not noticing her even though every natural impulse in his body was to notice every single, tiny, wonderful, precious detail of her. Unthinkable.

KK was not feeling the same mental dissonance; she was bored, lonely and feeling reckless. Besides, Micky had been an insufferable bore again last night. She skillfully caught the glance of the arrivist man as it rested momentarily on her café table and held it fixed in her eyes with a defiant smile. She knew he had noticed her the instant he came in of course, she was attractive and near his age, but he was desperate not to get caught noticing her in case she thought him creepy. She didn't think him creepy. The welcome he elicited on his entrance had revealed his kindness – special people are especially good judges of character and don't pretend to like dislikable people. He wasn't tall, he wasn't handsome, but he was quite cute looking, in a scruffy way. He also revealed, in the big grin he gave Carmen and the *'Alright Sunshine'* he gave Phil, that he had a bit of cheeky self-confidence to cover his shyness. He might be a bit of a rogue and a lot of fun. That's the combination that made her raise her hand, turn it over with an elegant flourish and indicate the empty chair opposite.

'You are welcome to join me.' She offered.

He had never had a better proposition – the sunlight that had framed his entry was equally wonderfully glancing off her serene face and he was completely smitten before he had even bumped into the chair, split her tea and wobbled the table vase as he sat down. He was all fingers and thumbs. It was charming.

So began the most exciting, all-consuming and utterly unsuitable romance of their lives, complete with torturous separations, tempestuous frictions, frustrations and frequent break ups. She would never abandon her kids, nor did he want to tell his own (away at University now), yet but they were both in deep over their heads. At that awkward first parting, when they both had to leave but didn't want to, and wanted to meet again but didn't dare to ask, he said, awkwardly,

'I've lost my mobile number – can I borrow yours?'

It was corny but it was cute. His mobile was sat on the table. They weren't eighteen anymore, so she took his phone and called herself. She answered her own call,

'Yes, I would love to. Somewhere unusual, somewhere cool and quiet. A photography exhibition at The Asia Society? Perfect. Sunday at 10 then.'

She put his phone back on the table, smiled coquettishly and glided effortlessly out the door. Alive.

Brick Head

On Remembrance Day, whilst old soldiers remembered past wars, young braves were skirmishing on the modern streets of Hong Kong and things were getting a trifle mediaeval. Students at Chinese U had just fought a battle deploying round banquet tables as shield walls, firing catapults, liquid fire petrol bombs and had even mobilized the archery club - black-clad Robin Hoods ready to fight guns with arrows. The students were now under siege at PolyU, completely surrounded by a solid ring of heavily armed police and the result was going to be as predictable as the valiant braves of the Sioux had discovered when faced with breech loading rifles and Gatling guns.

Whilst the city was gripped by the real-world conflict at PolyU, Jonny and Micky were involved in an equally vicious information war on Facebook. Jonny had shared a Be Water Facebook page clip of an elderly man, who had been killed when a brick hit his head during a melee at Sheung Shui. The video purportedly showed a lady in a skirt come up behind the unfortunate man, who was taking pictures on a break from street-cleaning rather than getting actively involved. The lady appeared to launch a brick at point blank range that, presumably accidently due to poor throwing, smacked into the back of the poor bloke's head and took him down. The Yellow Be Water comment blamed the Blue lady and the pro-Beijing mob.

Almost immediately Micky had posted another clip from YouTube, taken from on high at another angle which showed the killer brick coming from the front, from the protester side, and pole-axing the victim who collapsed straight backwards. The Yellow Be Water clip was a fake and swiftly discredited. The Police had called it a malicious murder, Beijing declared *'an atrocity against humanity that was inhumane and unforgivable.'* Despite having been beaten up by the police on Halloween, Micky despised the protesters even more. They were oiks and bad for business.

Micky had posted a comment. *'Fake news Locke. Here is the real clip. Yours is a fake. You can see the truth. The rioters threw the brick. The rioters started the mess, started the fight and are ruining Hong Kong. You bleeding-heart liberals don't know what the truth is.'* The two of them had then gone at each other like trolls in a bear-pit.

Ranald and Naz had seen it but both initially resisted the temptation to join in. This one was between Jonny and Micky; and whilst Micky was right on the initial issue, he was losing the online spat. Jonny knew he had been caught out, but his blood was up, and he proceeded to counterattack with everything from the Legco conspiracy, the surge in suicides, Tiananmen, Xinjiang, five demands, police brutality, PLA spies and agents provocateurs. Whilst his facts were oft debatable opinions, he was at least sticking to issues.

Micky's tactics were different; he was refuting Jonny's claim with statements that increasingly resembled something out of China Daily and ending each burst of rancor with a personal insult. Locke had been an idiot, libtard, halfwit, hippy twat, snowflake, left-wing wanker, moron and socialist parasite before Ranald and Naz had even scrolled down a page.

Ranald wotzapped Naz.

'Have you seen Jonny and Micky on Facebook? Proper cock-fight.' Naz immediately resorted to voice and made the phone ring. Ranald answered promptly,

'Alright Naz. Should we get involved or just leave them to it?'

'It's getting embarrassing. Everyone can see their scrap. I think we need an intervention buddy!' Naz was laughing, and Ranald joined in, but both were uneasy.

'Why don't you message Jonny and tell him to shut up and remove the posts; I'll do the same to Micky?'

'Good plan Ran. Let's do it.'

'Laters.'

Naz telegrammed Jonny, then seeing that Jonny had just posted another riposte and was looking suspiciously like he was just baiting Micky for the thrill of it, decided to call him as well.

'Hey Naz! What's up?'

'Facebook. Micky. Stand down Jonboy. It's getting out-of-hand.'

'Just a little political difference of opinion; nothing to it. I am remaining calm.'

'Micky isn't though is he? He's losing it. And you are twisting the knife. You are supposed to be a grown up. We are supposed to be considering a career in politics, not invective.'

'He's the one calling me rude names. I am being polite.'

'You are winding him up. Everyone can see the squabble. It's undignified.'

'Wellllll. Maybe a little.' Jonny chuckled. *'Alright. I'm tapping out.'*

'And I'd delete your posts if I was you. Political awareness my friend. You don't want to get disappeared.'

'Yeah, true enough. On it. Cheers mate.'

'Have you and Micky fallen out about something else? He seems proper raging.'

'No. I don't think. His Lordship just doesn't like being stuck up to. Stuck up folk are like that. He's always been a bit of cad that lad.'

'Hmmm. Alright. Be good.'

'Be lucky. Cheers Naz. I'm sat in PMQ having a coffee and there's

nothing much else to do than wind up the toff. See you in a couple of weeks for beers.'

'Gins next time I think – your neck of the woods innit?'

'Yep, I'm mother next time – Ping Pong for starters. See you then.'

Ranald's intervention wasn't going so well. Three WhatsApp messages and a Messenger text had not been read and Micky's Facebook posts were getting longer, more profane and extremely badly spelt. Ranald really didn't want to call but he didn't have much choice; the grammar was ghastly, it pained him. The first call was ignored. The second rang for a long time before being answered with the tersest snap of,

'Yes. What?'

'Hey Micky.'

'What Ran? I'm busy.'

'I can see.'

'What do you mean? Are you fucking stalking me?'

'Facebook.'

Silence.

'Micky? Are you there, mate?'

Silence.

Silence.

Then, *'The fucker.'*

'Come on. He made a mistake. He didn't know it was a fake.'

'He's a fucking, lying, cheating fake cunt!'

They were both men-of-the-world who swore in regular conversation all the time down the pub, but this was proper swearing, this was serious intent. Ranald tried to placate him. It didn't work. Micky began swearing some more and assassinating Jonny in every way possible from his background, profession, dress, looks, politics – you name it, he was slamming it. Ranald looked at his phone, Jonny's posts were gone already.

'Come on Micky. Let it go. You're making yourself look mental.'

'Fuck you Ran!' Micky hung up. The posts continued.

Red Right Hand

Micky finished his second Jade Cat cocktail, paid his exorbitant tab, and skulked out of the lavishly peacock feathered opium-den bar that reclined beneath his apartment block. The male dancer in silky black briefs and stockings gave him a wide berth as Micky swept past; he'd already found out that Monsieur was not in a playful mood. The girls behind the bar had realised the moment he scowled in that they were not going to be getting their normal tips from him that evening. He had sat, glared at and through them, lurking and menacing, hunkered down inside his bulky Top Gun bomber-jacket. He left without a word. Micky hadn't intended to take his bike just four stops down the MTR line to where he was meeting the boys, but he was sat on his Norton Commando and roaring out of the underground garage without even realising where he was. He could have been there in 7 minutes down Queensway but instead he found himself up on Bowen Road, winding along the face of the hill towards Robinson Road. He had worn his leather jacket but didn't have his helmet on. He hadn't noticed. He was looking to kick doors in and find himself a war.

Four hours earlier he had been stood in front of Big John's desk. His boss had his back to him, spun around on his office chair, feet on the windowsill, looking out across the harbour towards Lion Rock. John was reading from a folder, exquisitely neatly flagged and containing details of the figures that represented Micky's share of their firm's extensive property portfolio. The figures were mainly in brackets and mostly in red. May had prepared a detailed and thorough financial situation report. John was methodically scolding Micky with them. Micky protested,

'But everyone's figures are down. These protests are killing everything.'

'Aye well, it's a question of reputational risk you see.' Micky didn't really understand that remark and continued his plea.

'Come on John. The LTV thing will pull us back into profit. We've put together a great package there.'

'Ah yes, I'll be taking on that myself.'

Of course, he would be - the only project with any prospect of any good news and, with all the detailed, hard work done, it was time for Big John to stroll in and steal the glory. The master at work. John spun his chair around, trying his best to appear firm and menacing. Micky was well connected and had a wild streak, John was sweating, his eyes watered, and he was struggling to maintain his dominant Alpha act. Inside he was terrified about how this might go but was even more terrified of the CEO to have argued to save his key lieutenant of the past 7 years. He had received an accusation supported by evidence, reported it immediately, heard judgement and accepted his orders with an instinctive, *'Yes Ma'am!'*

'It's not just the numbers Micky. We are going to have to let you go and find somewhere else. It'll be a shame to lose the Cavendish-Tang family from the Firm, but we can't take any chances. Reputation you understand, lawsuits, very difficult.'

'What chances? Lawsuits? What? What!' Micky thought his fracas with the police in Mongkok was somehow out there.

'There's been a complaint Micky. Bit awkward. Harassment and bullying. Maybe a suggestion of a bit of, you know, hashtag me too type stuff.'

That didn't seem to fit the unexpected, random violence of a boozy night out. Micky reconsidered the threat,

'About who? You?'

'No! You!' John roared, outraged at the suggestion. John was extremely modern. Micky flinched as there was nobody more likely than Big John to be out of order with a female employee, whereas he himself was a bit of a cheeky rogue but surely not a creep. Was he?

'Who by? What? Who? What?'

'Can't say, but the evidence I have,' John tapped another folder on his desk, *'recordings as well, all a bit tricky.'* Micky looked at the folder - May's trademark blue cover and pink tabs. PA May. 7 years and she betrays him like this.

'That's rubbish! Bollocks! I've never touched her!'

John's PA had opened the door and no less than four security guards entered the room and arrayed themselves on either side of Micky. Three of them were over 60, the younger one weighed about 15 stone, all flab and no muscle, and all of them were dwarfed by Micky. They wisely decided not to take hold of his arms. The PA handed Micky a large cardboard box with two hands and Micky was neutralized, stood dumfounded with the box held in front of him like a supplicant. Face like a constipated trout, she spoke in a deliberate cut-glass, clear voice,

'I have arranged to send the rest of your things to the house. Your suits and sports kit will be delivered there, Sir. Goodbye.'

Big John had swung his seat back around, feet on the cabinet, looking out of the window again. Master of all he surveyed.

The Last Banter

Micky's bike had stopped. He had arrived. He pulled his Norton into the kerb where the double yellow line ended, a dead looking row of shuttered shops to his left. He sat, and he sat, then he looked across the road to the red door with the round window. He wasn't sure what he was going to do next, but he was going in.

The bar was semi-hidden behind a simple red door with white Chinese characters above it; it looked like a delivery entrance and the door opened onto a long staircase that dropped down into a cavernous hall-like space which, back in the day, had been a community ping-pong hall. Now it was a plush, trendy gin-bar with contemporary artists work on the walls, mis-matched bo-ho furniture and a beautifully lit bar running faux-bootlegged bottles high up the back wall.

Inside sat three other samurai and, despite their recent travails, the mood was high. The District Council elections had just delivered an absolute drubbing to the pro-government parties with democrats winning 17 out of 18 districts. Even Ranald, yet to arrive and previously a stalwart loyalist to the Establishment, had cheered the results; a police beating on a hospital trolley and being prosecuted on trumped up charges was liable to sway a man's opinion about the quality of the authorities he lived under. Unless you were Micky. Micky had assumed that they had deserved the chastisement but were too drunk to realise why. The boys were all relishing trading stories of the pro-Beijing bloc's humiliation and mocking the Party Machine's bitter politicians' finger pointing and dissembling obfuscations in defeat.

'That'll be you next year Naz!' Jonny slapped his buddy hard on the shoulder.

'Do what?' asked James. Naz grinned,

'Yeah, me and Jonny Sahib are going into politics.'

James thought that finally Naz had found his niche, *'Fuckin' ace! Yeah, good shout Naz, you'll be great at that! Still not gonna vote for you though. I always just go for the pretty one. You will definitely get in though with your PR skills.'*

Naz laughed, *'If it's like this year, as long as there is a D.A.B runner to beat, a blancmange on a potty could get voted in.'*

'That's the slogan – vote Naz, a blancmange on a potty!'

'Yeay!' Glasses of various fancy gins were raised. James kept the 'yeay' going with enhanced gusto as his eyes were looking up the steps. Ranald was coming down. He was still limping a bit, right wrist splinted, head mostly bandaged, but grinning inanely. The boys were on their feet and took it in turns to give the battered lad a big, but gentle hug.

Jonny took a step back from the table, *'I dunno what it is Damps, but there's something different about you...'*

'Yeah...' James took up the baton, *'... I know, no briefcase!'*

'You look like the fuckin' mummy mate. Does it sting?'

'He might look like your mummy, Jonboy.'

'Stings a bit to be honest.' Ranald was still tender.

'Does this hurt?' Naz pretended to slap his arm,

'How about this?' James mimed an elbow to his head, Ranald looked terrified and exclaimed hastily,

'Hey! I've had enough of police brutality for this year thanks, Mr Popo!' James grinned.

The boys settled back down and ordered Ranald a drink. Naz noticed that he was a little taciturn.

'Sup Damps?'

'Ummm. Before Micky gets here. Ummm. You know it's my fiftieth tomorrow. I've decided to change my life.'

Everyone went quiet. Ranald was clearly about to deliver significant news. News he was not quite sure he should deliver. His lips were sticky. Everyone held their breath, thoughts ran through their heads; Ran was the only one who had maintained as sylphlike figure and cancer was the prevalent thought - silently votes were split between prostate, bowel and lung. The last one was Jonny's guess. Ranald didn't smoke but Jonny still did and so was somewhat fixated in that one wearing death's cowl and coming a-reaping. Ranald continued, a pined look on his thin face.

'Well, talking about being on different sides, and batting and all that, it's my birthday tomorrow and my wife knows and ...'

The penny dropped for Naz first.

'Ohhhhh! You're not about to tell us you're a bit Bi are you Ran?'

Ranald stopped, eyes wide, mouth gulping and gazed around at his mates who were variously shrugging, tilting their heads, looking over their glasses rims and all wearing that wide, closed lipped smile of sympathy, amusement and understanding.

'Errr... I was going to say I'm probably leaving my job actually, maybe work for a charity, but...' Ranald stuttered, nobody said anything, but everybody's smile was opening out to a grin and James, sat to Ran's left, gave a mini-gasp and smacked his elbow into Ran's shoulder blade.

'Nuff said son. Case closed. Good luck with the job-hunting!'

They all broke into laughter together and looked at their buddy with a warmth that brought tears to Ranald's eyes.

'You know? You all know?' Ranald glared at Naz.

Naz shrugged, *'For decades mate.'*

James hadn't paid much attention in E and D training, *'Although if you're gonna cry then that actually makes you a total gayer and not just a half-an-halfie.'*

'You know that's homophobic, constable.' Levelled Naz.

'Not racist?' asked Jonny.

'Cultural appropriation?' James.

'Sexist! Are you trans too Damps?' Jonny was grinning widely.

Ranald brought the usual jibber-jabber-chat to a stop with a huge intake of breath and a,

'Well, is anyone going to actually get this poor war hero another drink then?'

'You've had one son, that's enough. You're on water now, doctor's orders!' Jonny pointed at the jug of lime water in the middle the table. Ran furrowed his brow,

'I'm wounded not dying. There'll be no need for those extremes yet muchacho. Besides, I drink Evian. I am a banker. Was a banker!'

James affected a deeply hammy look of puzzlement and then inquiry,

'Hey Ran. Now you are officially part-time hetero, does that mean your hot wife has some spare time and...' James wisely ducked before he finished speaking. He had no more interest in Eva than he did in 18th Century tea pots, but it was worth a punt.

The boys went about catching up on the news. Ranald had a few more doctor's visits to go but was recovering adequately. No sign of any charge for Micky and Jonny beating up the Mohawk cop, so Jonny had no special news to share. Neither had Naz, less having quit his consultancy job to prepare for a political career. He was rich enough and he could afford to take a few months' sabbatical. He had led a life of sabbaticals since leaving the service.

Ranald appeared to be the unlucky one. Coincidentally, he was the only ethnically Chinese one. Coincidentally. He had been charged with affray and soliciting prostitutes from Halloween as the Police sought to make false counter accusations to the CCTV captured footage of him being beaten and abused in the hospital by Chan 942 and Chan 832. His Bank had suspended him from work, and he was awaiting the result of a disciplinary investigation for bringing the Firm into disrepute. His CFO played golf with the Deputy Police Commissioner of Operations so they all knew what the result was going to be; it was just a question of whether he could sue for unfair dismissal. Unlikely, most judges were not as independently judicious as they used to be. James was more than embarrassed for his profession, he was ashamed. Only his silence in not identifying his friends on the CCTV kept him able to sit with them. That in itself was shameful, by rights he should have dobbed them in. Things were messy.

After the usual abuse for the amount of overtime pay James had received, James had succinctly explained to the boys that his missus was preparing to take the kids back to his parents' place in Marlborough at Xmas time - things were getting too nasty in Hong Kong for a young family like his. That left Micky who still hadn't turned up or answered any WhatsApp messages. Ranald's predicament and the news that James was planning to leave Hong Kong sombered the mood a little. Jonny broke the silence,

'Fuckin ell fellas, six months ago we were like pillars of the community, now look at us – rap sheet longer than the fuckin' Kray twins.'

'Not all of us, Mr Locke. I am not sure a respectable senior officer like myself should be consorting with miscreants and deviants like yourselves.' James mocked himself in his role as bastion of law and order.

'Waaaah! Forgive me Father for I have sinned! We've all been fitted up

with false charges, and you are the only real crook amongst us! Fascist!'

'Steady! Took the best decision I could at the time. Minimum force. And you haven't been identified yet Mr Locke.' Jonny wondered if it was the stabbing or the beating that he hadn't been caught for yet. He wasn't sure how to ask that question of James. James covered up the awkwardness with jabber,

'Chaotic and fluid situation.'

Jonny took the hint, *'Violent rioters'*

'Proportional response.'

They were all chiming in repeating various clichés from the five o'clock follies the Police Force press conferences had become. James had long since given up defending the propaganda amongst his friends and leant back in his chair, rolling his eyes at the heavens and then looking straight up the stairs opposite him.

Ping Pong Ding Dong

The tall silhouette of Micky, bulkier than usual in his Top Gun Maverick jacket, was coming very slowly, very deliberately down the stairs. He had sunglasses on, it was night-time, he was in a dark bar. Ordinarily they would have ripped him to pieces with scorn for that, but not tonight. James nudged Jonny, Ranald and Naz looked up and then at each other, teeth were sucked. Jonny looked around at them all and raised his hands, patting them downwards with the 'I got it, I know what I have to do' move. He stood up before Micky had reached the bottom of the stairs, the others sat still. Surely, Micky would forgive Jonny – he'd saved him from 'atchett 'ong in the alley. Ranald waved a weak *'Hi Micky*!'

Jonny came around the side of the table, palms raised,

'Mate, I am sorry about the Facebook thing.'

Jonny stepped forward and raised his hand to shake. Micky blanked him and walked past, took Jonny's empty chair, spun it round, sat legs splayed and leant forward on the back of it.

'Evening boys.'

He raised a long arm and waved and beckoned towards the bar.

'Yes please!' he called out in cut-glass tones and snapped his fingers.

Naz, Jonny and James shared a surreptitious glance and Jonny went and found another chair and sat at the far end from Micky. Ranald quietly slid Jonny's drink down the table towards him. Micky saw it and swept his hand forward to intercept it, knocking it over and spilling it towards Ranald's lap. Ranald leapt up, winced but said nothing. James spoke out though,

'For fuck's sake Micky!'

James put a straight hand and arm across in front of Micky's left shoulder and looked him in the side of the head. Micky didn't react at all. He just said,

'Whoops!'

Things were more than a tad awkward. Strained. Tense. A waiter came over to take Micky's order which was delivered curtly and rudely. The waiter spun on his heel and left without acknowledging Jonny's *'Sorry for the spill. Errrm, excuse me...'*

Things remained edgy. There was some attempt at conversation, but Micky's sun-glassed presence was unnerving; his derisive snorts, huhs and grunts strangled most topics, and he was chewing a tooth-pick – an irritating affectation of Hong Kong hard-men. After twenty minutes of this, Jonny lost patience.

'For fuck's sake Micky, get over yourself will ya? I made a mistake, big fucking deal. And take those stupid shades off, you look like a prick!'

Micky leapt to his feet, throwing the chair skittering forward as he rose. Everyone in the bar stopped and looked.

'Why don't you fuck off chav-boy? You don't belong here. These are my friends not yours. Fuck off back to whatever chip shop, pikey scum pit you came from!'

'Come on Micky!' entreated James and Ranald simultaneously.

'Why are you sticking up for him? He's not one of us.'

'What are you talking about? We've known him for 30 years, you dick. Stop being an idiot.'

Micky wasn't going to stop being an idiot. He was just starting. He picked up his glass and hurled it ferociously at Jonny's head. Jonny dodged and the glass, trailing its spewing contents behind it, sped across the room and smashed at the bottom of the stairs, sending some girls sat nearby shrieking. The barman was on his way to help them in a shot whilst two waiters were frozen with indecision as to whether to advance or retreat.

James shoved Micky hard away and sent the neighbours' table crashing. The three Chinese lads there leapt up shouting and Ranald started apologizing furiously. Naz had Jonny firmly by the arm. Ranald was in pain from his injuries and hoping that nobody or nothing would touch him at any point. Ever.

Micky's feet slid sideways on spilt drink as he righted himself, only to find James squarely blocking his path towards Jonny.

'Back down boy! Stand still!' commanded James. Pretty much everyone in the bar did exactly that. James could command. Everyone except Micky and Jonny, who was now struggling to escape Nazeem's grip and get at Micky.

'You're dead chav. I'm going to fuckin' kill you for what you've done!'

'Come on then, wanker, come on!'

Jonny was too fired up to think beyond their Facebook spat. But Ranald, having placated the Chinese lads had sat down again. With nothing to do but sit still and hope, he was guessing there might be more to this. But what?

Blocked by James, Micky turned to the tops of the hastily abandoned tables nearest to him and started hurling beer bottles and gin glasses at Jonny, and inevitably Naz and James who were stood between the two of them. People were shouting, bodies were disappearing behind the bar and vanishing swiftly out to the toilets. Somebody hit the fire escape door and several punters spilt out into the grubby alley behind. Because he was looking at Jonny trying to escape his grasp rather than paying attention to Micky, Naz had taken a bottle to the neck but it hadn't smashed. He had let go of Jonny who had wisely taken cover behind a pillar from the barrage of glass hurtling his way, rather than advance towards Micky.

'You're dead chav!'

Micky had run out of bottles, was panting and his sunglasses had disappeared. He still had a very resolute James facing him, but James was just about out of judicious restraint and working out which bit of big Micky would produce the quickest disablement. Jonny stepped out of the shadow of the pillar, crunching wide legged on the broken glass, time to fight back.

'Come on then, let's fuckin' see ya, you fuckin' Rupert!'

The door at the top of the stairs slammed open and two, blue shirted cops came crashing down the stairs and instantly clocked Jonny shouting. James looked back over his shoulder and went to intercept them telling them to calm down in Cantonese. Naz interposed himself back between Micky and Jonny. Ranald was apologizing to the bar staff, offering to cover the cost of the damage and trying not to move too much.

James, not sure if he was relieved or annoyed that his fellow police officers had arrived, strode confidently towards them, ready to brief them up and direct operations. He wasn't really expecting to get pepper sprayed in the face and knocked aside but he had enough about him to spin and avoid most of the blast of noxious gel. Miraculously the jug of lime water was still intact in front of Ranald sat at their table. He reached out a hand, Ranald slid the handle to him with the merest shift of his forearm and James sloshed the entire jug into his own face.

The two cops had been heading for Jonny but were pointed to their real target by the bar-staff whose heads had popped up from behind the bar, their arms gesticulating wildly. Micky wasn't going quietly. He ignored the baton strike to his forearm and dodged the pepper spray cop who had suddenly gone flying when he hit the ice/glass/drink smush that now coated the floor. The baton cop chased after him but slipped as well and smashed his chin on the bottom step – it really hurt.

Micky bounded up the stairs for the exit and made it out the red door and across the street to his bike, just as a police van came tilting around the corner. Micky was sat stock still on his saddle as the police van lurched up to a halt and eight riot cops piled out and stormed down into the bar. They didn't even glance Micky's way and he very gently started up and pulled away without attracting the van driver's attention who was on his radio and staring after his squad.

Inside, James had blinked the pepper out of his eyes and walked calmly up to the pepper spray cop who was sat on his arse in the wet, looking up after where Micky had gone. The cop turned his face and received the hardest open-handed slap he had ever imagined possible, knocking him sideways. The door burst open and the stairs boomed with riot booted stomps. Jonny and Naz strode over to James and propelled him towards the fire exit. They were gone in less than two seconds, exiting just as the lead riot cop literally ran over his blue-shirted colleague holding his busted chin at the bottom of the steps. Ranald was not going anywhere.

'We need to pay! Look at the state of this place.'

The room was suddenly engulfed by a torrent of riot cops. Within twelve seconds, the cops had everyone still in the bar up against the wall with their hands locked behind their heads. Less Ranald. He didn't move. Nobody moved him. 20 minutes later, all ID cards were checked and thirteen people who had been hiding in the loo were on their knees in the broken glass like everybody else. Another five minutes later, three unfortunate Chinese youths who had done nothing wrong but whose names had come up on the 'rioter' list were being marched up the stairs, hands cuffed behind them, to spend another night in the cells. Ranald had moved little but thought fast and given the impression that he was the bar owner and carried out a convincing performance in Cantonese, whilst wielding a broom he snatched from a corner. He convinced the police that all the trouble was caused by some gweilos he had never seen before, but sadly his CCTV was broken. The barman, knowing Ranald was going to pay, backed him up with some convincing

'Listen to my Boss please, Ah Sir,' play-acting. Not until the bar staff had the brooms and mops out did Ran quietly pay a large sum for the damage, thank the barman and, very gently, start making his steady way up the long stairs.

Tram Buzzin'

Naz, Jonny and James had torn down the alley and spilt out of a narrow doorway onto Queen's Road, adrenalin pumping, before flowing themselves down Water Street to Des Voeux. James immediately crossed to the middle of the road and swung himself into a passing tram. Naz and Jonny looked at each other in disbelief, and then shrugged and followed him in.

'Shortest night out ever!' James quipped, *'We must be getting old gentlemen.'* They all felt like they were 18 again and were buzzing.

'You hit an officer of the law, chief inspector.' Naz said through his teeth, deep in his throat.

'Superintendent if you please. I was merely acting in self-defence using minimum force in order to sustain a safe and secure environment your honour. And, to be fair, the twat deserved it. He fucking pepper sprayed me!'

'What are the chances of CCTV i.d-ing us?' Naz asked.

'100% if they had it on. I think I had better send a squad round to secure the evidence.'

'You can do that?'

'Shooting stars gotta break the mould son! The law isn't quite as flat-footed as it used to be my friend. Times have changed. Things are too busy for niceties. Doesn't make sense not to live for fun, Jonny boy!

Rules are bendier in fluid times.' James was enjoying himself. This was much more fun than babysitting 'so-called' riots.

James reached for his phone. Fenton was on duty and, despite his bravado, James was going to have to ask for an awkward favour and felt a flash of hesitation. This favour would require Fenton, Chewy and Fei to turn up fully masked and un-numbered to secure that CCTV within the next 15 minutes; no questions asked. This was a big ask. Fenton and team were loitering around Central, bored with nothing to do but wait, so Inspector Wong didn't consider it awkward at all, in fact he was grateful for a bit of skullduggery; things had been a bit dull since the Battle of PolyU to be honest. James was praying that plod would have been too careless to have got the footage already as that was a detective job not a riot job and the detectives wouldn't be round there until the next day or so. Plan B was that Fenton had the initiative to play the magic PTU card and relieve the beat cops of the evidence if necessary – he didn't have to spell that out, Fenton was a switched-on cookie.

As James finished his quick call, Jonny looked him straight in the eyes.

'So, Inspector Clouseau, pourquoi are we making our getaway in a tram? It does five miles a-fuckin' hour! Nobody in their right mind escapes the crime scene in a fucking tram!'

'Ah ha. Exactly Watson. Firstly, no CCTV on the tram. Secondly, nobody would ever suspect it as a getaway car and thirdly, and this is vital my man, it will make for a much better bar story.'

'Elementary.' Concluded Naz. *'My place for a night cap then? We can get a cab up by the Ferry Terminal, Eastern Tunnel, ETA 12 minutes.'*

'Good shout.' agreed James. *'This tram was a stupid idea Jonny.'*

Ho Man Ting

Back at Nazeem's place, a pristine, beautifully toned, minimalist bachelor pad, the boys sank into his deep, chocolate, leather sofa and jingled the ice cubes in their glasses of Talisker. Naz sighed and fixed James with a serious eye,

'You're proper done aren't you James? When you slapped that cop, that was it.'

'Yeh. I shouldn't have done that should I? He so deserved it though. I should be alright; Fenton got the CCTV and first offence, exemplary record, self defence and all that. Plod might not even report it – too embarrassed. Anyway, we're going back to UK at Christmas and Harry and the kids are gonna stay at my mum's in Marlborough, look for a place, find some decent schools, you know. Escape plan, phase one.'

'And you?' Naz asked. James suddenly looked exhausted,

'I've got just over six months to push to the pension point. I've had it mate. I love the lads, I still enjoy the job, most days. I've had the time of my life in the mob, but my Boss is a dick; his boss is a dick, they're all dicks. It's getting worse you know. Everyone hates us. Even the little old ladies hate us. I never joined the PLA man.' Jonny nodded slowly,

'I know you what you mean. I hit that point in the Army. The wrong people kept getting promoted, the bluffers and the bullies.'

'You mean the not you's!'

'Yeah! That too! I was robbed bruv! I burnt out though. The novelty had worn off you know?'

All three hmmm'd and nodded and looked into their whiskies. Jonny mused,

'Hong Kong has proper changed. They all thought it would change after

'97 but it's now that it's really changing. This is China. This a police state man.'

'It ain't that bad yet! It's just a little unpredictable right now.' James retorted, holding the conventional line. Jonny continued,

'We may love Hong Kong as much as the locals, maybe more cos we chose to come here, they have no choice. They're trapped here. But we'll never be wanted. We'll always be the aliens, the ex-pats, the gweilos.'

Naz interjected,

'And the brown boys. They don't like us either. I always get just that little bit of extra space on the MTR you know.'

'That's cos you smell.'

'Of curry.'

'Ha ha. Racist. Listen, the Commies may need our connections for making their money, for trade, but they'll never want us. This is real China now and China has always disdained foreigners. Even though we South Asians helped build the place, we aren't welcome in Hong Kong. We never have been really. I think our politics idea is dumb Jonny.'

Jonny nodded. James hmmd, then changed tack slightly.

'Violent too. As well as the riots, the low level aggro is getting worse. Man, no one ever even dropped litter but now they're jumping the barriers, spraying walls, smashing stuff up, petrol bombs, the lot. Someone was stabbed in Mongkok in broad daylight on a zebra crossing not so long ago. Victim was a scumbag like, a bit of a thug and a thief but it is unusual for a knifing to happen so openly.'

'Whodunnit? Triads?' Jonny asked.

'Word on the street is that it was a gweilo ..... weird.' James carried on,

'Dunno whodunnit, but with all the CCTV and facial recognition, people

stand out. White and brown people stand out – they don't belong in Mongkok. Aliens. The protests have messed up all the usual police work but it's only a matter of time before loose ends get tidied up. I expect there will be a few people heading for Taiwan – still no extradition treaty there of course. Politics boys. Avoid the politics.'

Jonny and Naz looked at James, who held their gaze. Secrets were not secrets for long in this town. Naz finished his glass; the others were already down to the shrunken ice-cubes.

'Better call it a day, fellas; we've got Ran's 50th tomorrow. You can kip here if you like.'

'Yeah, I will, cheers Naz. Posher than mine.' Jonny took the offer,

'Not for me chef, I'm going to stay at Damps tomorrow and Harrietta won't put up with two nights of freedom.' James started calling a taxi and asked as he did so,

'Do you think Micky'll come tomorrow?'

'Man, I hope not. He's lost the plot.'

"What have you done to get under his skin Jonny?'

'I have no idea mate. Been born common I s'pose.'

'You are common.'

'I like to say authentic. Special.'

'Needs.'

Breaking Glass

Micky was sat in the shadows on his bike, staking out Jonny's flat. He had been there 30 minutes. Maybe the bastard got arrested by all those cops that stormed the bar. How can he keep pretending he doesn't know what he's done wrong? Well, if he won't confess, KK will. Micky gunned his engine and roared off up Staunton, took a crazy fast left to hurtle precipitously downhill on Aberdeen Street. His front wheel bounced slightly at the change of gradient as it hit the flat yellow-box on Hollywood. Then the front wheel was hurling itself into the air, smashing through the tourist information post, ricocheting off a lamppost and then clattering a further 30 metres down the street. Micky parted company with his bike as they both hit the 'Dr Sun Yat Sen' museum pointer 6 foot up in the air, his legs spun like a windmill and he went through the plate glass shop-front head-first and ended up ten metres into the Gallery, face embedded in a wall mounted canvas. The heavy, flat fronted rubbish truck that had hit him came to a screeching halt, just alongside the window Micky had gone straight through and obliterated on his trajectory. Micky was not moving. Glass settled. The Pakistani driver sat stock still. It wasn't his fault, but he knew it was going to be.

Chapter 7

Grab the Lacy Part of the Training Shoe

Alive

Naz sat in Ranald's little Discovery Bay garden, looking out towards the beach, sipped his green tea and looked down with satisfaction at the way the marmite and butter were running thick and fluid into the pores of the toasted English muffin. He took a deep breath in and admired the self-discipline that had meant he'd woken early, clear headed and able to enjoy a fresh, winter's morning in the car-free, golf-carted, ex-pat paradise that was D.B. Jonny was ghosting about in the kitchen, another clear-headed man although his temperance had been heavily influenced by opposite behaviour the Friday night before at the gin emporium and Naz's whiskey cabinet.

James was in a corner of the garden wrapped in a jungle warfare hammock he'd brought with him, snoring like a belt fed wombat. Micky hadn't shown up. Nobody had chased after him.

'Man, this is nice. How the other half live eh Naz?'

'This place is very nice Jonny boy, but it's still a bit weird. S'a bit Stepford Wives meets The Prisoner innit? Be seeing you, Number 6!'

As if to prove it, two buff Asian taai taai's strolled past the bottom of the garden's low fence, all bobbing ponytails, tiny tennis skirts, toned calves and brightly, coloured racquet covers. A man in a Titleist baseball cap wheeled his golf trolley along just behind them. He was tall and very white. He no doubt had an expensive watch, waxed chest and washboard abs. This was a community for the clean, the keen and the successful; stockbrokers and pilots, investment analysts and insurance executives, an enclave of slim, trim, buffed and depilated early risers just a convenient 25 minute fab-fast ferry ride from Central with contemporary leisure and retail offerings for the active, modern family. Battered reprobates like Jonny and Naz did not belong here.

'Stepford wives!' they grinned at each other.

'Fit, but, my gosh, don't they know it!'

'I feel we should affect ourselves a natty striped blazer and jaunty boater old boy!'

They tucked into their muffins, instinctively glancing at their watches to keep a close eye on the time. Their daysacks were packed by their shins, tightly bound so nothing jostled or rattled. Their fancy dress had been chosen to be lightweight and worn with trainers – Beastie Boys, the bling was plastic and in the bin. The plastic, recycling bin. Both daysacks had a camel-bak tube sticking out the top for regular, on the hoof hydration. Their sports kit was low key, worn and comfortable, muted colours, Jonny's a bit shabbier and baggier than Naz's but both had the look of men who spent a lot more time pondering trees and getting their faces muddy than checking out Outdoor Extreme Catalogues.

The boys were going to leave at 0830hrs, sharp. They would tab up to the Tiger's Head, a tough start for a morning after, endless little concrete steps then a scrabble up a dusty, rocky hillside to the trig-point at the top. Then they had a gentle, winding descent down to the big rocks through the lush, scrapy vegetation to join the Nature Heritage Trail at a Pagoda. Jonny was going to break off left down to Mui Wo where he was meeting Barry, Arwyn and the hippies for lunch to plan their next noble, but hopeless, move in their Save Lantau and the Planet campaign. Naz would like to have joined them but had a family clan-cricket match to get to and so had resolved to go right at the pagoda and head down to Pak Mong and into Tung Chung on the Olympic Trail. He knew the trails well; he had lived in Tung Chung in a swanky new apartment when he had left the service and first come back to Hong Kong. He was an 'international businessman' and It was handy for the airport; plus, the complex was full of cabin crew so one of the few places in Hong Kong a slim, handsome man could go to the pool with another slim, handsome man and nobody cared less. The other advantage – nobody who was anybody in Hong Kong Society lived there.

The boys finished their breakfast, washed up almost silently, left a thank you note for Ran's missus Eva and slipped out the back-garden gate. It was the first time Jonny had met her, he didn't like her but was polite. The boys picked up their rucksacks and almost managed to resist giving James a kick in the arse from the underside of the hammock before they left; almost.

'Wah? Wankers!'

'Ciao Baby!'

'Fuck off.'

0909hrs, they were stood at the top of Lo Fu Tau, 465 metres higher than where they had started and collapsed down to sit on the little bit of concrete around the trig point.

'Google said 1 hour 3 minutes, we took 39 minutes,' Naz observed looking at his phone,

'Adequate,' replied Jonny, *'considering my bad knees and you being a fat, civvy wanker.'*

Naz smiled, and breathed in through his noble nose with great ostentation,

'I am a mountain god, my ancestral tribe grew up in hills ten times these teeny bumps from where they shot down your pompous, sweaty ancestors with a ten-rupee jazail.'

'Two thousand pounds of education? Them were not my ancestors, mate!'

They both sat and marveled at the amazing view. The sky was cobalt blue and for once there was no pollution haze, so they had a crystal sharp view all the way across the to the Island, over to Tsuen Wan and back up behind them to Lin Fa Shan and Sunset Peak. Their panting subsided, their sweat began to ease; they sat together in silence and felt blessed.

Five silent minutes passed. They both knew that this was possibly the last time they would enjoy this view together.

'It's all downhill from here brother.'

'Yep. Ready?'

'Ever Ready.'

They bounced, bounded and hurled themselves down the trail, moving so fast they were right on the edge of turning an ankle and careering off into the brush or the rocks. It felt like mountain biking or skiing when you are right at the zenith of your strength and ability to hold it together, keeping the speed and staying upright by faith, on the edge of your skill knowing you either have to brake a little, or wipe out. It felt like life. A party of Chinese hikers stood politely to the side as they charged past with a bright *'Jo Saan! M Goi!'* Both were relishing the trail, the drive, the competitive need to keep up with their wingman, the need to be the fastest and strongest up on the hill, two young cubs on the Tiger's Head trail. This rush, the flow, the motion, was what they lived for. Kite surfing, fast sailing on a precariously tilted close haul, go-karting, abseiling, rally driving; these were the pursuits that joined these two together; whatever was reckless and dangerous, entertained them.

They both knew that there weren't so many days left like these. They were never going to be pottering about that pristine golf course away down the wooded slopes to their left, but the knees were aching, the backs hurting, the ankles less robust and the balance less sure. The young tigers were in reality old wolves; but like old wolves, they could still hunt, with or without the pack, and their stamina and daring was their pride.

It felt like five minutes and they reached the pagoda that marked the highpoint of the Mui Wo trail, having dropped 200 metres in altitude over about 3 kilometres. Nobody was there and they crashed into the covered space, each swinging on a pillar and slamming to a halt, laughing and panting. They smashed forearms. Two veterans, fighting men who came alive in their wild element. They were just rogue, unwanted outsiders down there in civilization. They didn't belong down there. Never really had.

'Enjoyed that!'

'Me too. We don't do this enough. We must do it again before we really are too old.'

'Never too old bruv, sleep when you die!' They both laughed and slugged some water from their camel-bak tubes.

'How long to get to the MTR for you?' Jonny asked.

'An hour and fifteen I reckon, nice and easy downhill but quite a long way along the coast. You?'

'Mui Wo? 45 minutes to Bazza's easy. I shall beat Arwyn, he probably still ain't up!'

'Ran's lad would have got him up by now.'

'True. Annoying that Hamish. Right mate. Anon, anon, have a good one.'

'Be lucky son! Laters.'

'Toodleloo!'

As he set off at a gentle pace, Jonny checked his phone for the first time since yesterday afternoon. The little red circle on KK's Telegram icon (Kung Fu Panda) read 3. Ooops, he thought, been neglecting the tyranny of my social media too long and now my sweetheart will be in a mithering huff. How was he going to say that goodbye?

All the Gear

As the two friends parted ways at the pagoda, Big John McEwan was tightening up his turquoise laced, bright blue and orange La Sportiva Kaptiva trail running shoes, enjoying the compressed EVA midsole that would cushion his pace on technical ground. His green and black Lorpen T3 Trail-Running Ultralight Compression socks gripped his manly calves and his sleek, sheer MCS Run Lycra shorts stopped just above the impressive bulge of his vastus medialis muscle. He breathed in a little in the mirror as his Under Armour skin-tight running vest was failing to hide his amply bulging belly, even from the illusion maintained in his mind palace of incredible mightiness. Once he had inserted his wireless bud earphones, set the playlist to 'The Burn' and checked his app was poised, he headed out.

'Just going for a run; back in an hour!' he shouted out as he left.

Nobody answered. Nobody else was awake or cared. He reached his start point, the gate that led out behind the petrol station and onto the coastal strip. What once was a pleasant seaside promenade but was now bounded by water-filled, red and white crash barriers that demarcated the edge of the building sites and reclamation work progressing relentlessly. Big John's app kept a record of his runs, his heart rate, the routes, the average speed, the maximums, the minimums, the stats. It had a function that allowed him to share his exploits with his friends. He always shared; he posted his achievements to Facebook; nobody cared. He made the watch / fit-bit / digital wearable lifestyle tech gadget with advanced GPS, beep and set off at what was, in his mind, a majestic pace along the sea-front. He had done a Thought leadership blog on Linked-In about the importance of a healthy body. May had complimented him on it.

Coming down the hill, five kilometres away East, Naz didn't have an app or a record to beat or any interest in his last month's statistics. He had a G-shock watch and a phone that sat in his bag. No earphones, he listened to the birds as he walked. As the slope allowed, he would break into a gentle jog, but he was taking it easy now after his epic, hilltop gallivant with Jonny. The path was well found, the usual dull, functional concrete so he didn't have to concentrate on anything physical and could just enjoy the sky, the hills, the shape of Lin Fa Shan, the way the vegetation changed colour on the Lo Fu side, a bit like fire breaks. Suddenly there was a new section of path, beautifully dressed in stone with every polished rock artfully set. 'Wow!' thought Naz, amazing craftmanship performed in the boiling sun on the side of a hill, probably by some pensioners barely making the minimum wage. This society doesn't appreciate those who really add value.

The path fell down the hill quickly, criss-crossing a clear, tumbling stream full of smooth rocks which glinted with the occasional flash of fish. The villagers had put up unfriendly banners at various places, criticizing the Government for stealing their land and warning outsiders that trespassers were unwelcome. There was the smartest of public toilets at Ngau Kwu Long for passers-by, but the warning signs around the village meant that even Naz lacked the effrontery to step inside the low walls that marked the boundary to his left. Passers-by should use the loo, pass water and pass on by.

A small rise and fall and he was soon coming alongside Pak Mong, a village that the information sign told him had exceptional Fung Shui and again boasted a rather decent public toilet. The gateway into Pak Mong looked ancient and ornate, there were fierce looking gods and dragons painted and carved, but there weren't the 'get off my land' posters and banners that were found elsewhere along the trail. There were shops hidden amongst the sprawl of the skew-whiff village façade.

He walked through the gate and onto the broad, flat, square where the villagers had lain out their crops to dry and sort for centuries. There were few people, the place was tranquil and calm, the far end of the square guarded by a short, squat, stone tower that had been built to watch for pirates and had a brief moment of glory resisting the Japanese. The stones, the rocks, the trees around the village spoke of eons, grounded in their history and longevity. The village houses varied from bland, new 3 floored cookie-cut efforts to broken down old huts and pig pens. The place reeked of rich tradition, deep culture, venerable ancestors – and barely two bob ha'penny to spend. Naz was always moved when he came here to this valley. It was old Hong Kong, before the British, before the Civil Service, before the Capitalist Communists.

On the edge of the old village were larger, modern, vulgar houses. One in particular was high fenced and showy – the Headman or a Triad haunt, probably one and the same, thought Naz. The house had land and was more of a compound, a pound containing several smart, sleek, black cars and a small pack of matching sleek, black, forbidding guard dogs. Two dozed but one trotted towards the gates. Naz moved off quickly, not running, never run from a village dog, but move quickly away. He hated village dogs. Everyone hated village dogs, they were bred to be mean by their mean, small-minded owners and they would bite and snarl at strangers with no fear of being reined in. Real villagers hated outsiders and the fact that Naz's family had been in Hong Kong for seven generations still didn't make him local - Tang Dynasty makes one local. Just.

Naz moved swiftly down the road, past the dark, bricked furnace where the villagers used to burn the rubbish. People seemed to just chuck it in the verges these days. With his back to the hills, he was now staring at road bridges and elevated pillars, concrete monstrosities that had blighted the sky as the fabled Zhuhai-Macao-Bridge came ashore bringing the rich in their minivans, the workers in trucks and coachloads of compliant tourists, eager to fill their wheeled suitcases with luxury, branded goods from the soulless malls that had displaced the social and green spaces of old Hong Kong.

He could hear the dull roar of the dual carriageway now, and the occasional rattle and clattle of an MTR train or the Airport Express. He couldn't hear the pile drivers working on the foundations of housing blocks on reclaimed land for it was Sunday, the one day when the incessant metallic smashing of the piles stopped. That was why he had left Tung Chung and gone back to his family's neighbourhood of Kowloon Tong; Kowloon Tong was finished and not beset with building site dust, pile drivers, drills, trucks and the disheartening, relentless devastation that is progress. He noted the lake to his right and imagined how perfect the vista must have been forty years' ago, when he was a boy and Pak Mong looked down to the water instead of onto concrete, transport infrastructure. Back then it was a beautiful river valley opening out to the sea and looking across to Castle Peak, when Tung Chung was all rice paddies, water buffalo and a rickety little pier. Before the airport, before the new town, before the motorway, before all the progress happened there was just an Eastern stream.

Less than 200 metres away, and closing, Big John was contemplating the same scene from the opposite angle. That's impressive, he thought as he ran alongside the reclaimed land, only last year that was all just sea. The curving, concrete sweep of the highway junction caught his eye too, with this connection, you could develop the Pak Mong area, put some high value, luxury homes along the lakeside, some executive low rises going up the valley, turn that old village square into a marketplace with cafes and boutiques. This place has got potential, he thought as he jogged along. Now an MTR station just here and that would really push property prices up. He came up under the underpass below the motorway and turned right, blowing out hard before he started scaling the short climb of steps that led him onto the Olympic Trail.

Big John didn't notice Naz coming the other way. Naz was far enough away not to recognise the gweilo but close enough to know he was one, and one who was probably too 'well-built' for the skintight running god outfit he sported. Lycra should perhaps be left to the leaner, trimmer locals. A little flicker of competition ran through Nazeem's brain; maybe I should run a little myself he thought. He had strolled down from the pagoda and had plenty left in the tank, maybe I should burn this guy up a little, but wear him down first, rein him in. A little mischievous smirk played across his face as he took the other set of stairs up, the narrow ones through the overgrown trees. Naz picked up his pace, just a little.

Big John strode purposefully and manfully up the first set of stairs, came out on the flat and started along the narrow path. He noticed some rubbish, discarded lunch boxes and paper death money, on the edge of the path, 'disgusting locals,' he thought, 'no respect for cleanliness.' He didn't notice the graves up to his left, a small, overgrown path led up there, but he had never had the curiosity to deviate from his scheduled path; he had times to keep, goals to achieve, stats to post. The only thing that had ever stopped him was one of those ghastly, yellow striped banana spiders that had spun its web across the path and was sat, terrifyingly in the middle of it. Big John was not sure what to do. He had to run, he had to make a decent time, but he had an entirely sensible fear of spiders. Should he try and duck under or get a stick? He got a stick. A big stick. Smashed that web to pieces and the spider ran away. Ha ha! Who's the daddy? Who's Tarzan?

Naz passed by the graves a minute later, he paused respectfully alongside them, saluted for some instinctive reason, and noticed the squawking of a white cheeked laughing thrush. These birds gabbled and squeaked, chittered and gulped, in the most amazing way. He remembered finding himself in and amongst about twenty of them, hopping and chattering on The Peak. Cheeky birds. Might not actually be white cheeked laughing thrushes, might not actually be such a bird, but it seemed about the right description. Perhaps he should try i-Naturalist and find out. He noticed some rubbish, sadly the wind had scattered grave offerings about the bushes.

Naz headed onwards the main trail and reached the part with the 'perfect steps.' He considered them 'perfect' because the horizontal treads were measured and spaced at an ideal length for his stride, furthermore the vertical riser was modest and fitted his pace and knee-lift equally well. Whoever laid these steps was a genius thought Naz every time he came across them, not a craftsman like whoever had laid that path down the Mui Wo hillside near Ark Eden, that was classy stonework on an exposed, hot slope that would have required considerable graft and determination as well as skill. This was a simple exercise in concrete stairwork but still a thing to be admired and appreciated. This was great applied biometric mathematics.

Two hundred metre's ahead, Big John was flying now, his immaculate fitness and iron will propelling him powerfully up the steps and he was soon on the level again, passing under overhanging branches that were occasionally festooned with the fading ribbon markers of past trail running races. John had done a few events of course, completed one, had to retire from another with cramps and an ankle injury prevented him finishing a third. Nonetheless, he had still got all the money in for charity and been on the website and in the newsletter. He was an example to his staff in this regard. He had blogged about it. As John motored, he didn't notice any birdsong as he had a head full of the motivational hardcore, rocking beat of his 'The Burn' playlist – a bit of Phil Collins, Survivor, Bachman Turner Overdrive, ZZ Top. Every track a classic – the Jeremy Clarkson selection. He passed a white, incongruous sign that said 'Olympic Green, sign D7 689' oblivious to everything except his heart rate. 170 bpm. Better slow it down a bit.

Another kilometre and Naz had been up on John's butt for 2 minutes now. The big gweilo's saggy, lycra spanked arse was ponderously pounding along before him. John's protein-shaked arms were pumping away, and Naz could just tell that in this man's mind, he was a trail running legend. In reality, he was in the way. 'If that was me, I'd move over,' thought Naz five times before he realised that the runner before him had no idea that Naz was behind him; the classic rock anthems were too loud. John was also the type of man who would consider giving way a sign of weakness. He was also breaking wind at regular intervals. There was no space to overtake so Naz dropped back and settled into a steady jog. There would be two chances to pass him in a minute, the stream crossings where the path dissipated and a quick move across the boulders would easily outflank him. Then suddenly Naz recognised him. Big John. Big Construction Development Director Man John. Mr Mamamouchi.

Big John's ergo-moulded, noise cancelling ear-buds had just started filling his brain with the opening riff of Bonnie Tyler's 'Holding Out for a Hero' when he came round the corner where the trail dropped a little and hit a rocky stream that cascaded down the hill towards the motorway. Despite having done the route 26 previous times (personal best 54 minutes, 46 seconds, 669 calories), the wee brook and its scattered rocks caught him by surprise, his attention having been fixed on admiring the view of the reclamation off to his right. From here he had a great view of the dusty, flat, beige, land-that-was-sea dirt punctuated by derricks, cranes and pile drivers, idle now on a Sunday morning but full of the potent promise of progress and development, poised to slam into life again early on Monday. Only one sleep before the squat, hard hatted worker drones would be buzzing around building stuff again, with their tough, grippy, man hands and stoically lined faces, loyally and obediently putting in a twelve-hour shift for the minimum wage to create development, to build wealth, to make money for Lords of the Universe like him, Senior Director, Big John. Mr Business.

Big, bold John was not quite so sure on his feet as he was of his ego at that exact moment though. His 6mm drop, active grip, Sportiva Kaptiva Vibram soles, whilst beautifully engineered examples of action-oriented exercise shoes, could not possibly cope with 92 kilogrammes of teetering corporate legend, and his right foot gave way to a tiny slip. At the same micro-second, the swiftly moving presence of a leaping man registered in the left corner of his eye as Naz took the opportunity to bound left, upstream and overtake. Big John threw out a left arm to both counterbalance his starboard slip-shift and ward off the surprise 'attack' in his left peripheral vision. Amygdala was hijacked.

Naz, having been poised for this overtaking moment, was more concerned with whether to diss John as he swept past and how snarky he should be, or to just sweep by in condescending, superior silence. He had left a good metre's clearance to pass by but the sudden, out-flung left arm straight at his face made him instinctively raise his own right forearm to block. He landed on his left foot, as planned, but his next step was upset by the arm movements and he hit a rock just 17 centimetres to the right of that which he had sub-consciously aimed for with his silent, on-board running system that flowed so smoothly in his background software. It meant his block actually became a shove.

Big John, already off balance and, being heavy on top with a barrel chest and a solid centre of gravity-fed beer belly, had no chance of resisting the momentum that was about to hurl him down a metre of vertically rocked stream bed. His right arm came up and took the first impact, protecting his face and he half-bounced, half-spun, around so that his left shoulder went up and his butt and mid-shoulder blades connected with separate, jutting rocks. The rocks were smooth, but the impact was fierce, and the mid-riff blow knocked the wind explosively out of him. His generous arse saved his back from serious injury, but his right forearm was seriously bruised, albeit with no bones snapped. A knee had been knocked and smarted but was only slightly bumped. He was miraculously lightly damaged.

John was still tumbling though, at much reduced speed, and he now fell forward, head-first, towards the bottom of the crevice into which he had crashed. An outstretched left hand scuffed and lightly grazed the palm but stopped his head hitting the next rock. He came to rest in a sitting position, with the cool stream water running down his back and through his shorts, which for a moment made him panic that he was seriously bleeding. That moment didn't come for a few seconds though as the initial moments were entirely consumed with the gasping, whooping panic of being winded. As the blockage dissolved and oxygen flowed back into his system, all the other damage identification signals began bleeping, ringing and squawking into his nervous system's control centre.

Panic that he was going to die in a rocky stream suddenly welled up, then horror that his arm was broken overwhelmed him. As the air began recirculating in his system, he found he had enough energy to blurt out a swift, stream of vomit, psycho-somatically expelled from his body. He also farted savagely and half-shat himself, but the other sensations and the cold water masked any conscious recognition of that discharge.

Shock and confusion were paramount. There was nothing else but panting and blowing hard for at least seven, long seconds. Seven seconds is a long time for a man like Naz to consider what had just happened, whose fault it might be, how injured was the casualty, what options did he have for an immediate action, how should he call in help, what was the exact location for emergency crews to immediately deploy to, etc. He had a Plan A and a Plan B by the time he realised that the man in the damp crevice was probably not mortally wounded; in fact, he looked to be just a bit winded. Then he seemed to throw up a bit, cough and engage in some melodramatic huffing and puffing.

Naz looked down on him, the way Big John normally looked down on most everyone else, from a great height. The little miss mischief devil in his mind started giggling. Naz didn't have the bad manners and ill breeding to laugh out loud alongside his inner pixie, but he couldn't disguise a trace of a smile across his lips. *'Oh, how the mighty have fallen,'* he mused.

Mighty, fallen John had begun to recover. One ear-bud, despite being ergonomically designed to stay in under all conditions, had not. The other one was still there. Bonnie Tyler was still holding out for a hero, a bit tinnily though. He looked up and saw a lean, brown faced man looking down on him with a mixture of concern and amusement on his face. John only registered the amusement, the fucking smirk. His vigour and power began to surge back into him,

'You clumsy, fucking wanker!'

'Mate, it was an accident, I ...'

Big John regained his status and asserted himself, *'Shut up! You cunt! You, clumsy, fucking Pakki cunt!'*

That was enough for Naz. He turned away to his left and stepped across the remaining rocks onto the path and started moving gently away. A steady walk, then a faster stride then a jog. He just wanted to get away from that odious man. Behind him, with a stumble and a splash and a roar and a hundred *'Fuck, fuck, fucks,'* John got himself up and back onto the path. He checked himself out; right arm hurt a bit, left palm scratched, shoulder blades ached, arse burned and was weirdly squelchy, knee throbbed, but nothing broken it seemed. Playing rugby for decades had made him invincible. 'That fucker did it on purpose, I bet. What's that noise? My headphones. One of my headphones is missing. Bastard! I am not going down there again, I'll never find it. That fucking Arab owes me; that fucker is going to pay me for new ones, or I'll fucking kill the dirty, skinny, little prick.'

Fueled by rage and revenge, Big John started moving. He lost his balance again at the next piece of uneven ground, putting his left hand out against the sheer, dark, grey rock wall that rose up to his left, his little cuts smarting further when they touched the rough, dried up lichen. *'Bastard! Fucker!'* He pushed himself on, the path leveling out and he started to jog, gingerly at first as his knee still throbbed, but gradually speeding up. Naz was a good 200 metres ahead, his head full of thoughts about what had just happened, was he at fault, should he have helped more, or did the bloke deserve it?

Damn, that bloke deserved it. He is a bully and a danger to the planet. He is a symbol of everything that is wrong with this town; no not a symbol, he is a protagonist, an instigator, a cause. He and his cronies have colluded with the Government for years to exploit and manipulate the people to enrich themselves. He had insulted Naz, bullied Micky, shown himself to be homophobic, racist and sexist. Even more, he was clearly incompetent and one of those toxic leaders who survive by bluster and threat. Christ, maybe he should have pushed him. Maybe he should have followed him down the mini-chasm and found a rock to finish him off. That would be true justice. I hope he is hurt.

In his reverie, Naz had emerged from the narrow path and turned onto the broad, concrete road that ran up to the hillside public works that sought to control the risk of landslides and flood waters crashing down the hill and onto the motorway below. He had reached the end, the dead end, before he realised his mistake. It had been a few years since he had been on this trail, he forgave himself and turned about to go back again. As he found the crossing point and turned left back onto the right path, Big John was taking a sharp right 20 metres uphill and caught a glimpse of Naz's legs ahead of him. The sight gave him renewed strength and passion and he surged forward on the slight downhill.

The path was narrow at this stretch, closely bound by metal barriers on both sides, and it wended its way along a contour, jigging in and out as it crossed the cuttings of streams that cascaded down into the huge, concreted drainage system that protected the road with stepped waterfalls, solid walls and blocks that looked like D-Day tank obstacles designed to break the force of flash floods and catch tree debris. Naz turned left and from the corner of his eye noticed the looming, puffing, lycra-bulging brute closing in on him like a wounded rhino covered in spittle and sweat. Naz smiled to himself and broke into an easy lope, gliding up the short steps that led up to each 90-degree left which heralded a stream crossing, ducking under typhoon felled branches, switching right to drop down the few steps back onto the contour. Be the bigger man, walk away, turn the other cheek.

100 metres later, the path veered half-left and uphill, maybe ten metres vertically up. He stretched his legs up this rise, confident of putting some distance between him and the blustering, blowing fury that chased him. The steps ended with a half right and Naz found himself on a long, gently curving terrace that swept across the slope between beautiful stands of cowskin and paper-bark trees where years ago he had first noticed their peeling, splendor and then been astounded by the myriad of butterflies that fluttered by in this secret forest just 30 metres from the howling scar of the motorway. He took a casual glance

over his right shoulder and saw Big John puffing and blowing halfway up the steps, bent forward, a hand pushing on his knee trying to keep his legs going. 'He's blown out.' Naz thought. 'Why am I running anyway, maybe I should turn around and deck him? Nah, he's going to have an endless sulk about this, I shall keep composed and go on about my life, happy in the thought that this will make him rage for weeks.'

Naz opened his stride and moved easily, along the curved path. Two men were at the end. One, super skinny with glasses and wearing a purple adidas t-shirt, was coming down the 527 steps to the left, a camera in hand. The other, overweight and sweating, was looking up at the steps, his bags dumped on the path besides him. There was no way the fat lad was going up there. Naz didn't want to be seen but couldn't avoid having to step over the bags and come close by them both, stepping in between them and keeping his head down. They didn't really pay him much attention. The big, white guy who followed him though was more remarkable. He was a bit of mess, he stank, and he swore,

'Get ooota l'fockin' way!' as he bowled past.

The two men looked at each other and shrugged. Gweilos, think they even own the hills.

The fence ended and the path crossed a road that ran up from the main road to one of the catchwater forts that defended the road from the mountain. The path cut back in a triangle and Naz went lazily around it, up a little then down from the apex to cross the last stream over a little, hand-railed bridge. He loved this last stream. There was a tumble of rocks which caused little pools to form that housed tiny fish and frogs, dragon flies hovered and alighted around them. At the back, twenty metres up and into the brush, there was a tiny, hidden farm; three terraced fields, or rather allotments, each the size of two double beds, no more, where some mysterious person had founded a secret garden to grow their herbs and vegetables in a town where the Government and the trillionaire landlords owned and proscribed every available bit of space for their own development needs. He never saw anyone there when he had explored, but he always admired the perpetrator of such a gentle land-crime. Despite his pursuer, he was tempted to go and have a look. Perhaps he could vanish up there and let the honey monster amble by? Did he have time? He resented the fact that his trip down memory lane, his quiet time, his me-time, had been hijacked by the obstacle, then impediment and now threat of a man he despised.

His freedom to choose was denied him though, much to his surprise. In a last-ditch effort, Big John had closed the gap and was at the bottom corner of the triangular switch-back. He could see that if he cut across the base of the triangle, across the rocks and a little bit of fallen brush, he could intercept his prey. John launched himself forward, snatched and missed by a good two metres as Naz skipped past him and alighted on the centre of the bridge. John overshot and ended up sprawled on his knees just off the path. Down again.

'*Waargh!*' The noise he made was primeval, savage. Naz took a quick glimpse back. His pursuer, the predator, was on his knees. Why was he running from this, this abomination of a man? He stopped. Turned full about and stepped very slowly, very deliberately forward. He wasn't breathing hard, he slowed his breath further but sucked in deep, through the nose and mouth. He relaxed his shoulders, his right falling naturally into a slightly advanced position as befitted his southpaw preference. He didn't need to think now. He had stopped thinking. He was just being. The big man was up, glaring, spitting, fuming, both fists raised, all of his body shaking and shuddering with exertion, fury, indignation,

'*You're gonna pay, you're gonna pay.*'

John was talking about his headphones. Naz had no idea about that, his switch had thrown. Naz had blanked the raging insults and threats out, he heard nothing. All he had to do was execute the attack protocol. That was the only conscious decision and move he had to make. Everything else would flow as it had a thousand times on the bag, a hundred times in the ring - throw the right for range, fast, flashing and distracting. The feet would be wide, knees bent, a skip, a shuffle propelled forward off a fast, pushing rear leg, the bent knees lifting, the potential energy driving into kinetic force; feel the left arm rising, the punch coming up from the solid ground, driven by the legs, power enhanced through the hips, up through the stomach and into the chest, to the arm, to the fist, to the target.

The blow connected with sharp kinetic force, driving upwards and spinning the big man away uphill. They had both moved through 90 degrees, Naz had his back to the drop into the stream, John was spinning but the momentum of his own punch, a right-handed, clumsy, bear of a swipe had counter-balanced some of the exquisite precision of Naz's focused energy and the sheer momentum of it stopped John falling off to his left and instead kept him whirling to crash back into Naz's right shoulder. Ninja Naz was undone.

They both stumbled, slipped then dropped into the catchwater channel. It was a chest high drop down a dirty, green painted wall to the pale, tan concreted bed, strewn with rocks and branches that had come down the flood channel. The nullah bed lay flat for three metres, before the walls angled in to a two-metre wide, fifty-centimetre step, then a narrower one, then a third and a fourth step to hit the bottom where a drop-tank type pool lay at the mouth of a large, round, concrete pipe that tunneled under the rest of the slope ready for its final drop to the roadside gutter. The mouth of the tunnel was half obscured by hanging vegetation, a plant that had worked out how to grow across and down the surrounding concrete and fall gracefully across the orifice, breaking its outline and obscuring anything within from the bridge and the path.

They didn't fall that far though. They smacked down onto the wide, angled nullah bed, legs entangled, upper bodies sticking out from each other in a Y-shaped splay of wrath and rage. Two ultimate fighting machines, in a shambolic pile. John sat up and expelled everything from his mouth – spit, blood and hate in a furious filthy spew that splattered into Naz's face. Naz was a very clean man. An obsessively, fastidiously, hygienic man. Something in his inner depths, his base psyche, squirmed and whipped with revulsion along his nerve-ways and attack channels to his hand, bypassing his conscious brain entirely, and his fingers clenched around a small, hand sized rock with a cleft, chipped, jagged edge. John was dead before he knew it. One, whirling, high overhanded blow to the temple came in from above, and he dropped backwards pole-axed, his head coming to rest just in mid-air over the lip of the top of the four steps.

Naz was still sat. His legs under John's heavy and now inert limbs. He looked up at the bridge. Nobody there. He lost a second, then another. He sparked on the third. *'Think Fast.'* He scuffed himself out from under the dead limbs, dropped down two steps, took hold of the shoulders and heaved. The weight was significant, but the running water lubricated the motion as he went backwards, slipped down the next two steps and ended up knee deep in the plunge pool. He shifted to one side, got the body's head and shoulders onto the lip of the tunnel and then clambered into the pipe himself, his day-sack scraping the rough, roof wall. Once in, he heaved again, his feet wide to stay out of the water and get some grip. Haul, drop, haul, drop, haul, drop, haul drop. Four lugs and he was into the middle of the pipe. The water gurgled. There was a faint rush of traffic and the fierce rasp of his breathing. Water trickled. Dead John was silent and sodden.

Most people would have frozen at this point; gone catatonic in horror and disbelief. He had just murdered a man. He hadn't meant to murder a man, so maybe it was manslaughter, but it was a killing. Fortunately for Naz, it wasn't his first. Granted, it was one of a very short list of unintentional killings, or at least unplanned ones, but experience counts. Most of his killing had not only been officially sanctioned by the Secret Intelligence Services, but meticulously planned and prepared for. There hadn't been many official kills either, he wasn't James Bond, just three shootings and nine air-strikes and missile call-ins to be precise. Not excessive in twenty-two years' service. There had been two, accidental, or spur-of-the-moment killings; those two drunk HOS thugs behind a bar in Bosnia and that sharp-witted Ishaqzai drug runner who Naz was certain had just sussed him out as a spy in a filthy compound just North of Gereshk. Then again, the Isahqzai might have been working for ISI or the CIA and just recognised a fellow traveler; he never knew, never asked and always felt the doubt. The HOS duo, however, were straight forward neo-Nazi scum who had decided to beat him up for being the wrong colour in the wrong place. He had taken a severe bollocking for that one. Unprofessional apparently. Not a shred of guilt for those two.

Naz was a professional though and everything was clicking in smoothly now. Escape route needed without being seen. A way back home without showing up on CCTV. An alibi. A way to move without attracting attention. His fancy dress in his backpack was dry and unstained by sweat but a shiny, black and red tracksuit might not be as run-of-the-mill as it was in the late Eighties. Coming out the way he went into the tunnel risked being seen by passers-by, the other way might lead onto the road but was worth a look. He needed to decide whether to come back and dispose of the body; it would be found eventually by any decent search or flushed out in the next rainstorm – not that the Popo were likely to do a decent search as they would have no idea where Dead John vanished on his running route and it wouldn't rain hard for months yet...

Doh! Where he vanished! He had to have a phone on him, they could see exactly where he vanished and when his pulse stopped. Fucking tech! He probably had it tracking. Fuck! Idiot. He backtracked back down the tunnel and started to methodically search the body. Fitbit watch needed to come off, be gentle, no DNA transfer, keep washing hands in the stream. Phone found, in the fancy, shoulder-belt posers wore on the hill. The light was dim but enough to determine there was nothing else electronic. He took a limp hand and placed the right thumb on the phone sensor to unlock it. Wet. Dry it. Done, in, turn off run tracker. Turn off all apps, turn off location tracker. He was going to have to take the phone and drop it in the ocean, but perhaps he should first turn it on again somewhere else and lay a false trail. Might make sense, buy a few days, make the police think John had gone off to somewhere else and vanished there, buy time for passers-by to forget any runners they saw, dislocate him from the scene. Alternatively, should he keep it simple, just take the phone, turn it off and dump it in the harbour? Bollocks, tech made everything tricky.

He was pretty confident there was no CCTV between where he had left DB and here. His own phone though had left a trail, which would show him static at this grid for at least ten minutes. There needed to be a link to him for the cops to even examine his phone trail as they wouldn't be monitoring this area routinely to pick up phone signals. They would be concentrating electronic surveillance on protesters and urban areas not hikers. The only threat to him was a passer-by who described him and then being picked up by CCTV somewhere in Tung Chung. There had only been those two lads by the steps, and they would have moved on by now.

OK, so course of action 1 – phone on, tracker on, false trail, course of action 2 – phone off now, head for MTR, dump phone in harbor somewhere mid-ferry ride later on. Decision, course of action 1.5, turn on Corpse John's phone, avoid Tung Chung, go up the 527 steps to Por Kai Shan, hit the highlands to Lin Fa Shan pass, take selfies, and then drop off left down to Nam Shan, turn off phone on South side to send searchers over there, drop into Mui Wo, round to Barry's, join the gang, alibi sorted with a little help from Jonny to fill in the gap if necessary. That'll work. Fucking hard slog but worth the effort. 527 steps, sounds on, '*Dem a shoot, dem a loot, dem a wail,*' start sweating double-oh-seven.

And Dead.

There was a ferry coming in across the bay, the haze was absent for the first time in what felt like a year and the view was sharp and clear. There were tears deep inside Jonny's eyes, but they were being kept down by a mixture of disbelief, fury and confusion. He was sat on a rock, looking down over Mui Wo, the gentle rise of Butterfly Hill below him, the hidden waterfall off to his right, where he had planned to take Kay as soon as the school holidays kicked in and they could steal a day together. It wasn't looking so likely now. Her messages were short:

'We have to stop.'

'Everything changed.'

'Finish.'

He had texted back, *'Why? What happened? He found out?'* 'He' was the only thing he knew about KK's husband, his pronoun. Jonny had never seen a picture or known his name. She had made him promise never to try and find out, never to pry, stalk or investigate. She made him promise and his oath to her was sacred. It sometimes drove him crazy, he sometimes asked her, sometimes had a go at her about it, but he never betrayed his promise. He had walked for 30 minutes and sat for thirty more before he got an answer.

'No.'

He shot back, *'What then? Come on, tell me.'*

'No. Give up. Bye.'

He tapped the screen and then hit her number. It rang twice then stopped. Call declined. He tried again. Call blocked. He went back to the Telegram and started typing but she was faster.

'Stop. Give up.'

He typed *'I don't understand. We have to talk. Meet me.'*

It wasn't delivered. He was blocked. Overwhelmed. There was no one he could tell. It was supposed to be him telling her that he had to go.

Peer One

Ranald brought the tray gingerly over to the table, saucer and spoon rattling in his shaky hand. He took a chair, table for five. Four empty seats.

'You'd be a shit waiter Damps.' Jonny would have said and grinned at him.

'True, true.' Ran would have stayed on his feet and with a flourish started handing out the goodies,

'Good at maths, shit at football. Now messieurs, iced lemon ginger honey soda and blueberry cheesecake, for the exotic one.' he would have served Naz who would have looked away from contemplating the big wheel or the sky and given Ran a thankful nod and the kindest of smiles.

'Orange rooibos and lemon tart for ...'

'The tart, yeah, yeah, yeah I know!' Micky would have got it in before Ranald did.

'Well, it's harsh but fair Cavendish. When are you ever going to keep it in your pants son?'

'When the Viagra runs out, hombre.'

'Ah, the little, blue pill of happiness.'

Instead, Ranald put his own Tiramisu and Chai Latte on the table and put the empty tray on an empty table. Monday afternoon at Pier 8, the best sea-side café on Hong Kong island and he had it to himself. Ranald puffed and groaned as he sat down and invisibly his ghost friends laughed and said in unison,

'You're not proper old til you make a noise sitting down!'

Ranald asked himself, *'So where are you Jonny boy? Taiwan, I suppose. Looking for a job, I guess. Visa denied. Banned from the SAR. Seditious foreigner.'*

'How about you Naz? Zero, zip, nada. Nothing. He's just vanished again. He'll reappear. He always does. Mr Benn. Or is it the shopkeeper?'

Ranald looked up at the sky, *'You fool Micky. Impetuous, beautiful arrogant fool.'* Tears filled his eyes. He pulled out his phone, WhatsApp announced *'Inbound. ETA 1325hrs.'*

'Tactical Tim.' Ranald rolled his eyes and wondered, *'Do you think he'll abseil in off the IFC or drop in by parachute?'*

He looked over the balcony along the waterfront past City Hall and Tamar Barracks towards where Police HQ was, obscured by Legco. He hoped to see James strolling towards him. He didn't. The sea front was empty. James would leave town soon, as well. Just him left. The Chinese one. The view reminded him of the tear gas and riots of the past six months. It had all calmed down. Since the elections. For a bit. But it'll start again when the Government won't change. The protesters were regrouping but Ranald felt the pain in his wounds and knew The System would win. This is China. I am Chinese. They're just rounding people up and jailing them, all quietly, quietly. The long game mate, China always plays the long game.

Ranald knew it would be a while before he had his day in court. The lawyer said it'll be months, maybe a year. She reckons they'll try and do a deal – we drop the charges against the Chan Chan brothers and they'll drop their bullshit ones against me. His lips moved sub-consciously and he spoke out loud,

'No chance. Wankers. They need to get done.'

Ranald's head went up, his back straightened, he was embarrassed to have spoken aloud but there was nobody there to notice. Nobody except James, who had seen him call out and loved him for it.

'What Ho Chap!'

Ranald checked his watch, 1325hrs.

'Did you abseil or parachute in?' asked Ranald.

'Actually, Chewy dropped me off by speedboat, he's just switched to Maritime. Great boat! I'll take you out.' James wasn't joking, that was how he'd got there. He was cool. He looked at his friend.

'Cheer up Damps! Sun is out, sky is blue. Two arms, two legs, we're alive mate!'

Ranald relaxed and smiled.

'I've got a bit of good news actually, you know that wank bank fired me for no reason? Well, I met one of KK's friends at the wake...' Ranald's tongue stumbled and he paused, mouth open, eyes far away, without any realization of what was physically happening as grief kicked in, then he un-glitched and went on,

'... and turns out her mate's the CEO of WWF and they desperately need a Finance dude, and I'm going to be that dude. I am no longer a jobless vagrant.'

'Yaahey!' James was buoyant in his delight. *'Welcome back to the light side Kylo Ren! I knew you could the escape evil world of corporate finance. Maybe you'll be less dull now too!'*

Ranald grinned, he actually felt enormous pride, a sense of purpose and self-worth that had been absent for decades. He had a small tear in his eye and looked away from the table towards the sea to hide it – grief and pride.

'Just us two? Fuck.' James looked up and away, up to the Peak then away to the East along the harbour. Bottom lip wobbled, voice trembled ever so slightly.

'We're bleeding Ran, but we're still the lucky ones. Absent friends.' James raised his smoothie glass, the boys stood.

'Absent friends.'

The Naam

Jonny stood looking out from a rooftop terrace in Hue. He had no friends here. He spoke no Vietnamese. He had no job. He had told everyone he was going to Taiwan. He was a wanted man. Probably. He had a beer bottle in his hand, his old, battered, red-starred cap on the back of his head and a new phone. Two arms, two legs and he had wifi. He had typed a cryptic clue to KK but couldn't send it; she had blocked him, so the message sat on his phone screen, clasped in his hand as he looked at the sky.

> *This is the end. My sweetest friend.*
>
> *You have no idea how sad you have made me; how much I miss you.*
>
> *I let you down, but I don't know how.*
>
> *I stare at the phone, checking it, checking it again, willing it to give me a message, a sign, a something.*
>
> *It's just silent but I imagine such bitterness and contempt and irritation in your every utterance, every look, every too high, too loud, too pitched, too spiteful little laugh.*
>
> *I want to write to you, but you will hate it, wail and rail and complain and despise and condemn.*
>
> *Your cold heart breaks the sneer of men.*

'I should delete it,' he thought, 'it's mean. It's really harsh. I am mean.' He looked down at his screen to delete it.

A red alert told him he had a Signal message from an unknown caller. 'How the fuck can I have a message? Spam already? I just got this phone.'

'Nice view. Crap hat. Beer cold?'

The End

About the Author

I like to sit on the grass, under a tree in the park, and write. It's a bit like work but slacker. To relax, I love the hills and trails, especially when it rains a little and nobody else is about.

About the Reader

Thank you for reading my book. You might be unique. I showed some early drafts to friends. Some said it's good; others that it was too descriptive, too many adjectives, too complex, too clunky, too confusing, less is more, show don't tell, etc. Nobody really read it. If a critic ever reviewed it, they might hate it; the troll-bots would. But I hope somebody likes it, some day. You'd be the odd one, the weirdo. Hi! Write a book in return. People will discourage you; don't care. Just do it. For you. And at least one other nutcase ;)

www.ingramcontent.com/pod-product-compliance
Lightning Source LLC
Chambersburg PA
CBHW022200170626
46807CB00005B/2286

* 9 7 8 1 8 3 8 1 7 2 4 3 5 *